LUKE JENSEN
BOUNTY HUNTER
BURNING DAYLIGHT

LUKE JENSEN
BOUNTY HUNTER
BURNING DAYLIGHT

WILLIAM W. JOHNSTONE
WITH J. A. JOHNSTONE

PINNACLE BOOKS
Kensington Publishing Corp.
www.kensingtonbooks.com

PINNACLE BOOKS are published by

Kensington Publishing Corp.
119 West 40th Street
New York, NY 10018

PUBLISHER'S NOTE
Following the death of William W. Johnstone, the Johnstone family is working with a carefully selected writer to organize and complete Mr. Johnstone's outlines and many unfinished manuscripts to create additional novels in all of his series like The Last Gunfighter, Mountain Man, and Eagles, among others. This novel was inspired by Mr. Johnstone's superb storytelling.

All Kensington titles, imprints, and distributed lines are available at special quantity discounts for bulk purchases for sales promotions, premiums, fund-raising, educational, or institutional use. Special book excerpts or customized printings can also be created to fit specific needs. For details, write or phone the office of the Kensington sales manager: Kensington Publishing Corp., 119 West 40th Street, New York, NY 10018, attn: Sales Department; phone 1-800-221-2647.

PINNACLE BOOKS, the Pinnacle logo, and the WWJ steer head logo are Reg. U.S. Pat. & TM Off.

ISBN-13: 978-0-7860-4404-7
ISBN-10: 0-7860-4404-7

First printing: July 2019

10 9 8 7 6 5 4 3 2 1

Printed in the United States of America

Electronic edition:

ISBN-13: 978-0-7860-4405-4 (e-book)
ISBN-10: 0-7860-4405-5 (e-book)

The Jensen Family
First Family of the American Frontier

Smoke Jensen—*The Mountain Man*
The youngest of three children and orphaned as a young boy, Smoke Jensen is considered one of the fastest draws in the West. His quest to tame the lawless West has become the stuff of legend. Smoke owns the Sugarloaf Ranch in Colorado. Married to Sally Jensen, father to Denise ("Denny") and Louis.

Preacher—*The First Mountain Man*
Though not a blood relative, grizzled frontiersman Preacher became a father figure to the young Smoke Jensen, teaching him how to survive in the brutal, often deadly Rocky Mountains. Fought the battles that forged his destiny. Armed with a long gun, Preacher is as fierce as the land itself.

Matt Jensen—*The Last Mountain Man*
Orphaned but taken in by Smoke Jensen, Matt Jensen has become like a younger brother to Smoke and even took the Jensen name. And like Smoke, Matt has carved out his destiny on the American frontier. He lives by the gun and surrenders to no man.

Luke Jensen—*Bounty Hunter*
Mountain Man Smoke Jensen's long-lost brother Luke Jensen is scarred by war and a dead shot—the

right qualities to be a bounty hunter. And he's cunning, and fierce enough, to bring down the deadliest outlaws of his day.

Ace Jensen and Chance Jensen—*Those Jensen Boys!*
Smoke Jensen's long-lost nephews, Ace and Chance, are a pair of young-gun twins as reckless and wild as the frontier itself . . . Their father is Luke Jensen, thought killed in the Civil War. Their uncle Smoke Jensen is one of the fiercest gunfighters the West has ever known. It's no surprise that the inseparable Ace and Chance Jensen have a knack for taking risks—even if they have to blast their way out of them.

CHAPTER 1

Luke Jensen froze with the glass of whiskey halfway to his lips as he heard the metallic ratcheting of a gun being cocked above and behind him. He glanced at the nervous-looking bartender and asked quietly, "He's on the balcony, isn't he?"

The man's lips were tight. His double chin bounced a little as he gave a short nod.

"I'd get down, if I were you," Luke advised, then he dropped the whiskey and threw himself to the side as a gun roared.

The deafening blast filled the saloon. From the corner of his eye Luke saw a bullet gouge out a piece of the hardwood bar and send splinters flying.

By the time he hit the sawdust-littered floor a split second later, his long-barreled Remingtons filled both hands. The guns roared and bucked as he triggered them. The .44 slugs smashed into the chest of the man standing on the balcony and rocked him back a step before he stumbled forward against the railing.

Luke recognized the man who had just tried to kill him. His name was Son Barton, a West Virginia mountaineer who had fled his home state because he had a habit of shooting people who annoyed him. He had headed west, fallen in with several other killers and outlaws, and ridden the dark trails for the past few years. Luke had tracked the gang to this Arizona Territory settlement and intended to collect the rewards on them.

The wanted posters said DEAD OR ALIVE, but it looked like Son Barton was going to be dead because life was fading fast in his eyes. The gun he had fired at Luke slipped from nerveless fingers and fell to the saloon floor. As Barton tipped forward over the railing and followed, he turned over once in the air and landed on his back with a resounding thud. He gurgled once but didn't move and didn't make any more sounds after that, either.

Still holding the Remingtons, Luke put a hand on the floor, pushed himself to one knee, and tried not to groan from the effort. These days, he felt every one of his years. He stood the rest of the way up and glanced out the window.

The four horses he'd been looking for were tied up at the hitch rail outside. Barton's three friends were still unaccounted for.

The bartender poked his bald head up enough to gaze wide-eyed over the hardwood. The few men who had been drinking in the saloon had stampeded out as soon as the shooting started.

Luke said, "The other three upstairs, too?"

The bartender shook his head. "Just two of 'em. Only got three girls workin' for me. The fourth man said he was goin' over to the store to pick up some supplies."

Since the settlement was small that man was bound to have heard the shots. He'd be heading to the saloon to see what had happened, but it would take him a while get there, so Luke didn't worry about him for the time being. The other two upstairs concerned him more. And with good reason.

A man burst through the door of the room where he'd been frolicking with one of the soiled doves and began spraying lead from a Winchester as fast as he could swing the barrel back and forth and work the rifle's lever.

The bartender ducked again.

Luke dived forward and slid through beery sawdust underneath a table. Bullets whapped against the wood above him. His head and shoulders emerged from the other side. He tipped the Remingtons up and fired two more shots. One missed, but the other caught the rifleman in the throat and jerked his head back as it bored on up into his brain. Blood shot out a good three feet from the wound as he went over backward.

The rifleman's frenzied firing had served as a distraction, Luke realized. The third member of the gang had made it almost all the way down the stairs while Luke had been dealing with the rifleman. And this hombre held a shotgun. He leveled it and squeezed off one barrel as Luke desperately tried to roll aside.

The buckshot hit the floor, except for one piece that plucked at Luke's shirtsleeve. He wasn't hurt, though, and as he came up on a knee again, he thrust the Remingtons out in front of him and triggered them.

The shotgunner jerked. Luke bit back a curse as he saw that his aim had been a little off. He'd hit the varmint in the left arm and left shoulder. He might bleed to death eventually, but he was still on his feet and still had hold of that scattergun.

Luke jammed the revolvers back into their holsters and grabbed hold of another table. As he swung it up, the wounded outlaw fired the shotgun's second barrel. Luke felt the table shiver as the charge struck it. Then he lunged forward and shoved the table out in front of him. It hit the shotgunner and knocked him back against the wall behind him.

Luke rammed the table into the man twice more, then, panting from the effort, shoved it aside and drew one of the Remingtons, even though the outlaw wasn't a threat any longer. He had dropped the shotgun, which was empty, and slumped to the bottom of the stairs, stunned. Luke twirled the Remington around and rapped the butt against the outlaw's head, knocking him out cold. No point in taking any chances.

Outside, a swift rataplan of hoofbeats sounded in the street. Luke hurried to the entrance and shoved the batwings aside. Only three horses stood at the hitch rail. The fourth one was making tracks out of town with a cloud of dust curling up from its hooves. The rider leaned forward over the animal's neck and frantically swatted his hat against its rump to urge it on to greater speed.

"Well, hell," Luke said.

The bartender stuck his head up again. "Is . . . is it over?"

"Yeah. The fourth one lit a shuck, and I don't feel like chasing after him. Reckon I'll have to be satisfied with the three I got . . . for now." Luke started reloading the Remingtons, keeping an eye on the man he had knocked out. "You have any law in this town?"

The bartender stood up. "Got a marshal. A deputy sheriff from Singletary, the county seat, swings by now and then, but you can't ever tell when he's gonna come through."

"A jail?"

"Well . . . a smokehouse where Marshal Hennessy locks up fellas when he has to."

Luke pouched the iron he'd been reloading and took out the other revolver. "I suppose a telegraph office would be too much to hope for."

"I'm afraid so. The railroad didn't come through here, so we never got a telegraph line. Summerville is just a sleepy little place, mister."

"That's the name of this town?"

"Yes, sir. Summerville, Arizona Territory."

Footsteps sounded on the boardwalk. A middle-aged, leathery-faced gent peered over the batwings and asked, "What in blazes is goin' on in there, Doolittle? Sounded like a damn war broke out."

The bartender waved a pudgy hand at Luke. "This fella came in and was about to have a drink when some of my other customers started shootin' at him."

The newcomer pushed the batwings aside and took a step into the room, revealing the lawman's star pinned to his vest.

Luke holstered the second Remington. "You'll take note of how this gentleman phrased that comment, Marshal. All three of those men shot at me first. That makes this a clear-cut case of self-defense."

The bartender, Doolittle, nodded, making his double chin wobble again.

"I take it they had a good reason for trying to ventilate you?" the marshal asked.

"They considered it a good reason. They knew I've been tracking them and planned to collect the rewards that have been posted for them."

Marshal Hennessy's lips tightened. "Bounty hunter, eh?"

"That's right." Luke gestured toward the body lying on its back. "That's Son Barton. The one over there at the bottom of the stairs is Jimmy McCaskill. He's just knocked out. You'll find another dead one up on the balcony, but I don't know which one he is. Didn't get a good enough look at him, and I didn't see the fourth man, the one who got away, at all. But Barton and McCaskill ran with Ed Logan and Deuce Roebuck, so I'm sure the dead man will turn out to be one of them."

As if he hadn't heard what Luke was saying, Marshal Hennessy said, "I don't like bounty hunters."

Luke sighed. "Most lawmen don't. I understand that, Marshal. But we do serve a useful function, you know."

"Yeah, so do buzzards, but that don't mean I got to cozy up to 'em."

"I'll be satisfied if you'll just agree to lock my prisoner up for the night. I'll have him out of your hair tomorrow morning. We'll ride up to the county seat where I can turn him over to the sheriff there."

Hennessy rasped his fingers over his beard-stubbled chin, then nodded. "All right, I suppose I can do that. You're responsible for feedin' the varmint, though. I'm not gonna ask the town to stand the cost of that."

"Fair enough." Luke went over to McCaskill, bent and took hold of his collar, and started dragging his senseless form toward the door. "Lead the way, Marshal."

Hennessy did, trudging along Summerville's only street until he came to a small but sturdy-looking smokehouse. Brackets had been attached on either side of the door, and a thick beam rested in them. He struggled to lift it, saying, "I keep telling the town council . . . uh . . . they oughta build me a real jail . . . but they say the town can't afford it."

Luke let go of McCaskill's collar and reached to help the marshal. "I don't imagine you have much call for one."

"Nope. I have to throw a liquored-up cowpoke in here every once in a while, but that's about it."

Luke motioned for Hennessy to step aside. He took hold of the beam and lifted it out of the brackets. When he started to lean it against the smokehouse wall, he spotted McCaskill trying to crawl away. The outlaw had regained consciousness. Luke wondered how long he'd been shamming.

McCaskill must have thought he could crawl off for a few yards, then leap to his feet and make a dash for his horse. He tried to jump up, but Luke tossed the beam and it caught the outlaw across the back. The weight was enough to knock McCaskill facedown on the street and brought a groan from him.

Luke planted a booted foot on McCaskill's head and said, "You're a determined one, aren't you? I suppose I can see why, since you're bound to hang. But you're starting to annoy me, Jimmy." He drew one of his Remingtons. "It would be a lot easier just to haul your carcass to the county seat."

"Here now," Marshal Hennessy blustered. "Gunning a man when he's trying to shoot you is one thing, but that'd be pure murder, mister."

"Don't worry. I'm a patient man . . . within reason." Luke stepped back and kept McCaskill covered while the outlaw climbed to his feet and stumbled into the smokehouse. Luke replaced the beam, effectively locking him in.

Now that he had a thick door between him and Luke's guns, McCaskill regained some of his bravado. "You're gonna be sorry, you damn bounty hunter. Deuce is gonna get me outta here, and we'll see to it that you die slow and painful."

"Deuce Roebuck, you mean?" Luke said. "I hate to break it to you, Jimmy, but the last I saw of Deuce, he was fogging it out of here and never looked back. I expect he's at least five miles away by now. By nightfall, he'll have gone twenty miles and completely forgotten about you."

"You just wait and see," McCaskill said, but his voice had a quaver in it that revealed his confidence was slipping.

Luke turned back to the marshal. "Do you have an undertaker here in town?"

"Yeah, but I didn't figure you wanted to have those other two buried. Don't you have to take them to the county seat, too, to collect the bounties on them?"

"Yes, but I thought maybe he could clean them up a little. Blood attracts flies, you know."

Hennessy pursed his lips. "He'll do it . . . but he'll charge you for it."

"If it makes the ride a little more pleasant, it'll probably be worth it." Luke paused. "Of course, I suppose I could just cut their heads off and throw them in a gunnysack . . ."

CHAPTER 2

Summerville's undertaker was a tall, cadaverous man who introduced himself to Luke as Clifford Ferguson. Luke had wondered sometimes why undertakers all seemed to be either thin to the point of gauntness and dour or fat and jolly. He hardly ever ran into one of normal size, with a normal demeanor. He supposed the most likely explanation was that some men who dealt with death all the time lost their appetite, while others coped with the strains of their grim profession by embracing the pleasures of life, including plenty of good food.

Ferguson agreed to clean up the bodies of Son Barton and Ed Logan. A search of their saddlebags turned up a spare shirt and trousers for each man, so Ferguson would dress them in those duds and burn the blood-soaked clothes. He named a price of two dollars per corpse for the service.

Luke handed over a five-dollar gold piece he had also found in one of the saddlebags and got a silver dollar in change.

"I ain't sure I ever saw a bounty hunter quite so

picky about the carcasses he hauled in to collect the blood money on 'em," Marshal Hennessy commented as he and Luke stood on the boardwalk in front of the saloon watching Ferguson and his stocky Mexican assistant load the bodies onto a wagon.

"It's summer, and Singletary is half a day's ride away," Luke said. "I actually considered asking Mr. Ferguson to go ahead and embalm them, just to cut down on the stink, but I decided that would be too much of an expense. The bounty on the three I'm taking in only adds up to eighteen hundred dollars, eight hundred for Barton and five hundred apiece on the other two, and they had less than twenty dollars between them in their saddlebags. They went through the loot from their recent jobs quickly."

"Eighteen hunnerd bucks is a damn fine chunk of money." Hennessy added sourly, "The town only pays me sixty dollars a month, plus half the fines I collect. That's better than cowboying, but not by much."

"In that case, Marshal, let me buy you a drink," Luke suggested.

Hennessy shook his head. "My stomach won't take whiskey no more. They call it rotgut, and it surely lived up to its name." He inclined his head toward a small frame building diagonally across the street and went on. "I've got a pot of coffee on the stove in the office, though, if you're of a mind."

"Thank you, Marshal. That sounds good."

The coffee probably *wasn't* good—Luke had come across very few local lawmen who could brew a decent cup—but he didn't figure it would hurt anything to accept Hennessy's invitation. The likelihood that he would ever pass through Summerville again was small. He couldn't rule it out, though, and being on good terms with the local star packer sometimes came in handy.

They walked across to the marshal's office. The coffee actually wasn't as bad as Luke expected, although it would be a stretch to call it good. He thumbed back the black hat on his head and perched a hip on the corner of Hennessy's paper-littered desk while the marshal sagged into an old swivel chair behind it.

"Jensen," Hennessy said musingly. "I reckon you get asked all the time if you're related to Smoke Jensen, the famous gunfighter they write all those dime novels about."

"From time to time," Luke admitted.

"Well . . . are you?"

"As a matter of fact," Luke said, "Smoke is my brother."

It was true. For many years, his younger brother Kirby—known far and wide as Smoke—had believed that Luke was dead, killed in the Civil War. In reality, violent and tragic circumstances had led to Luke carving out a new life for himself after the war, with a new name as well. Only in recent years had he gone back to using the name Jensen, but he kept the profession he had chosen—bounty hunting.

Hennessy stared at him for a couple of seconds, then said, "You're joshin' me."

Luke shrugged. "It's the truth, Marshal. I haven't seen Smoke for a while. Mostly he goes his way and I go mine. He has a successful ranch over in Colorado to look after, you know."

"And you're just a driftin' bounty killer."

"We each have our own destiny. Some philosophers

believe that our fates are locked into place before we're even born."

"Well, I don't know about that. Seems to me that a fella's always got the choice of takin' a different trail if he wants to."

"It's certainly nice to think so." Luke took another sip of coffee and looked idly at the papers scattered across Hennessy's desk. Most of them were reward posters. "You get these dodgers when the stagecoach brings the mail?"

"Yep. Sheriff Collins sends 'em to me."

Luke moved some of the papers around and then tapped a finger against one of them. "There's the reward poster for Son Barton. It's possible the posters for the other three are somewhere in here, too."

Hennessy frowned. "What are you gettin' at, Jensen? You think I should've known those boys were in town and tried to arrest 'em myself? I know Summerville ain't a very big place, but I can't keep track of every long rider who drifts in and then back out again."

Luke had a feeling the marshal didn't want to know when outlaws were in his town. That would mean going out of his way to risk his life for a salary that certainly wasn't exorbitant. As long as visitors to Summerville didn't cause any trouble, Hennessy was perfectly content to let them go on their way.

Luke couldn't blame him for that. "That's perfectly understandable, Marshal."

Something else among the papers caught Luke's eye. He pushed some of the reward dodgers aside and picked up what appeared to be a piece of butcher paper. The writing on it hadn't been done with a printing press, like the other wanted posters. Someone had used a piece of coal to scrawl in big letters at the top *WANTED*, and below that in slightly smaller letters *Three-fingered Jack McKinney*.

"What's this?" Luke asked.

Hennessy leaned back in his chair and grinned. "Reckon the sheriff thought I'd get a laugh out of it. He sent a note sayin' that they been poppin' up around the county. Homemade wanted posters ain't exactly legal."

"'Wanted for being a thief and a killer and a no-account scoundrel'," Luke read from the poster. "'Reward'"—he looked up at Hennessy—"'Reward $1.42 and a harmonica. The harmonica is only six months old.'"

The marshal chuckled. "It's a joke. Some kid wrote it. You can tell by the writing. He's probably got a friend named Jack McKinney and figured it'd be funny to fix up a wanted poster with his name on it."

"Maybe. But you just said Sheriff Collins told you they'd been posted in other parts of the county. Seems like an awful lot of trouble to go to for a joke."

"You can't never tell what a kid will do. It can't be real. Who'd ever go after an outlaw for a measly $1.42 bounty?"

"And a harmonica," Luke reminded him. "Don't forget the harmonica."

"Well, if you want to go after this Three-fingered Jack, whoever he is, you just feel free to take that dodger with you. You might need it to collect the ree-ward." Hennessy slapped his thigh and laughed some more about it.

As Luke finished his coffee, he folded the hand-made wanted poster and slipped it into his shirt pocket.

The marshal didn't even seem to notice.

* * *

After leaving the marshal's office, Luke went by the undertaking parlor to see how Ferguson was coming along with the job on Son Barton and Ed Logan. Ferguson promised they would be done by evening, but since Luke wasn't planning to leave until the next morning, the undertaker suggested, "I can put them down in the root cellar if you'd like. Keep them cooler overnight. That might help with the smell tomorrow."

"I'd be obliged to you for that."

"Only cost you another dollar."

Luke smiled as he handed back the silver dollar Ferguson had given him in change earlier. He suspected the undertaker had had that in mind all along.

That left Luke at loose ends. Summerville didn't have a hotel, so when he gathered up his own horse and the mounts belonging to the three outlaws and led them to the town's only livery stable, he asked the hostler, "What are the chances that I can sleep in the hayloft tonight?"

"If you've got four bits to spare, mister, I'd say the chances are real good," the man replied. "And four bits for each of the horses, so that adds up to, uh . . ."

Luke dropped three silver dollars in the callused, outstretched palm. "Give them a little extra grain and we'll call it square."

This stop in Summerville was getting expensive, but for now he was using the money he had found in the outlaws' saddlebags. If the total wound up going over that amount, he would recoup the funds when he collected the rewards in the county seat.

With that taken care of, he drifted back to the

saloon. Doolittle was still behind the bar. Somebody had mopped up the blood that had been spilled earlier, and the customers who had been chased out of the place by gunplay had returned.

In addition, three soiled doves in shabby dresses sat together at a table, their services not in demand at the moment. All of them showed the wear and tear of the hard life they led. No amount of paint could cover that up.

Doolittle cast a nervous glance across the bar at Luke. "You're not plannin' on shooting up the place again, are you?"

"I wasn't planning on it the first time." Luke's voice hardened as he added, "And I'd sort of like to know how Son Barton even knew I was here."

One of the doves spoke up. "I can tell you that, mister. He had just finished with me—and mighty damn quick, I might add—and got up to look out the window. He said, 'It's that damn bounty hunter' and some other things that I'm not even comfortable repeatin'. Then he yanked on his clothes, grabbed his pistol, and ran out of the room. Nobody who works here tipped him off, if that's what you're thinkin'."

Luke nodded slowly. He hadn't been aware that the outlaws knew he was on their trail, but he supposed someone he had questioned regarding their whereabouts could have gotten word to them to be on the lookout for him and described him.

"Felicia's right, Mr. Jensen," Doolittle said. "We don't mix in our customers' affairs. Anybody's got a problem with anybody else, we try to stay out of it."

"A wise way to be," Luke said.

Doolittle reached for a bottle and a glass. "Since you

didn't get to finish that drink earlier, how about you have another one now, on the house?"

"Thank you, Mr. Doolittle. You're a gentleman and a scholar."

Doolittle filled the glass and pushed it across the bar. "Not hardly, but I can pour a drink."

That was the only thing anybody in Summerville had offered to do for Luke without charging him for it.

A little later, the soiled dove called Felicia went over to the bar and made it pretty clear she wouldn't mind if Luke took her upstairs, but he wasn't sure if she intended for it to be a business transaction or not.

He had always had pretty good luck with women. They seemed to find him attractive despite his craggy features and the gray that was starting to appear in his dark hair. But unlike some men, being involved in a shooting scrape didn't leave him puffing and pawing at the ground like a bull, so he diverted Felicia's veiled suggestion as politely as possible.

The only eating place in town was a hash house owned by a pigtailed Chinaman. Luke had supper there, then went back to the stable, climbed into the loft, and settled down to sleep.

He wasn't sure how long it was after he'd dozed off that an explosion woke him.

CHAPTER 3

The blast was powerful enough to shake the ground a little. Luke felt it through the hayloft floor. He rolled over and grabbed his boots. Along with his hat and his gunbelt, they were the only things he had removed when he turned in.

He yanked the boots on, jerked the Remingtons from their holsters, and stuck them behind his belt, not taking time to buckle on the gunbelt. The explosion might not have anything to do with him or his prisoner, but that seemed unlikely if Summerville really was such a sleepy little place as the townspeople claimed. Hell had a history of breaking loose just about everywhere Luke showed up.

He went fast down the ladder.

The hostler stumbled sleepily from the office and living quarters at one side of the barn. He said in a groggy voice, "What the hell—" as Luke ran past him to the double-doored entrance.

Luke pulled one of the big doors open and stepped out into the street, resting his hand on a gun butt. His hunch was right. The explosion had gone off down at the smokehouse where Jimmy McCaskill was locked up.

As he pounded toward it, Luke noticed the squat building was heavily damaged. Flames shot up in places from what was left of its walls.

A man holding the reins of two horses hopped around anxiously, darting closer to the smokehouse and then jumping back from the fire's heat. "Jimmy! Jimmy, where are you? Come on! I'm bustin' you out! Hurry!"

Luke came to a stop about fifteen feet away and filled both hands with the Remingtons. "Roebuck, you damned fool. You probably blew him to kingdom come."

The flames cast enough garish light for Luke to recognize Deuce Roebuck's angular features from the reward dodgers, but he would have been sure Roebuck was responsible for the explosion even without that. Nobody else had a reason to try to break McCaskill out of jail.

"How many sticks of dynamite did you use, anyway?" Luke went on as Roebuck dropped the horses' reins and whirled toward him.

He didn't really expect an answer to the question, but Roebuck yelled, "Four, you son of a bitch!" as he clawed at the gun on his hip.

Luke lifted the right-hand Remington and fired first, just as the outlaw cleared leather. Roebuck slewed halfway around. The gun in his hand blasted as he jerked the trigger, but the bullet went into the ground only a few feet away from him. He tried to stay upright but fell to both knees and struggled to twist his head toward Luke. His mouth opened and closed a couple of times as he tried to form words, but no sound came out that Luke heard. Roebuck swayed once and then toppled forward on his face.

Marshal Hennessy yelled, "What in the all-fired Hades!" as he ran up behind Luke. The lawman wore boots and a nightshirt that left his bony knees sticking out. He carried a shotgun. His white hair, askew from sleep, made him look a little loco.

Luke used one of the Remingtons to point at the man he'd shot. "That's Deuce Roebuck, the one who got away this afternoon. I guess he got to feeling bad about leaving his pards behind, because he turned around and came back. Must have talked to somebody and found out McCaskill was the only one still alive. He got the bright idea of using dynamite to bust him out of the smokehouse."

"Good Lord," Hennessy muttered. "Looks like he blew the hell out of the place."

"And out of McCaskill, too, I expect."

A number of townspeople had straggled up behind the marshal to find out what all the excitement was.

Luke looked at them and went on. "If somebody will fetch a lantern, I'll have a look in there."

Someone handed him a lantern. As Luke had predicted, Jimmy McCaskill was dead. The explosion had filled the air inside the smokehouse with huge flying chunks of wood from the thick beams. At least half a dozen of them had punched holes through McCaskill. Luckily for Luke, none of them had struck the outlaw in the face, so his corpse was still recognizable.

After Luke dragged the body out of the rubble and left it lying next to Roebuck's, Hennessy asked,

"You gonna have Clifford Ferguson clean up these hombres, too? He's liable to charge you extra, it bein' night now and all."

Luke didn't answer the question directly. He just said, "The way things are going, stopping over in your sleepy little town is going to wind up costing me money, Marshal."

Luke left Summerville early the next morning. He had strung the outlaws' horses together with lead ropes so they trailed behind him single file, each carrying a blanket-wrapped burden draped over the saddle and tied in place. That made for a grim procession as Luke rode north toward Singletary, leading the first horse in line. He wasn't sad to be leaving the settlement behind him.

There wasn't much to see out on the semiarid plains, and the company wasn't very good, of course, so Luke was also glad the ride wasn't that long. By midday he spotted smoke rising from chimneys and not long after that, the buildings of the county seat. He saw church steeples and even a few two-story buildings.

A man leading four horses obviously carrying dead men was going to attract a lot of attention anywhere, and that town was no exception. By the time Luke had traveled a block along the main street, he had a sizable audience of small boys and dogs trailing him. Men and women on the boardwalks stopped whatever they were doing and gawked at him.

The street stretched for a dozen blocks to a redbrick railroad depot at the far end. Luke didn't have to go that far. Right in the middle of town stood a stone courthouse on the street's left side behind a lawn that was fighting to stay green in the summer heat.

As he headed in that direction, Luke saw several men running the same way, drawing ahead of him as he moved along at an easy pace with the horses. He knew those townies were hustling to see who could get to the sheriff first and break the news that a man had just ridden into town with four corpses.

By the time he drew rein in front of the court-house, a stocky, middle-aged man in a sober black suit was striding across the lawn toward the street. He came closer, stopped, planted his feet, and hooked his thumbs in his vest pockets. A neatly clipped, gray-ing brown mustache decorated his florid face. He glared up at Luke and said, "You'd better have a damned good reason for parading through town like that and making a public spectacle of yourself, mister."

Luke rested easy in the saddle with his left hand on the horn and used his right thumb to push his hat back. "I have a very good reason, Sheriff. I have the bodies of four wanted outlaws here. I'd like to turn them over to you and file a claim on the rewards posted for them."

"I thought it had to be something like that. You should have left them outside of town and come in to report them. The undertaker could have gone out in his wagon and brought them in with the proper amount of discretion instead of subjecting the citi-zens to such a repulsive sight."

Luke waved a hand toward the bodies. "I wrapped

them up in blankets, Sheriff. That's more than I had to do."

A pudgy young man wearing a deputy's badge hurried up, puffing and panting.

The sheriff snapped at him. "Go fetch the undertaker, Tom. Tell him there are four bodies for him to take charge of."

As the deputy trotted off, Luke said, "I hope that boy doesn't have heatstroke."

"You let me worry about my deputies," Sheriff Collins said. "What's your name, anyway?"

"Jensen," Luke answered, his own voice harder and flatter in response to the lawman's obvious dislike.

"You had no call to do things this way," Collins said peevishly. "Folks don't like seeing such grisly displays."

"Are you serious, Sheriff?" Luke asked with a frown. "Fifteen years ago, the people who came this far west to settle had to worry about Apache war parties raiding through these parts, not to mention vicious gangs of outlaws and bushwhackers. No man ever stepped out his front door without taking a gun with him, and he was ready to use it to defend his family. The railroad was still just a dream. Are you telling me that the citizens have changed so much, have gotten so soft since then that the wrapped-up bodies of a few owlhoots are enough to give them the fantods?"

Collins flushed, turning his face even redder than it had been to start with. "Don't you go judging these townfolks. Not all of them were here during pioneer days. Most came in after the railroad did. Arizona is a civilized territory now, this part of it, anyway."

"Civilization is a wonderful thing," Luke said, "but some things are lost with it, too."

The creaking of wagon wheels made him look over his shoulder. A big wagon with a black-painted wooden cover over its bed rolled along the street toward him. Six black horses were pulling it and a black-suited man was handling the reins. That would be the undertaker.

Luke dismounted and watched while the man, another thin and gloomy sort, supervised a couple of strong-backed assistants as they lifted the blanket-shrouded bodies from the horses and deposited them in the wagon. Collins, still seething, watched, too, as did the crowd that had gathered.

Luke said, "That's Son Barton, Ed Logan, Jimmy McCaskill, and Deuce Roebuck. I caught up to them yesterday in a place south of here called Summerville."

"I'll wager that Oren Hennessy wasn't any happier to see you than I am."

"He didn't fall all over himself slapping me on the back in good fellowship, but he *did* give me a cup of coffee."

"Don't expect the same here," Collins said. "I'm pretty sure I've got dodgers on all four of those names you mentioned. I'll take them down to the undertaking parlor here in a few minutes and confirm your claim, Jensen. You can come by the office later this afternoon and I'll sign the paperwork for the rewards. You can take it over to the bank and they'll handle things from there."

"I've done this a time or two before, Sheriff. I know how it works."

"It may take a day or two to get the money. While you're waiting for it, you'll stay north of the tracks unless you're down here on official business. There are places up there for the likes of you."

Luke had to bite back an angry response. He didn't like the sheriff any more than Collins liked him, but the lawman had the upper hand. He could hold up those rewards if he wanted to be a bastard about it.

Anyway, Luke had an idea how he was going to deal with Collins's obnoxious attitude, but that could wait. He just nodded noncommittally and said, "I'd like to sell these horses and rigs. Can you recommend a stable where I might do that?"

"Harwell's," the sheriff said with grudging cooperation. "Two more blocks north on the other side of the street. You'll see the sign. Once you've done that, keep going until you're north of the tracks."

"Because having the citizens of your fair town exposed to a dangerous ruffian such as myself might make some of them faint dead away."

Collins scowled and turned away, no longer willing to continue the conversation.

Luke would have let the lawman go, but something else occurred to him, and he gave in to his curiosity. "Just one more thing, Sheriff." He reached into his shirt pocket and pulled out the folded piece of butcher paper. He unfolded it and held it out. "What do you know about this?"

Collins looked over his shoulder, then swung to face Luke again. He stepped close enough to snatch the paper out of his hand and demanded, "Where did you get this?"

"Marshal Hennessy gave it to me. He said you'd sent it to him as a joke."

"Joke, hell! I was warning Hennessy to keep his eyes open for that crazy kid. He's going to get himself or somebody else hurt riding around all over the county raising hell like he's been doing!"

CHAPTER 4

Luke frowned at the red-faced lawman. "You're going to have to explain that, Sheriff."

"I don't have to explain anything," Collins snapped. "I don't see that it's any of your business."

"Humor me."

"Why? Are you thinking about going after that bounty? The whole dollar and forty-two cents?"

"And the harmonica," Luke said with a wry smile. "Everyone keeps forgetting about the harmonica." He paused. "I'm sure I can find someone else to tell me all about it if you don't want to, Sheriff."

Collins looked disgusted, but he jerked his head toward the courthouse and said, "Let's get out of the blasted sun. It gets hot in the middle of the day like this."

After tying the five horses to a hitch rack at the edge of the street, Luke followed Collins into the courthouse. Behind the building's thick stone walls, the sheriff's office was a lot cooler. A coffeepot sat on a stove in the outer office, but true to his word, Collins didn't offer Luke a cup.

He said, "Don't bother sitting down. You won't be here that long."

"Such hospitality," Luke muttered.

Collins hung his hat on a hat tree, revealing only a few lank strands of brown hair on a liver-spotted head. He pointed to a stack of papers on his desk. "I've got half a dozen more of the blasted things right there that folks have brought in, complaining about them. The kid tacked them up on walls and boardwalk posts all over town. He's been putting them on trees along the roads and trails, too. He's a damn nuisance, that's what he is."

Luke recognized the butcher paper and the crude charcoal printing. With a slight frown, he asked, "Why do people have a problem with these posters? They seem harmless enough."

"Because nobody wants Three-fingered Jack McKinney to see something like that on his place of business or out front of his house. McKinney might get mad, and there's no telling what he might do."

"Wait a minute. There actually *is* an outlaw named Three-fingered Jack McKinney?"

"Well, I suppose the part about only having three fingers on his left hand probably isn't written down in the family Bible, but the Jack McKinney part is. As for being an outlaw . . . he didn't used to be, but he sure is now." Collins sat down behind the desk and sighed. "Up until about five years ago, he had a place north of here, close to the county line at the edge of the hills. A ranch and a farm, both. He raised some crops, but he had nice little herds of cattle and horses, too. And a nice family. Mighty pretty wife and two fine boys."

"I have a feeling that this story isn't going in a pleasant direction."

"One day McKinney rode off and didn't come back. His wife insisted that something must have happened to him, like maybe his horse threw him and he was hurt. She asked me to lead a search party, and I did. We scoured the whole northern half of the county and never found a trace of him. His horse's tracks led west from the ranch but petered out after a mile or two in a rocky stretch. I may not be the best tracker in the world, but I'm good enough I could tell he was being careful not to leave a trail. He *wanted* to disappear."

"If his life was as good as you say it was, why would he do that?"

"Why in blazes does any man do anything?" Collins scowled. "Nobody ever knows what ugly things are crawling around in another man's brain. Even a nice, friendly fellow like McKinney can have all sorts of secrets, and most of them would look like what you see wiggling around under a rock when you lift it up."

"'A man may smile, and smile, and be a villain,'" Luke quoted. "*Hamlet.*"

"Never heard of that fella," Collins replied with a shake of his head, "but that describes Jack McKinney pretty well. Always had a smile on his face and a friendly word for anybody who crossed his path. Everybody who knew him liked him, including me. When he disappeared, none of us ever thought that the next time we heard of him, it'd be because he was leading an outlaw gang up in the Dakotas."

That explained why McKinney's name had been unfamiliar to Luke. He hadn't been up in that area for quite a while. Anyway, not even the most dedicated bounty hunter in the West could be expected to keep up with every owlhoot between the Mississippi River and the Pacific Ocean.

"The stories were bad," Collins continued. "The McKinney gang held up banks, robbed trains, looted towns and then burned them to the ground. When folks around here first started reading about those outrageous things in the newspaper, nobody figured the Three-fingered Jack McKinney the stories talked about was the same man as Jack McKinney, the rancher who'd vanished. I mean, Jack McKinney's not an unusual name."

"No, it's not," Luke agreed. "I take it something happened to let everyone know it *was* the same man?"

Collins nodded and pointed to a bulletin board on one wall of the office. "A wanted poster showed up . . . a real one. The drawing on it of Three-fingered Jack didn't leave any doubt. The outlaw was the man we'd known, all right."

Luke walked over to the bulletin board. A dozen or so reward dodgers were tacked to it. He needed only a moment to pick out the one for Three-fingered Jack McKinney. The drawing underneath the big word *WANTED* showed a man probably in his thirties, with dark hair, a close-cropped beard, and a lean face with quite a few wrinkles around the eyes. He appeared pleasant, even mild-mannered, certainly not like the sort of hombre anybody would expect to be guilty of murder, robbery, arson, and all the other crimes the wanted poster listed.

But Luke knew from experience that you couldn't go by appearances. He had seen too many baby-faced youngsters who'd turned out to be vicious killers.

Gruffly, Collins said, "If it had been up to me, I

might have put that in a desk drawer and kept it to myself, but one of my deputies saw it before I could do that, and he spread the word around town. By nightfall everybody knew about it, so there was no point in trying to hide it."

Luke turned back toward the desk. "Why would you have done that, Sheriff?"

"For Amelia's sake. McKinney's wife. She's a fine woman. Everybody likes her as much as they did him. And for the boys, too. Bad enough their pa disappeared like that. To find out he's a no-good outlaw, to boot . . ." The sheriff's voice trailed off as he shook his head.

Luke dropped the homemade wanted poster on the desk. "That doesn't explain this. What kid were you talking about who made these?" A possibility occurred to him and made him raise his eyebrows. "One of McKinney's boys?"

Collins nodded. "The younger one. Aaron. He was about seven, I guess, when McKinney disappeared. Twelve years old now."

"He's offering a reward for his own father's capture? Why would he do that?"

"You don't give up, do you? Haven't you heard enough about that poor woman's troubles?"

"You mean Mrs. McKinney again."

"Who else would I be talking about?" Collins leaned forward and his voice took on some heat as he said, "Her husband runs off and becomes an owlhoot, her older boy chases after him, and now her youngest is riding all over the countryside, tacking up wanted posters and stirring up more trouble—"

"Wait a minute, Sheriff," Luke broke in. "What's that you said about the older boy?"

"You're not going to be satisfied until you get the whole story, are you? I should've gone ahead and chased you north of the tracks and told you not to come back until I sent for you."

Luke had heard a note of admiration in the lawman's voice when he spoke of Amelia McKinney. Maybe it was more than admiration, Luke mused. Maybe Collins had some other feelings for Mrs. McKinney, feelings he couldn't do anything about while Three-fingered Jack was alive. Luke couldn't be sure, though, and it was none of his business anyway.

"I just figured you'd rather give me the straight story, rather than whatever gossip I could pick up around town, Sheriff. But I can think of only one reason somebody would offer a reward of a dollar forty-two and a harmonica. That's all the earthly riches the boy has to his name."

Collins grunted. "You'd be right about that. Mrs. McKinney has tried to keep the spread going since her husband vanished, but it hasn't been easy. She had to sell off their stock, bit by bit, just for the family to survive. They've scraped by doing that and raising a few crops, but I doubt if she's got two nickels to rub together. Now, with Thad gone, too . . . Well, damn it, it's just not right what that poor woman's had to go through."

"You said the older boy ran away?"

"Ran off to take up the owlhoot trail with his worthless pa. That's what he said he was going to do, anyway, when he got mad and left."

Luke understood why Collins felt sorry for Amelia

McKinney, whether there was any other reason for the sheriff's concern or not. It sounded as if the woman had indeed had more than her share of troubles.

"The older boy . . . Thad, you called him . . . he went to the Dakotas to try to find his father?"

Collins shook his head. "No, McKinney is back in these parts, and his gang is with him. Has been for about a year. They raided some settlements the other side of the hills and held up a couple of stagecoaches. Witnesses got good looks at McKinney. They haven't gone after the bank here or tried to hold up any of the trains, but I figure it's just a matter of time until they work their way this far south. When Thad heard about that, he got the idea that he wanted to be an owlhoot, too." Collins snorted. "I suppose he thought that would be better than the hard work around the spread. After he left was when his little brother started making those wanted posters and sticking them up."

"You don't think that's going to cause anyone to go after McKinney who wouldn't already be doing so, do you? That seems pretty unlikely."

"Maybe not, but Aaron doing it keeps people worried and stirred up anyway. Like I said, nobody wants to draw the gang's attention or get McKinney mad at them. He might decide to get even with them. But the worst of it is, McKinney might come after the boy himself. If anything happened to Aaron, I reckon that would be more than his ma could take. I don't think Amelia could stand it." Collins scraped his chair back and stood up. "There. You've wormed the whole blasted story out of me, and I don't know why you're interested unless you plan to go after McKinney yourself."

Luke looked at the actual wanted poster again. "There's a regular reward on him. Twenty-five hundred dollars. I'm sure there are rewards out for some of the other members of his gang, as well. A man would clear a good payoff if he brought them all in."

"What a man would do is get himself killed like the damn fool he'd have to be. One man, no matter how good he is, can't go up against fifteen or twenty bloody-handed outlaws and expect to survive."

"Those are pretty bad odds," Luke admitted. "Anyway, I haven't said that I'm going after anyone or anything, other than the reward money I've already earned. And now I really have to deal with those horses. Harwell's Livery Stable is the best place to take them, I believe you said?"

"That's right. Give me an hour or so to find those wanted posters and check out the bodies down at the undertaker's, and I'll fill out the claim forms so you can pick them up and take them to the bank later."

"I can save you some time," Luke said. He pulled out more folded reward dodgers, these from one of the hip pockets of his trousers. He unfolded them and handed them to Collins. "I knew you'd need them, so I got them out of my saddlebags before I left Summerville this morning."

"You were prepared."

"Like I said, I've done this before."

Collins grunted as he unfolded the wanted posters that bore the likenesses of Son Barton, Ed Logan, Jimmy McCaskill, and Deuce Roebuck. "Give me a while anyway. If I'm not here when you come back by,

I'll leave the forms with whatever deputy is on duty out front."

"Thank you, Sheriff." Luke left the courthouse and walked to the hitch rail where he had left the five horses.

Twenty minutes later, he had arranged for his own mount to spend the night in one of the comfortable-looking stalls in Fritz Harwell's livery barn, as well as selling the other four horses to Harwell for a decent price, along with their saddles and tack.

Their business concluded, Luke asked the stableman, "What's the best hotel in town, Mr. Harwell?"

"Why, that'd be the Rycroft House, I guess," Harwell replied as he scratched his head. "Just in the next block. But didn't the sheriff tell you to stay north of the tracks? He don't cotton to bounty hunters, and that's what he tells every stranger in town he don't like."

"The sheriff has misjudged me," Luke said with a smile. "Good day to you, Mr. Harwell."

"Yeah, uh, good day, I reckon."

Luke was whistling softly to himself as he left the livery stable. He had some things to think about while he waited on that reward money, and he intended to do that thinking—and waiting—in comfort.

He spotted the Rycroft House in the next block on the opposite side of the street, and his steps carried him toward the impressive, two-story hotel.

CHAPTER 5

"I'm not sure the sheriff is going to like this," the young, slick-haired hotel clerk said nervously as Luke signed his name in the registration book.

Luke replaced the pen in its holder.

"He shouldn't be upset with you. A business that caters to the public can't be expected to turn away customers for no good reason." He slid a ten-dollar gold piece across the counter. "I've paid in advance for a week's lodging, including meals in the dining room and a tub of hot water A simple transaction that harms no one."

"Well, I suppose you're right, Mr., uh, Jensen. You want that bath now?"

"Please," Luke said.

"I'll send a boy up with the tub right away and tell them in the kitchen to start heating water." The clerk handed Luke a key. "You'll be in room eight. Top of the stairs and around to the front. One of the nicest rooms in the house."

"I'm obliged to you."

Luke had his saddlebags over his left shoulder, his Winchester tucked under that arm, and his war bag in that hand as he went up the stairs. The hotel room looked comfortable—a nice four-poster bed, rugs on the floor, a couple of chairs, and a mahogany wardrobe. The curtains were pushed back and both windows were open to let in some air, as well as the noises of the main street they overlooked.

A gangling, redheaded teenager arrived mere moments after Luke did, toting a tin washtub. He set it down and said, "I'll fetch the hot water, mister."

Luke tossed him a coin and nodded in thanks.

"Make sure it's good and hot. I need to soak off a considerable amount of trail dust."

The boy grinned, nodded, and hurried out.

Luke was ready to leave the room an hour later. At first glance he didn't appear to be the same man. Soaked and shaved and brushed, he had traded his black trail clothes for a gray suit and a white shirt. A silk cravat around his neck was held in place by a pearl stickpin. Instead of buckling on the gunbelt with its holstered Remingtons and sheathed bowie knife, he had tucked a small, ivory-handled pocket pistol into a holster rigged under his coat beneath his left arm. A .41 caliber over-and-under two-shot derringer went into the coat pocket on the right side. A dagger made in Italy rested in a sheath sewed into the top of his right boot.

A gray beaver hat rested on Luke's head. He looked in the mirror, adjusted the hat to a slightly jauntier angle, and chuckled. He hardly ever put on this garb, and when he did, he was usually in San Francisco or Denver to take part in one of the high-stakes poker games to which he occasionally treated himself. He had never dressed like that in some hot, dusty prairie town, and he probably wouldn't have done it today if Sheriff Collins's attitude hadn't annoyed him.

The desk clerk perked right up when he saw Luke coming down the stairs. He said, "Sir, I"—he stopped short and frowned. "Why, you're . . . I mean . . ."

"That's right," Luke said. "Is there a good place in town where a gentleman can get a drink?"

"The, uh . . . I guess . . . the Plainsman Saloon is the best in town."

"And when is dinner here at the hotel?"

"The dining room starts serving at five."

Luke nodded and went out, leaving the clerk to stare after him in consternation.

It seemed to Luke that he had been walking back and forth across the street ever since he rode into town, and finding the Plainsman Saloon required more of the same. It was on the other side of the street from the hotel, a block and a half from the railroad depot. That was a good location for it to pick up trade from those waiting for a train, or disembarking from one.

The hour was just past midafternoon, so from then until dark, the Plainsman would steadily get busier. Luke pushed through the batwing doors at the entrance and saw that a dozen men were already in the place. Six stood at the bar, drinking, while four sat at a table playing poker. The remaining two men shared a table and a bottle.

Only one woman was in sight at the moment. She stood behind one of the poker players with her hand resting on his shoulder. Honey blond hair flowed around her face and over her shoulders. She wasn't dressed particularly provocatively, other than the fact that the light blue gown she wore was cut a mite too low for wearing to church. Nor was her face painted.

But her smile had a kick to it as she turned toward Luke, and her walk as she left the poker table and came toward him gave off an undeniable air of sensuousness that Luke noted . . . and appreciated.

"Welcome to the Plainsman," she greeted him. "I didn't think it was time for a train to pull in."

"I didn't get off a train," Luke told her as he smiled.

"Surely you didn't *ride* in."

"As a matter of fact, I did. A little more than an hour ago."

Her eyes, which were a slightly darker shade of blue than her gown, widened in surprise.

"You're the bounty hunter who brought all those bodies in!"

"That's right." Luke pinched the brim of the beaver hat. "Luke Jensen, at your service, ma'am."

She introduced herself automatically in return. "I'm Glenda Farrell."

"It's my pleasure, Miss Farrell. You work here?"

"It's Mrs. Farrell," she said, "and the truth is even more shocking. I own the place. I inherited it from my late husband."

"My condolences on the loss."

"I appreciate that, but it's not necessary. Gifford has been gone two years. I've long since stopped mourning him, and to tell you the truth, I wasn't all that broken up when he passed. We worked together quite well, but that doesn't mean our marriage succeeded as much as our business did."

Luke shrugged. "Sometimes that's enough."

"In our case it was." She looked him up and down. "I didn't get that good of a look at you earlier, Mr. Jensen, but I'll admit I stepped out onto the boardwalk to see what all the commotion was about when you rode into town earlier. I never would have taken you for the same man. Didn't our illustrious sheriff give you his usual speech about staying north of the tracks?"

"He did," Luke admitted, "and I have to say, I'm a bit curious about what attractions that area might hold."

Glenda laughed. "Nothing you can't get down here that's even better."

The poker player whose shoulder she had been resting her hand on threw in his cards just then and said, "Damn it, Glenda, you took my luck with you when you walked away."

She half turned toward the table. "I could have told you you weren't going to fill that straight, Clint. The odds were too high against it."

The man scowled. "That wasn't it and you know it You stole my luck."

He had a shock of black hair above an angular face. A black Stetson hung on his back by its chin strap. He was dressed in black trousers, black vest, and a red shirt. As he scraped his chair back and stood up, he went on. "You had to abandon me and run off to make eyes at this fancy dan."

Luke saw that Clint had a black gunbelt strapped around his waist. The wide belt sported some elaborate tooling, as did the holster attached to it. A pearl-handled, nickel-plated revolver rested in that holster.

"I'd suggest that you're not really one to be throwing

around terms like *fancy dan* in such a derogatory manner, my friend," Luke said.

Clint's lips twisted in a sneer. "Seems like he's in love with the sound of his own voice, too. Why don't you come on back over here, Glenda? I'll forgive you for ruinin' that hand for me. There's always another shuffle and deal."

"I don't think so," the blonde said coolly. "I was just about to offer Mr. Jensen a drink. On the house, since it's his first time in the Plainsman, of course."

"I appreciate that," Luke said. "And I accept the offer."

"Wait just a damn minute," Clint snapped. "You can't ignore a good customer like me who's been comin' in here for a long time just because some new fella wanders in off the street."

"I can ignore whatever and whoever I want," Glenda said. "This is my saloon, remember? Just settle down, Clint. It's not like you actually have any sort of claim on me, no matter what you might believe."

Clint's face flushed with anger.

Luke knew that he had been making people mad ever since he rode into town, but he wasn't responsible for anyone else's hot temper and he hadn't done anything to apologize for . . . so the thought of doing so never entered his mind. Instead he said to Glenda, "I hope you'll have a drink, too."

"You know, I believe I will," she replied with a smile. She linked her arm with his and turned them both toward the bar.

The sudden rush of footsteps behind them was plenty of warning for Luke. He disengaged from Glenda and whirled quickly, while Clint was still several feet away, rushing toward him. The man swung a clenched fist at Luke's head.

Luke leaned to the side, reached up, and grabbed Clint's arm. Pivoting smoothly, he heaved. Clint was off balance and couldn't stop himself as Luke's powerful muscles sent the poker player flying toward the bar. A couple of the drinkers who'd been standing there jumped out of the way.

Clint's belly struck the hardwood's edge with enough force to double him forward over the bar. He knocked over a half-full mug of beer someone had left there. The collision with the bar drove the breath out of his lungs. He gasped for air as he staggered back away from it.

"Damn . . . you!" he managed to say as he clawed at the pearl-handled revolver on his hip.

The derringer leaped into Luke's hand so fast it seemed like magic. He hoped Clint would see that he was beaten and stop that draw while he still had a chance.

Clint wasn't backing down, though. The fancy gun cleared leather and started to rise. Luke triggered the derringer's upper barrel.

The shot was louder than most folks would expect from such a small weapon. The .41 caliber slug ripped into Clint's right shoulder and drove him back against the bar. He cried out in pain as the pearl-handled gun slipped from his fingers. He sagged against the bar and clutched his shoulder with his other hand. Bright red blood welled between his fingers. His chest rose and fell heavily.

The hum of conversation in the saloon had come to a complete stop. Glenda, the bartender, and all the customers stared, their rapt gazes shuttling back and forth between Luke and Clint.

Luke kept the derringer trained on the wounded man and said in a loud, clear voice, "All of you will have noted that I gave him the chance not to push this to such an extreme. It was his choice, and he started his draw first. Even then, he could have stopped short of gunplay, because I didn't fire until his gun was out of the holster. I'd appreciate it if each of you would remember those things when you talk to the sheriff about this incident . . . which I'm sure you will."

"If you mean you want us to say that it was Clint's own fault he got shot, I don't think any of us are going to deny that, Mr. Jensen," Glenda said. "You're right. We all saw what happened."

Several of the customers nodded, as did the bartender.

"You . . . you shot me!" Clint grated through clenched teeth.

"But I didn't kill you, which I would have been well within my rights to do," Luke pointed out. "I believe you'll live."

"My arm may never be the same again!"

"That's the risk you run when you go around picking fights with men you don't know."

"I'll kill you—"

"Nobody's killing anybody!" Sheriff Collins bellowed as he slapped the batwings aside with his left hand and strode into the saloon with a shotgun in his right.

Luke could tell that the lawman had hurried up the street to the Plainsman because he was breathing hard. The town was so civilized these days, he probably didn't hear many gunshots.

The sheriff used both hands to steady the Greener as he continued. "What the hell is going on here? You there, in the fancy suit, put that derringer—Wait a minute. *Jensen?*"

"That's right, Sheriff." Luke set the derringer on an empty table beside him. "I fired one shot in self-defense—"

"Shut up," Collins snarled as he leveled the shotgun at Luke. "You're under arrest!"

CHAPTER 6

"What!" Glenda exclaimed. "Sheriff, have you lost your mind? Mr. Jensen didn't do anything wrong."

"He's south of the line, after I gave him orders not to be unless he had a good reason."

Luke said, "I consider a comfortable hotel room, a hot bath, a drink amid pleasant company, and some decent food to all be good reasons, Sheriff."

"I don't care if you got cleaned up, you're still a bounty hunter, and they bring trouble! That's why I'm holding you responsible for this."

"That's right, Sheriff," Clint put in. "He's a mad dog! He shot me without any warnin'!"

One of the men who'd been drinking at the bar, who had the look of a tough old cattleman, said, "That's a damned lie, Clint Norman, and everybody in here knows it." He faced the sheriff. "Norman started acting like a jackass when he lost a poker hand. Blamed it on Glenda because she'd been standin' beside him but went over to talk to this other fella when he came in. This fella—Jensen, you say his name is?—tried to talk sense to him, but Norman wasn't havin' any of it. He reached for his iron first. Jensen beat him to the draw six ways from Sunday. If Norman had had any sense, he would have let his gun drop back in its holster and saved himself some pain. But he forced Jensen's hand." The rancher snorted in disgust. "If you ask me, Norman's a mighty lucky hombre. Jensen could've put that bullet in his brain just as easy."

"That's the way it was, Sheriff," Glenda said.

Collins glared furiously, but he slowly lowered the shotgun. He looked over at Clint Norman, who was still holding his bleeding shoulder. "How bad are you hurt?"

"I don't know, but I need a doc!"

"You'll get one."

Glenda asked the sheriff, "Are you arresting him for starting the trouble?"

"You let me worry about who I arrest and who I don't," Collins snapped. "Kick that gun over here and then come with me, Norman."

Sullenly, Clint complied with the order. Collins picked up the pearl-handled revolver, then used the shotgun to motion him toward the saloon's entrance. Before leaving, the sheriff pointed a finger at Luke and said, "I want you north of the tracks, pronto."

"Sorry, Sheriff. I've already paid for a room at the Rycroft House, and I intend to use it tonight." Luke smiled. "I'm told that the food in the dining room is quite good."

Collins fumed, but he didn't say anything else, and marched Clint toward the doors.

Just before he pushed through the batwings, the wounded man glanced back at the bar and called,

"I'm gonna remember that big mouth of yours, Stanton." Then he bulled out and the sheriff followed him.

Luke turned to the white-haired cattleman. "I'm sorry if this altercation causes any trouble for you."

Stanton snorted again. "I've been threatened by a lot worse than that cheap gunman. When I settled out here, there was nothing for miles around but hostile Indians, Mexican bandits, and bushwhackin' renegades. No-accounts like Clint Norman don't worry me." He stuck out a big, work-roughened hand. "Ben Stanton."

"Luke Jensen." He shook hands with the rancher.

Stanton introduced him to several more of the men, all of whom had cattle spreads in the area.

"You gentlemen don't seem to have any qualms about associating with a bounty hunter," Luke commented.

"That's because we're all still a mite rough around the edges ourselves," one of the men said with a grin. "Civilization keeps trying to smooth 'em out, but I'm not sure it ever will."

"I hope it don't," another man added, bringing a round of laughter.

"Have a drink with us," Stanton suggested to Luke.

"I'd love to, but I was about to have one with Mrs. Farrell, and I should honor that commitment first."

"I don't reckon any man here will hold it against you if you do, amigo."

Glenda turned to the bartender, who seemed to know what to do. He brought a bottle and two glasses from under the bar and handed them to her. She led Luke to a fairly large table in the back of the room, where they sat down in well-upholstered chairs.

"I take it this is where you regularly hold court," he said as he took off his hat and placed it on the table.

"I'm not sure I'd call it that, but it's my personal table." She poured the drinks. "I hope you like cognac. You strike me as the sort of man who would."

"I do, indeed." They clinked their glasses together, and he added, "To a visit more pleasant than it's been so far."

They drank, and Luke licked his lips in appreciation of the smooth but fiery liquor.

Glenda said, "I hope you don't judge us too harshly. This is actually a pretty nice place to live . . . most of the time. It's just that Clint Norman is . . . headstrong."

"Reckless and arrogant and hot-tempered, you mean."

She shrugged.

"Thinks of himself as slick on the draw," Luke went on. "Any man who'd walk around with a gaudy gun rig like that would have to. Does he have any justification for feeling that way?"

"He's killed two men in gunfights," Glenda said. "They both drew first. So I suppose he has some speed and skill, if you want to call it that."

"He has saloon speed. I'm guessing that in both of those fights, the other men had been drinking?"

"That's what I've heard," Glenda said. "They were north of the line, so I wasn't there to know for sure."

Luke raised an eyebrow. "So Sheriff Collins lets Norman go back and forth across the line with impunity?"

"His uncle owns a large ranch west of here. That spread and the men who work there are important to the town."

Luke nodded and said, "I thought it might be something like that."

Glenda refilled the glasses. "Don't get the wrong idea about the sheriff. He can be opinionated and inflexible, but he does a good job of keeping the peace. Giff and I weren't here when the town was still the railhead, but from what I've heard, it was wide open and a dangerous place to live in those days. It's a lot better now, and Collins deserves most of the credit for that."

"I'll bear that in mind," Luke said. "Anyway, I don't intend to be here for long. I'll probably be riding out tomorrow or the next day, depending on how quickly that reward money comes through."

"And that's the only reason you'd have to stick around?"

Luke smiled at her over the rim of the glass. "Well . . . perhaps not the *only* reason."

Luke called a halt to the drinking after the second brandy, promised Glenda he would stop back by the Plainsman later in the evening, and went to the Rycroft House for dinner. A plump, pretty waitress took his order for roast beef with all the fixings and delivered a tray of food that smelled and tasted delicious. The coffee he used to wash it down was good, too.

As he ate, Luke was aware that some of the other guests in the dining room were casting careful glances at him. He knew that word had gotten around. Not only was he the bounty hunter who had brought in the bodies of four dead outlaws earlier in the day, he had also been mixed up in a shooting scrape since then. They weren't used to having the likes of him around these days. But they would just have to put up with his presence until he was ready to ride out.

Ben Stanton walked into the dining room, hat in hand, and looked around. He met Luke's eyes and then walked toward the table.

"Mind if I join you?" he asked as he rested his free hand on the back of the empty chair on the other side.

"Please do. The food is excellent, but I was just thinking I might want to linger over another cup of coffee and let it settle for a bit. I wouldn't mind some company while I'm doing that." Luke smiled. "Good conversation always improves the digestion."

Stanton dropped his hat on the table and sat down. The waitress was there immediately. He told her, "I'll have the roast beef, too, with all the fixin's." When she left he said to Luke, "I met your brother once."

"Is that so?"

"Yeah. Back in Kansas City. We were both selling some cattle. Big Ben Conyers from down Texas way was there, too. Smoke's one hell of an hombre."

"I can't argue with that."

Stanton clasped his hands together on the table and leaned forward. "I just heard that Collins didn't arrest Clint Norman. Just got him patched up at the doc's and told him to get out of town and not come back for a few days. He's trying to give you time to get gone so if Norman does try to get even with you, it won't be in the sheriff's bailiwick."

"You think Norman will do that?"

"I think Clint Norman is a craven cur who wouldn't be above backshooting a man," Stanton said bluntly.

"So you'd best have eyes in the back of your head, Jensen." He grunted. "Of course, I imagine you do, being in your line of work."

"A habit of being careful is one reason I've lived as long as I have."

"I just thought I'd say something, and I remembered you telling the sheriff you intended to eat supper over here."

"I'm glad you did. Maybe I can ask you something."

Stanton shrugged burly shoulders. "Go ahead. Don't guarantee I'll know the answer."

"Did you know Jack McKinney?"

"Three-fingered Jack?" The cattleman looked and sounded surprised. "Matter of fact, I did know him. Sold him some stock at a good price to help him get his herd started when he and his wife and young'uns came out here."

"Did he strike you as the sort of man who would turn owlhoot with no warning?"

Stanton shook his head. "I couldn't hardly believe it when we heard about that gang he was leading up in the Dakotas. Like a lot of people around here, when he first disappeared I figured something bad had happened to him. I was right worried, in fact. Then, when it looked like he rode off and *wanted* to drop out of sight, I was puzzled, sure enough. But I still never would've dreamed that he'd turn lobo like that." He frowned across the table at Luke. "Why are you interested in Jack McKinney?"

Luke smiled and said, "I got hold of one of those wanted posters his son Aaron made up."

"That boy! You can't really blame him for being mad that his father abandoned the family, but to put up a bounty on your own pa . . . I know it doesn't amount to much . . ."

"A dollar and forty-two cents," Luke said, "and a harmonica."

Stanton laughed. "Yeah. Loco, ain't it? But it's kind of the principle of the thing, I guess. Those two boys, they sure wound up goin' in opposite directions. Thad took off to try to find his pa and join the gang, and Aaron wants 'em all brought in, dead or alive." He paused. "Say, are you thinking about going after Three-fingered Jack?"

"I haven't made up my mind," Luke said, "but I'll admit, the situation interests me. What about Mrs. McKinney? How's she handling things?"

"As well as she can, which is to say, not all that good. It's been hard on her. Some of the other ranchers and I have tried to lend her a hand now and then, you know, without hurting her pride too much, but it's not easy."

"I got the feeling your sheriff is interested in her."

"Ross Collins?" Stanton blew out a disgusted breath. "He may have some crazy notions in his head, but he'd better not hold his breath waiting for Amelia McKinney to return any feelings he has for her. That ain't gonna happen, and if Collins had a lick of sense in his head, he'd know it. Anyway, Miz McKinney's still got a husband. Of course . . . if a bounty hunter was to bring in Three-fingered Jack, say . . . and the wanted posters, the real ones, all say dead or alive . . ."

"If I were to go after McKinney, you've just given me a very good reason to bring him in alive, Mr. Stanton. I don't believe I'd want to do anything to make it easier for Sheriff Collins to start courting that poor woman."

Stanton guffawed at that, then dug in on the plate of food the waitress set in front of him. She filled his coffee cup and refilled Luke's.

Luke lingered as he'd said he would, enjoying the next half hour as he listened to Ben Stanton spin yarns about the early pioneer days in Arizona Territory. It had been a bloody, dangerous time, and the settlers who had come through it were tough as leather, men and women alike.

Luke finally said his good-nights.

"Going back up to the Plainsman to have another drink with Glenda Farrell?" Stanton asked.

"I promised her I would. But first I intend to stop by the sheriff's office and pick up some papers he promised to have ready for me."

"Collins will have gone home by now."

"That's one reason I had supper first," Luke said. "I don't think the sheriff is that anxious to see me again, and the feeling is mutual."

He left the hotel and stepped out into the darkness of early evening. Most of the day's heat still hung over the town, but a breeze was beginning to break it up. Far out on the plains, lightning flickered. Probably just heat lightning and nothing would come of it, Luke thought, but it was always possible that a storm really was building out there.

The courthouse windows were dark except for the corner where the sheriff's office and jail were located. Luke paused at the edge of the street under the cottonwoods before starting across the lawn toward the large stone building. He slipped a cheroot from his coat pocket and put it in his mouth, then took out a match as well and held it in his left hand as he stretched his arm as far as it would reach. His iron-hard thumbnail flicked the match to life.

Colt flame bloomed redly in the shadows as a shot roared.

CHAPTER 7

Luke heard the wind-rip of the slug as it passed through the air a couple of feet away from him. The man who'd fired the shot had aimed it at the match flare, just as Luke intended. He hadn't been absolutely certain someone was stalking him, but his instincts told him that was the case.

As he dropped the match, he palmed out the little pistol from the shoulder holster. It spat fire and lead as he triggered twice, using the muzzle flash he had seen as a target. Someone grunted, then footsteps slapped rapidly against the ground. The bushwhacker was running.

Luke went after him. He caught flickering glimpses of movement in the shadows but nothing plain enough to shoot at. He was confident he had hit the man who'd ambushed him, but evidently the wound wasn't bad enough to slow him down much.

Somewhere ahead of him, a horse blew out a startled breath. Then hoofbeats pounded. Luke slowed and then stopped as the swift rataplan diminished in the night. The bushwhacker had had a horse ready and waiting and had made it into the saddle before Luke could catch him. Now there was no chance of that.

It didn't really matter, he told himself. He already had a very good idea who had just tried to kill him.

He replaced the pistol in the shoulder holster and walked back toward the courthouse. He chewed on the cheroot but left it unlit. A yellow blob of light suddenly bobbed in front of him and quickly resolved itself into the glow from a lantern.

As the light reached Luke, the man holding the lantern stopped short and called, "Hold it right there, mister! I'll shoot!"

Luke took the cigar out of his mouth and said, "I'd rather you didn't." He kept his hands in plain sight. "I'm not looking for any trouble."

As the man with the lantern came closer, Luke could see him well enough to recognize him as the chunky deputy who had been with Sheriff Collins earlier in the day. Tom, that was his name, Luke recalled.

"It's Luke Jensen, Tom. You're exactly the man I was looking for."

"I am?" The deputy had the lantern in his left hand and a Colt in his right, but he kept the gun pointed at the ground in front of him. "What for?"

"The sheriff said he was going to leave those reward claim forms with whoever was on duty when he left for the day. That would be you, correct?"

"Uh, yeah, and I know he put some papers on the desk he said to give you if you came by." A frown creased the deputy's forehead. "But what was all that shootin' a minute ago?"

"Somebody took a potshot at me, and I returned fire."

"Are you hit?"

"No, he missed."

"What about the other fella?"

"Bring that lantern on over here," Luke suggested, "and maybe we can find out." He led Tom to a spot about where he thought the bushwhacker had been lurking underneath one of the cottonwoods, and sure enough, as the lantern light washed over the ground, Luke pointed out a splash of fresh blood. "I hit him, but he was moving pretty fast when he ran away from me. He had a horse waiting for him and galloped off before I could do anything else about it."

"Did you get a look at him?"

"I never did," Luke said, "but you and I both know it had to be Clint Norman."

Tom frowned again and shook his head. "You shouldn't go around accusin' folks if you didn't actually see 'em."

"No one else in this town has any reason to want me dead," Luke pointed out.

"Maybe not, but you still couldn't testify in a court of law that it was him who took that shot at you."

"I suppose not. But a diligent sheriff would take a ride out to Norman's uncle's ranch tomorrow and demand to see him. It should be pretty easy to tell whether he has a fresh wound in addition to the one in his shoulder that I gave him in the Plainsman this afternoon."

"If you think I'm gonna tell the sheriff how to do his job, you're loco, mister. He don't take kindly to that."

Luke shrugged. "No, I don't imagine he would. But bear in mind what I told you anyway, Deputy."

A few men came closer on the street and hailed them. "Hey, what's goin' on down there?"

"Nothin'," Tom called back. "Just go on about your business."

"I suppose we should go get those papers," Luke said.

"Yeah, I guess," the deputy agreed grudgingly. He and Luke walked into the courthouse.

Luke looked over the four claim forms on which Sheriff Collins had stipulated that the bodies Luke brought in had been positively identified as those of Son Barton, Jimmy McCaskill, Deuce Roebuck, and Ed Logan. As soon as the bank had sent wires to the territorial capital to confirm the rewards, Luke would get his money and he could move on.

He had a pretty good idea about where he would go next.

"I heard a rumor that you were mixed up in that shooting earlier," Glenda Farrell said as she and Luke sat at her table in the Plainsman.

The saloon was crowded with men lining the bar and several poker games going on. Short-skirted serving girls moved among the customers, laughing, flirting, and delivering drinks. None of them took men upstairs, though, Luke noted, so evidently the Plainsman didn't conduct that sort of business. He was sure establishments that did could be found on the other side of the railroad tracks.

"Someone took a shot at me while I was down by the

courthouse," he said. "Luckily, I was halfway expecting an attempt on my life and was being careful. You might even say I was trying to draw out whoever it was."

"Humph. We both know who it was. Clint Norman's pride was hurt worse than his shoulder was."

"But he *was* wounded," Luke pointed out. "I doubt if he could have used a gun with his right hand."

"I've seen him shoot left-handed, showing off. He's not as good with that hand, but good enough to try to ambush somebody."

"I'll take that as more proof," Luke said, "not that I needed convincing."

"Ross Collins should have arrested him after what he did. The only reason he didn't is because he's afraid of old Buck Norman."

"An elected position such as sheriff attracts politicians, and politicians always know who has the most power and influence. It's like the old story about the nature of the scorpion. You can't blame Collins for being what he is."

Glenda shrugged. "I suppose not. You weren't hurt when Clint ambushed you?"

"Not a bit."

"What about him? I know you must have shot back at him."

"There were signs that I hit him. Not badly enough to keep him from getting away, but he lost some more blood."

"If he dies, his uncle Buck is going to be looking for you," Glenda said with a worried frown.

"I'll deal with that when and if it happens."

"Why don't we talk about something more

pleasant, like what you intend to do with the rest of your evening?"

"I thought I'd spend it here with you, if that's agreeable."

That put a smile on her face. "I think that's more than agreeable, and by the time the evening is over, I'll bet you will, too."

Luke was dressed in his trail clothes again when he picked up his horse at Fritz Harwell's stable, late the next morning.

"Leavin' town, Mr. Jensen?" Harwell asked as Luke finished cinching up his saddle.

"That's right. My business here is done. Your bank operates very efficiently. It took only a couple of hours to conclude my affairs." By that he meant that he had collected the reward money for the four outlaws.

Harwell had to be able to figure that out. The stableman nodded. "I know that some folks won't be sorry to see you go, but I just want to say I got nothin' against you. You were a good customer, and it was a pleasure doin' business with you."

"I appreciate that, Mr. Harwell." Luke shook hands with the man, then swung up into the saddle. He ticked a finger against his hat brim and rode out of the livery barn.

He could have stayed and had lunch in the hotel dining room. If his supper the night before and breakfast that morning were any indication, the meal would have been very good.

He could have stopped by the Plainsman and said good-bye to Glenda Farrell, too, but their farewell the previous evening had been quite satisfactory for both of them, Luke believed, and sometimes it was best to leave well enough alone. He heeled his mount into a trot that carried them up the street at a good pace.

Along the way, he passed Sheriff Ross Collins, who was standing on the boardwalk in front of a general store. He glared as Luke rode past. Luke thought about tipping his hat to the man, but again, decided to leave well enough alone.

He circled the depot and walked his horse across the railroad tracks. It was the first time he had seen the part of town where Collins had wanted to banish him. It didn't look that bad. The buildings were a little more run down, most of the people on the streets were not quite as well dressed, and there were a lot more saloons, at least half a dozen that Luke saw. He had been in a lot more disreputable-looking places, though.

The main street turned into a trail that led almost due north toward a range of low, rugged peaks several people had mentioned. To his left was a green line that marked the course of the river that watered the broad, shallow valley and made it possible for ranches and farms to exist in the area. Farther west, everything dried up and the terrain flattened out into a desert that stretched for forty or fifty miles, broken up by badlands that less than ten years earlier had been strongholds and hiding places for Apaches who refused to go to the reservations in the southeastern part of the territory.

Gradually, those renegades had been either defeated by the army or driven into submission by hunger and other hardships. Most people believed the days of the Indian Wars were over. Luke wasn't so sure about that. There were still places deep in the wilderness where the holdouts against civilization could take refuge and wait for the right time to strike against the white invaders once more.

He rode for a couple of hours, gnawing on some jerky from his saddlebags to make up in part for the meal he had missed by riding out when he did. The trail angled to the west, closer to the river. Luke hadn't asked for directions to the McKinney place, but he figured it couldn't be too far from the stream since Sheriff Collins had said that Jack McKinney and his family raised crops as well as horses and cattle. Creeks trickled across his path here and there, feeding into the river, and when the hills loomed close in front of him, he followed one of them on a hunch.

The bottomland along the creek looked like it could be cultivated, and enough grass grew on the rolling terrain nearby to support a limited amount of livestock. It was far from the best country Luke had ever seen, but with enough hard work, a man could make something of it.

A man . . . and his family.

On the other hand, maybe it was the prospect of that never-ending hard work that had driven Jack McKinney to ride off and disappear and eventually turn outlaw, Luke mused as he rode along the creek's south bank. No matter what McKinney might do, his spread would only ever be so good and no better. If he knew anything at all about what he was doing, he would be aware of that, and the knowledge could have been too much for him to accept.

Those thoughts were running through Luke's head as he approached a cluster of boulders surrounded by some scrubby mesquite trees. He looked them over, purely out of cautious habit, and suddenly pulled rein as he spotted a glint of sunlight from metal among the rocks.

The next instant, a rifle cracked and a bullet kicked up dirt and pebbles twenty feet in front of him.

As the shot's echoes died away, a voice called, "That's far enough, mister! Come any closer and the next one won't miss!"

CHAPTER 8

Holding the reins in his left hand, Luke raised both hands to shoulder level and replied, "Hold your fire, son. I mean you no harm." He could tell that the voice belonged to a boy and had a powerful hunch that boy was Aaron McKinney. He didn't say as much just yet, though, preferring to let the youngster proceed at his own pace. If Aaron felt like he was in control of the situation, he'd be less likely to start throwing lead around wildly.

"You'd better be more worried about me intendin' harm to you," the boy said from his hiding place in the rocks. Luke could tell that he was working hard to put plenty of bravado in the words, but the faint tremor in his voice told a different story. "You're trespassin'."

"That wasn't my intention, I assure you."

"You talk like a schoolmarm!"

Luke laughed. "I've been called a lot of things, but I don't believe a schoolmarm was ever one of them. Is it all right if I lower my arms? I give you my word that I'm not looking for trouble."

"Well . . . all right, I reckon. But don't you try

nothin'. I can shoot the eye out of a Gila monster at a hundred yards!"

"I believe you," Luke said as he brought his arms down and rested both hands on the saddle horn. "My name is Luke Jensen. Why don't you come out where we can see each other and you can introduce yourself, man to man?"

For a moment, there was no response to that, but then brush rustled a little and mesquite beans rattled as the boy pushed through the growth around the boulders and stepped out into the open. The somewhat ragged brim of an old felt hat shaded lean, freckled features. Rust-colored hair stuck out from under the hat. If this was indeed Aaron McKinney, Sheriff Collins had said he was twelve years old. Luke judged the youngster to be a little tall for that age, and on the gangly side, to boot. He wore boots, canvas trousers with crossed suspenders, and a homespun shirt of faded red. All the clothes looked slightly too big for him, which made Luke think they probably were hand-me-downs from that older brother. The ease with which the boy held an old Henry rifle told Luke he was accustomed to handling the weapon.

It was still aimed in Luke's general direction, so he said, "I'd be obliged if you'd point that somewhere else, son."

"Ain't your son," the boy snapped, but the Henry's muzzle sank toward the ground. Not so much that he couldn't raise it again in a hurry, though.

"What's your name?" Luke asked.

"Aaron," the boy said, confirming Luke's hunch. "Aaron McKinney. You said your name's Jensen?"

"That's right."

"I don't know any Jensens, and I don't reckon you got any business on my spread."

"This range is yours, is it?"

"Mine and my ma's. You feel like arguin' about it?"

Luke had to laugh again. "You really do have a burr under your saddle, don't you, Aaron? Look, I think we got off on the wrong foot here. I'm just passing through. I'm not a rustler or a road agent or anything like that." He patted his horse's neck. "I think my friend here could use a drink, though, if your place is close by."

"There's the creek," Aaron said with a nod toward the stream. "Nobody stoppin' you from usin' it."

"And I certainly wouldn't turn down a cup of coffee," Luke went on.

"You just invite yourself to have coffee with folks?"

"I can pay."

Luke saw the temptation in the youngster's eyes. If everything he had heard was true, Aaron and his mother were just about broke. Even a little bit of money could be important to them.

To reinforce the offer, Luke reached slowly into his shirt pocket and took out a silver dollar. The coin flashed in the sunlight. "What do you say, son?"

Aaron scowled. "I done told you, I ain't— No, never mind. Put your money away, mister. My ma raised me right, and that includes bein' hospitable. Our place ain't far from here, and I reckon you'd be welcome to sit and rest a spell. Ma will have a pot of coffee on the stove, too." The Henry's barrel came up a little. "But if you try anything funny, I'll blow you right to hell, and don't think I won't."

"Nothing funny," Luke promised. "I give you my word."

"Wait there a minute, then." Aaron went back into the rocks and emerged again a moment later leading a rangy mule that had plenty of years on him. The boy stepped up onto a boulder and from there climbed onto the mule's back. He held the reins in his left hand and carried the rifle in his right. "Come on," he said to Luke as he turned the mule to follow the creek.

They rode for about half a mile along the stream's winding course. The farther west they went toward the river, the more trees and grass grew along the banks. Luke saw about a dozen rather scrawny cows grazing along the way and asked, "Your stock?"

"That's right," Aaron said. "They may not look like much, but they're ours. See? They've got the MC brand on 'em."

Luke couldn't help but wonder if those dozen head were the entire MC herd these days.

They rounded a bend in the creek and Luke saw a log and stone cabin built near the base of a hogback ridge with stunted pines growing atop it. To the right of the cabin and even closer to the ridge was a barn with a pole corral next to it and beyond that a garden patch. Across the creek was a field that appeared to have been cultivated at one time but was lying fallow. An orchard of fruit trees stretched along the creek beyond the field. The trees were clinging to life but didn't look healthy to Luke's eyes, although he was far from an expert on such matters.

As the two riders came closer, a woman stepped out of the cabin onto a porch that sagged a little from disrepair. Her hair was red, too, although a darker shade than the rusty thatch on Aaron's head. She had a square-shouldered determination about her that Luke could see even from a distance. The shotgun she held reinforced that impression.

"That's your mother?" Luke asked the boy.

"Yeah, and you see that scattergun she's got? She knows how to use it."

"I never doubted that," Luke murmured.

The two of them drew rein in front of the cabin as the woman asked, "Who's this?"

"Says his name's Jensen," Aaron replied. "Just a saddle tramp passin' through, or so he claims." The boy paused. "But he's got at least a dollar, and he says he'll pay for a cup of coffee. I told him he didn't have to."

"Good. This is a ranch, not a café. Western folks don't put a price on hospitality." The woman's jaw was square, like her shoulders, and her face seemed permanently set in stern lines. It softened a little, though, as she looked at Luke, nodded, and went on. "Welcome to our home, Mr. Jensen. Get down from that horse and come inside out of the sun for a spell."

Luke swung down from the saddle and twisted his reins around a hitching post.

"I'm obliged to you, Mrs. McKinney, and like I told your son, I really don't mind paying—"

"I wouldn't hear of it," Amelia McKinney interrupted him.

"Well, in that case, maybe I could split some firewood for you. Or if you'd like, I could try my hand at shoring up that porch. I'm not really a carpenter, but I've done a little work along those lines, here and there."

"Now, we might could talk about that. But after you've had that coffee. Come in, please."

Luke stepped up onto the porch, took his hat off, and smiled.

Amelia McKinney said, "Aaron, did you check on those cows?"

"I was doin' that when I heard Mr. Jensen ridin' along the creek," the boy said. "They're right where they're supposed to be, Ma."

"That's good. We can't afford to have them wandering off."

She ushered Luke into the cabin. The walls were thick enough to make the air pleasantly cool inside. The trees on the ridge provided some welcome shade, as well.

The curtains on the windows were faded, as if they hadn't been replaced in quite a while. The furniture was still sturdy. It looked like a fairly comfortable place to live, although it was far from luxurious. On the other hand, Luke mused, anybody who settled in such an isolated part of Arizona Territory probably wasn't all that interested in luxury to start with.

Amelia nodded toward the table with a blue-and-white-checked cloth on it. "Have a seat, Mr. Jensen, while I get that coffee for you."

Having already taken his hat off as soon as he stepped inside, Luke placed it on the table and sat on a ladderback chair. Taking a tin cup from a shelf, she filled it with coffee from the pot on the big cast-iron stove. She set it on the table in front of Luke.

He said, "You'll join me, I hope?"

"Well . . . there's always more work to get done around here than there are hours in the day to do it . . . but I suppose a few minutes wouldn't hurt anything." She poured a cup for herself and sat down at the far end of the table.

Aaron stood in the doorway and leaned his shoulder against the jamb. "Pa ought to be gettin' back any time now, shouldn't he, Ma?"

"Yes. Yes, that's right." She smiled at Luke. "My husband should be riding in soon, Mr. Jensen. I hope he gets back in time for you to meet him, but I understand if you'll need to be moving on."

"I hope so, too," Luke said as he returned the smile. He understood why the two of them had lied about the possibility of Jack McKinney showing up.

They didn't want to admit that they were out in the middle of nowhere with no grown man around and none likely to be there any time soon. While it was well known that most Westerners, even the most hardened outlaws, wouldn't harm a respectable woman, especially one who was married, that didn't extend to every drifter who came along. Some of them could be dangerous.

"What are you growing over there in the orchard across the creek?" he asked. "It's been a while since I've seen fruit trees."

Amelia brightened a little at the question. "We have apple trees and peach trees. Keeping them alive has been a challenge, I'll admit, but I think we're going to have a good crop this year."

"I hope so. Nothing much better than fresh apples and peaches."

"We didn't get the corn and beans and potatoes in, but from what I've heard, it doesn't hurt anything to let fields rest for a spell. We'll have a good harvest next year, and until then, we have our cattle."

Luke had seen those cattle and knew they weren't going to amount to much, but he didn't say that. All he had to do, though, was look around the spread to know that Amelia and her son were fighting a losing battle, especially with just the two of them to keep the place going.

If he went after Jack McKinney, it wouldn't do a damned thing to help them. He wasn't sure why that idea had been in the back of his head ever since he'd seen that homemade wanted poster. Nor could he have said what drove him to ride out and find McKinney's family, other than sheer curiosity. Why would a seemingly happy man suddenly disappear and then turn outlaw? True, keeping the spread going would be a hard row to hoe, but McKinney had had an attractive, seemingly pleasant wife and a couple of strapping sons. Luke could only assume that the older boy was like Aaron. As a man who had lived life on the drift as a bounty hunter for the better part of two decades, Luke knew that he never could have settled down to such an existence, but most men would have welcomed a life like that, even if a lot of hard work came with it.

One thing he knew: Aaron ought to be helping his mother, instead of making wanted posters that served no real purpose and riding all over the countryside tacking them up.

"Aaron, you should go out to the barn and check on Fanny," Amelia said. "I think she's just about ready to calve. We're liable to have a busy evening."

Aaron frowned at Luke. "I don't know, Ma, I think I ought to stay here—"

"No, you go on and make sure she's comfortable. Mr. Jensen and I will be fine."

Clearly, Aaron didn't like it, but he picked up the rifle he had leaned against the wall and turned to leave.

"I might be able to give you a hand with that birthing, too," Luke offered. "I've brought a few calves into the world, although I admit, it was back on my family's farm in the Ozarks, before the war."

"Were you in the war, Mr. Jensen?"

"I was," Luke said. "It's not something I speak of often, though."

"I understand. Neither did my father and my uncles. My husband was too young to have served."

"He didn't miss much except a lot of hard times, on both sides."

"I hope something like that never happens again."

"I couldn't agree more, ma'am." Luke took another sip of coffee. "This is very good."

She smiled again. The expression transformed her face even more than he had realized earlier.

"Thank you. I'd ask you to stay for supper, but we're a bit low on supplies at the moment . . ."

He held up a hand to stop her.

"Don't think a thing about it. A man like me, it's mighty nice just to be able to sit for a spell at a table with a cloth on it and talk with a lady."

"I'm glad you stopped by—" Amelia fell silent as a heavy footstep sounded on the rickety porch. She looked at the open door and resumed, "Aaron, you're back from the barn already—"

The stocky figure that loomed in the doorway didn't belong to Aaron McKinney. Sheriff Ross Collins stood there pointing a Colt at Luke. "Jensen, what the hell are you doing here, you bastard?"

Amelia started to her feet, saying, "Sheriff, for heaven's sake, you don't need to—"

"Miz McKinney, don't you know what this man is?" Collins interrupted her again. "He's a no-good bounty hunter after the blood money he can get for killing your husband!"

CHAPTER 9

"You don't need that gun, Sheriff," Luke said into the stunned silence that followed Collins's words. "I don't have any intention of causing trouble for Mrs. McKinney."

"No?" Collins snapped. "What do you think coming in here and lying about who you are is going to do?"

"I didn't lie." Luke sipped from the cup and then set it on the table. "I told her my name is Luke Jensen, and that's the truth."

Amelia found her voice again. "You didn't say anything about being a bounty hunter."

"You didn't ask me about my job. I suppose you might consider it a lie of omission, but even that is stretching the matter, in my opinion." Luke looked at the lawman and added, "What are *you* doing here, Sheriff?"

Collins flushed even more. "I like to check on the folks in my county. That's part of my job. Thought I'd ride out here and see how Miz McKinney and the boy are getting along. You put me in mind of 'em with that damn wanted poster you waved in my face yesterday."

"Wanted poster?" Amelia repeated, clearly surprised again. "Sheriff, has Aaron been up to that again? I've talked to him about not wasting his time doing such things."

Collins looked uncomfortable. "I don't know if he's still at it or not. He put up enough of the things, and they're still circulating around the county . . ."

"Sheriff," Luke said again, "please put that gun away. You're going to frighten the lady."

Amelia looked at him. "It's going to take more than the sight of a gun to frighten me, Mr. Jensen."

Luke inclined his head in acknowledgment of her point. He'd been able to tell right away that she wasn't the sort of woman who spooked easily. Despite that, he didn't cotton to the idea of the sheriff—or anybody else—waving a gun in his direction.

Luckily, Collins didn't aggravate the situation. He jammed the Colt back in the holster on his hip and said, "I still want to know what you're up to, Jensen."

"Yes, I'd like to know that, too, considering I shared our coffee with you," Amelia said. "Are you going to hunt down my husband? Is that why you came out here? To see if you could get a lead on where he might be? If you did, you're wasting your time. I haven't laid eyes on Jack in five years!" A little muscle twitched in her jaw as she added, "And it'll be all right with me if I never do again."

"You don't want him found?"

She shook her head. "I don't care one way or the other."

Luke nodded slowly. "I didn't come here thinking I would find your husband. If anything I was just trying to understand him, to get an idea of how his mind works. Admittedly, that might help me track him down, but really I was just satisfying my curiosity."

"Trying to see why he ran off? To find out if I'm such a horrible woman that he just couldn't stand to be around me anymore?"

"Miz McKinney, don't say that," Collins said. "Nobody ever thought you were to blame for Jack leaving, or for what he did later. That was all his responsibility, not yours."

As if she hadn't heard the sheriff, the woman looked across the table at Luke and said, "I've asked myself those same questions, Mr. Jensen. Over and over again, in fact, on more dark nights than I can count. But I have no answers. I don't know why my husband did what he did."

"I do!" That angry exclamation came from Aaron, who pushed past Collins into the cabin. "He left us and ran off because he's no good! My pa's an outlaw. He's a terrible man, and whatever happens, he's got it comin' to him."

Amelia came sharply to her feet. "Aaron, stop that! You know better. Your father always took good care of us—"

"Until he wasn't here anymore. You know somethin' went bad in him, Ma. It had to for him to run off the way he did."

Collins said, "You speak to your mother with respect, boy."

Aaron whirled on him. "You can't tell me what to do. You're not my pa! I don't have a pa anymore!"

"Aaron!" Amelia's voice was like the crack of a whip. "You go on back out to the barn now. I want you to watch that cow, and you come get me when she starts to calve. Do you understand?"

Aaron's face was pale. He looked like he wanted to continue arguing, but after a moment he jerked his head in a nod and stalked out of the cabin, past the sheriff who had come a few steps into the room.

"I don't reckon you can blame the boy for being upset," Collins began in a mutter.

"I don't blame anybody," Amelia broke in. "What's the point in blame? It doesn't change anything." She turned her head to look at Luke. "And you still haven't told me what you're going to do. Don't you think you owe me that much, since you accepted my hospitality?"

"What do you *want* me to do?" Luke asked. "There's a bounty on your husband's head, and going after men like that is my job. But if I do, there's a possibility it won't end well for him."

"I don't care," Amelia said in a flat, hard voice. "After all this time, I don't care what happens to Jack. Anything that was ever between us is long since over."

Luke glanced at Collins and saw the sudden flare of hope in the sheriff's eyes at Amelia's words. He wanted to turn the trouble that had befallen Amelia and her sons to his own advantage. That made Luke dislike Collins even more.

"But . . ." Amelia went on.

"What is it?" Luke prodded when her voice trailed off.

She drew in a breath, blew it out through her nostrils. "Thad."

"Your other son."

She nodded. "A few months ago, he left, too. He

said he was going into the hills to find Jack and his gang and join them. I don't suppose I can blame him, either." She sighed and sank back into the chair. "He wasn't facing anything here except a lot of hard work for nothing. We were never going to be able to keep this place going."

Collins said, "Now, that's not necessarily true."

"It is, and you know it, Sheriff. Sooner or later you're going to be standing out there on the porch— if it hasn't fallen down by then—selling the place at auction for the taxes."

"It might not come to that."

Amelia ignored him again and turned back to Luke.

"I want my son back, Mr. Jensen. Even if we lose this spread, I don't want Thad spending the rest of his life as an outlaw . . . and I don't want him being gunned down by some other bounty hunter or lawman who doesn't understand that he's just a boy who's upset because he thinks his father's abandoned him."

Jack McKinney *had* abandoned his sons and his wife, Luke thought. No matter what his reasons might have been, there was no getting around that fact. But reminding Amelia of it wouldn't accomplish a blasted thing.

"Are you asking me to find Thad and bring him back?"

She nodded. "I am. If you have to kill Jack, then so be it. Kill him and every one of those men who ride with him. But spare my son and bring him back here to me."

Collins said, "Amelia, you don't know what you're doing. You can't trust a man like Jensen—"

"Will you do it?" she asked Luke, ignoring the sheriff's protest.

A tense silence hung over the room for a moment, and then Luke nodded and said, "I'll do my best. But ma'am, I can't give you my absolute promise to save your son. He may not even be with your husband. He may not have found the gang. Something else could have happened—"

"He's with Jack," she said. "I can feel it in my bones."

"If he is," Luke said, "I'll do everything I can to bring him back to you safely. That much I *can* give you my word on."

"So you're going after Three-fingered Jack?" Collins said with a sneer. "Funny how that worked out, isn't it, Jensen? You come in here pretending to be a gentleman, and you take advantage of this poor woman's emotions, and it still winds up with you going after a pile of blood money. That's what you wanted all along, isn't it?"

Luke didn't bother answering that. He stood up and reached for his hat. "I'm obliged to you for your hospitality, Mrs. McKinney. Looks like I won't get around to working on that porch for you after all, or helping you with the calving. Perhaps the sheriff would like to pitch in." He slanted an ironic glance toward Collins, who scowled back at him. "Is there anything you can tell me that might help me locate your husband and . . . your other son?" He had started to say *his gang* but changed it to emphasize his promise to try to find Thad.

Amelia shook her head. "No, I don't know anything except the same rumors that everyone else around here has heard. The gang's been seen on the other side of the hills and have raided some ranches and settlements up there."

"That's rugged country. Plenty of places for a hideout."

"I wouldn't know about that. Maybe Sheriff Collins can tell you more."

Judging by the obstinate look on the lawman's face, he didn't intend to tell Luke anything except maybe to go to hell. But that was all right. Luke was used to not getting any cooperation from the authorities. Most star packers had no use for bounty hunters.

"Thank you again. I'll be in touch." Luke walked out of the cabin, leaving Amelia McKinney sitting at the table with what he thought was probably an uncharacteristic slump to her shoulders. No matter how strong a person she was, sooner or later carrying the weight of the world had to have an effect.

Collins stomped out after him and closed the door as Luke paused on the porch to put his hat on. "You've got a hell of a lot of nerve. I ought to arrest you—"

"On what charge?" Luke interrupted coolly.

"Making that poor woman's life even harder."

"How am I doing that? By giving her hope that maybe I can bring her son back to her?"

"You know damn well that if you get the chance, you'll kill him, just like you'll kill McKinney and the others."

"Why would I do that?" Luke asked.

Collins glanced at the closed door and lowered his voice. "Because there's a reward on *all* the men riding with the Three-fingered Jack gang. Some of them by name, with higher amounts, but there's a blanket reward of two hundred dollars for anybody caught riding with him."

"You're talking about a boy who's, what, sixteen or seventeen years old?"

"Since when did that ever stop a man like you? Thad's worth two hundred bucks to you, dead or alive, and that's all that matters."

Luke looked narrow-eyed at the sheriff for a moment, then shook his head. "You're awfully quick to jump to conclusions, Collins. You think you know me, but you don't. Well, listen. I don't expect you to like me—"

"Good, because that'll sure as hell never happen."

"But you'd better stay out of my way," Luke said. "And if you really want to help that poor woman in there, as you call her, you'll tell me anything you know that might give me a lead on finding the gang."

Collins glared at Luke and chewed his upper lip for a few seconds, then said, "Have you ever heard of a place called the Black Castle?"

Luke frowned. "No, I . . . Wait a minute. I do recall hearing someone mention it a while back. Supposed to be some sort of sanctuary for outlaws, isn't it?"

"I've never laid eyes on the place myself, don't even know if it really exists. But if it does, it's up there in those hills"—Collins nodded toward the low, rugged peaks—"maybe twenty miles north of here. Out of my jurisdiction, so I've never gone looking for it. But if I was an owlhoot operating in this area and needed a place to lay low for a while, I reckon I'd see if I could find out whether the rumors are true."

"Thank you, Sheriff. That might actually come in handy."

"If you could find Thad and bring him back here, it'd make his mother happy. That's all I want for her."

Luke still didn't like Collins, but the obvious sincerity in the sheriff's voice at that moment made it a little more difficult to dislike him.

That brief respite in the hostility between them didn't last.

Collins went on. "And if you go up there and find yourself in some robbers' roost and get shot full of holes . . . that won't bother me one damned bit, either."

CHAPTER 10

Luke rode back along the creek the way he had come, hoping to find a better trail north toward the hills. After a couple of miles he turned in that direction. He could have gone all the way back to the main road he had followed from Singletary, but that would have been out of his way after the detour to the McKinney spread. The path he chose was smaller and only dimly marked, as if lone riders passing that way every now and then had made it.

As he moved along at an easy pace, he thought about the rumors he had heard concerning the Black Castle. Such places were scattered throughout the West, the most famous—or notorious—being the Hole in the Wall. But there were other owlhoot havens, legendary sanctuaries like the Dutchman's and Zamora and Robbers Roost. Luke had no idea how the Black Castle had gotten that name, or honestly, if it even existed. If it did, paying a visit probably wasn't a very smart thing for him to do, given the fact that he made his living by hunting down outlaws. There was a very good chance he would run into somebody who had an old grudge against him, a score best settled with hot lead.

He was going to have to take that chance, Luke thought. After all, he had never expected to die peacefully in bed. In many ways, he had been living on borrowed time these past twenty years, ever since he had come so close to dying during the war.

The terrain grew more rugged as the trail twisted like a snake into the hills. The landscape was rock and bare sand, with only an occasional clump of hardy grass or a lonely, stunted bush. Saw-toothed ridges jutted up and formed sheer canyon walls on either side of the winding trail. It was dangerous country, Luke knew, perfectly made for an ambush.

That thought had barely gone through his mind when some instinct made the skin on the back of his neck prickle. Like a physical touch, he felt eyes watching him. And when a rock clattered somewhere ahead of him, he suddenly yanked his horse to the side.

At that same instant, the flat crack of a rifle shot echoed from the looming ridges. Luke felt as much as heard the slug whine past his ear. He slid his Winchester from its sheath as he hauled the horse around in a tight turn. More shots blasted as he kicked the animal into a run.

More than one bushwhacker had been waiting for him, he realized as he bent forward in the saddle. Bullets cut sizzling paths through the air around him. It was a good two hundred yards to the most recent bend in the trail. As many shots as were flying around him, he couldn't hope to cover that much ground without one of the bullets finding him.

His gaze fell on a fissure in the ridge he had passed a few moments earlier. It was coming up fast on his left and offered the only cover anywhere close. Without stopping to think too much about what he was doing, Luke let his instincts guide him and kicked his feet free of the stirrups. Holding tightly to the Winchester, he went out of the saddle in a rolling dive.

He landed hard enough to knock the breath out of him, but his momentum carried him on over and back up onto his feet. Bullets kicked up dust around his heels as he dashed into the crack in the rock. The horse galloped on down the trail, but the bushwhackers weren't shooting at it anymore. They concentrated all their fire on Luke.

The rifles fell silent as he disappeared into the crevice. He pressed his back against the rock and stood there with the Winchester held at a slant across his chest, which heaved as he tried to catch his breath. His heart slugged heavily, and he felt his pulse beating inside his skull.

The thought he'd had more than once over the past few years crossed his mind. *I'm getting too old for this . . .*

After a minute or two, he began to recover his breath and his composure. Now that the echoes of gunfire had rolled away, an eerie silence descended over the hills. The sun hung high overhead, and the baking heat that enveloped the landscape made beads of sweat pop out on his forehead. He sleeved them away and thought about his next move.

He considered popping out of the crack long enough to crank off a few rounds in the direction of the ambushers, just to let them know he still had some fight in him, but he discarded that idea. Let them wonder if they had hit him. They might get curious enough to come and check on him, and that would bring them out in the open where he would have a clear shot at them.

Or they might try to wait him out. He had no water, and the heat and thirst would get worse as the day went on. If they had shade and full canteens, they could afford to be patient.

He turned his head to look along the cleft, which was narrow to start with and grew even narrower as it penetrated into the ridge. One side was almost sheer, but the other side had more of a slant to it and was rough enough that Luke believed he could climb it. That was his best bet, he decided. If he could get to the top of the ridge, he might be able to circle around behind the bushwhackers and get the drop on them.

Of course, if they caught him while he was climbing, they wouldn't have any trouble shooting him off of there like a fly on a wall. That was a risk he would just have to run, he told himself.

Climbing with the Winchester wasn't easy, but he didn't have anything he could use to rig a sling for it. He moved carefully, trying not to let the rifle bang against the rock. If the ambushers heard it, they might figure out what he was doing and move quickly to stop him. Sweat coated his face and trickled down his back before he had ascended ten feet. Somewhere not too far away, men's voices called quietly to each other, but he couldn't make out the words. They were closing in on his hiding place, he thought.

With no warning, his left foot slipped. He had good holds with his right foot and left hand, so he was in no danger of falling, but several small rocks rattled down the steep slope beneath him, alerting the men stalking him.

"Go!" one of them shouted.

Luke pulled himself up, drove with his feet, and scrambled toward the ledge five feet above him. Rapid footsteps slapped against the ground nearby.

"There he is!" a man cried.

A split second later, a shot blasted. The slug smacked into the rock a few inches from Luke and whined off. He grabbed the ledge, hauled himself up and over as more shots rang out. He came up on his knees, leaned out, and fired three times back down the slope as fast as he could work the Winchester's lever. He caught a glimpse of movement as men shouted in alarm and dived for cover, but he didn't think he'd hit any of them.

Still, he had the high ground. He might not have a horse or any water and a limited amount of ammunition, but the men trying to kill him were at a strategic disadvantage. He backed off, got to his feet, and started working his way along the ledge, which rose gradually toward the top of the ridge.

"Get back to the horses and spread out!" a man called. "He's got to come down from there sometime, and we'll be waiting for him."

The voice was familiar to Luke. He paused and shouted, "You brought help with you this time, didn't you, Clint? You couldn't kill me alone, even when you tried to ambush me, so you got some of your uncle's cowboys to come along and hold your hand!"

Clint Norman bellowed a curse. Shots slammed out one after another as Clint emptied a revolver in Luke's general direction. The angle at which he was firing ensured that all the bullets sailed harmlessly into the sky.

Luke laughed harshly. "You're going to have to do better than that, Clint!"

"One of you climb up there after him!" Clint ordered.

"I don't know about that," another man said. "That fella's a bounty hunter. He's used to shootin' it out with hombres who want to kill him."

"Do what I told you, damn it!"

Luke called, "If I were you boys, I'd take my chances with Clint's uncle. It's bad enough he tried to turn you into murderers. Keep following his orders, and some of you are bound to get killed."

Clint continued cursing and ranting. Luke dropped to one knee and trained the Winchester on the part of the ledge he had climbed onto a few minutes earlier. He heard rocks clattering and knew Clint had browbeaten one of the men with him into making the attempt to get behind their quarry. Luke waited patiently until he saw the crown of a hat case up into view.

He squeezed off a shot. The hat sailed wildly into the air as a man yelped. Luke caught a glimpse of a gun barrel and knew the man had lifted the hat on it in order to draw his fire and find out just how dangerous it was going to be to continue climbing.

Now he knew. Luke heard more rocks clatter down the slope, followed by a man exclaiming, "The hell with this!"

Clint said, "Rooney, get back up there, or you're out of a job on the Circle B!"

"Then I'm out of a job," the man responded. "I'll draw my time and ride right now! Jensen didn't know whether my head was in that hat when he shot it. I could have a bullet through my brain just as easy."

Luke grinned to himself for a second, knowing that he didn't have to worry about an attack from the rear. None of the men with Clint Norman were going to risk that. He resumed his careful path along the ledge.

Men were still arguing below when Luke came out on top of the ridge. He could see a couple of hundred yards in both directions. His horse had galloped off to the south, and he wanted to recover the animal, so he headed that way even though it was the opposite direction from his ultimate destination. His shirt was soaked with sweat as the sun beat down on him.

The ridge was maybe a hundred yards wide, littered with boulders, and cut through with crevices, some of them wide enough that he had to detour around them. The ground was so rough that he couldn't afford to hurry. If he did, he stood a good chance of spraining or even breaking his ankle.

"There he is!" shouted a man from behind Luke. One of the men with Clint had found another way to the top.

Luke ducked and twisted and brought his Winchester up as a shot blasted. He didn't know where the bullet went, but it didn't hit him and that was all that mattered. He spotted the man about a hundred yards away and triggered a shot of his own. The man stumbled and dropped his rifle, fell to his knees and caught himself with one hand. He was hit, but the way he bawled curses made Luke think the wound was painful but probably not too bad. Enough to put the varmint out of the fight, though. At least, Luke hoped so.

As he resumed his hurried passage along the ridge, he wondered how many men Clint had brought with him. During the ambush, he hadn't been able to tell how many men had been shooting at him—only that it was more than one.

With one of his allies wounded and another too spooked to continue the fight, the odds might be getting too close to even for Clint's taste. Knowing that, Luke wasn't surprised a few minutes later when he heard hoofbeats. He paused, looked back, and saw that the man he had shot was gone. The fellow had been able to make it down off the ridge crest and was probably one of the men riding away.

Again, Luke couldn't tell for sure how many horses he heard, but several, no doubt about that. Had all the bushwhackers fled . . . or was that just a ruse to get him to drop his guard?

He came to a spot where the ridge fell away in a much gentler slope. He had to get back down to the trail somewhere, so it was as good as any, he decided. From up there he could see the tops of some trees about a quarter of a mile farther on and recalled from when he rode past them earlier that some grass grew as well. His horse might have stopped there to graze.

Luke took a handful of .44-40 cartridges from his pocket and thumbed them into the Winchester to replace the rounds he had fired. Then he held the rifle ready for instant use as he picked his way, sliding in places, down the angled slope to the trail.

Nobody shot at him while he was descending. When he reached the bottom, the silence continued. His gut told him that Clint Norman and the other bushwhackers had fled, but he was still careful anyway. He walked south along the trail toward the trees he had seen from the ridge crest, pausing every few moments to listen intently. His eyes never stopped moving as he searched for any sign of another attack.

Peace still reigned over the hills.

Relief went through Luke when he came in sight of the trees and spotted his horse standing in the shade underneath them, head down. The animal cropped at the grass growing there. Luke spoke softly as he approached. He'd been riding that mount for a while, and the horse was used to him, but horses sometimes spooked for no apparent reason.

He caught hold of the dangling reins, slid the Winchester back into the boot under the right saddle fender, and checked the horse over to make sure none of the flying lead had struck it earlier. Seeing that the horse appeared to be unharmed, Luke swung up.

"I'm glad you didn't run all the way back to the McKinney spread," he said. "That would have been embarrassing, trudging back on foot."

He turned the horse and set out in the same direction he'd been going earlier. Before he had gone fifty yards, something bothered him and he reined in. He hipped around in the saddle and gazed back along the trail. Nothing moved, not even a bird or a lizard. Frowning, Luke faced forward and heeled the horse into motion again.

He wasn't convinced that he wasn't being followed . . . but if he was, whoever was back there probably would try to kill him sooner or later, and he would deal with it then.

CHAPTER 11

A short time later, Luke passed the spot where Clint Norman and the men with him had sprung their ambush earlier. Nothing happened. Maybe Clint would give up the grudge he held. Luke didn't really believe that would happen, but it was something to hope for, anyway.

He rode deeper into the hills, climbing steadily. The higher elevation helped some with the heat, but the sun was still brassy in the sky overhead. Luke gnawed on a piece of jerky, washing it down gratefully with swigs of water from one of his canteens.

Late in the afternoon he spotted buzzards circling lazily ahead of him, riding currents of heated air. His eyes narrowed as one of the carrion birds dipped down low to the ground, then swooped up again. Two more buzzards repeated the maneuver and came to the same conclusion as the first. Whatever they were keeping their beady, avaricious little eyes on was still alive.

Probably an animal, Luke thought, but on the off chance that it wasn't, he nudged the horse into a slightly faster gait and came in sight of a huge pile of slab-sided boulders. A flash of bright color at the base of the rocks caught his eye. He pulled the Winchester from its scabbard, cranked a round into the chamber, and rode forward carefully. As he came closer he made out a human shape sprawled on the ground. It appeared to be a man lying on his back with a yellow bandanna draped over his face.

Luke thought the man was dead, but then he moved a little. That was enough to spook the buzzards again. The big, ugly birds had been circling gradually lower, but they soared up at that sign of life.

The man lifted a trembling, gnarled hand and tugged the bandanna off his face, revealing a brush of gray whiskers that jutted up from his jaw. He tried to push himself into a sitting position but slumped back down with an audible groan. Luke figured the man had heard hoofbeats approaching, and that had roused him from his stupor.

The man wore brown canvas trousers tucked into high boots and a fringed vest over a red-checked shirt open at the throat to reveal long red underwear. An old, battered brown hat lay nearby. A gunbelt was strapped around the old-timer's scrawny waist, but the attached holster was empty.

Luke reined in when he was still twenty feet away and kept the Winchester's muzzle pointed in the man's general direction. He didn't believe the man was setting a trap, but until certain of that, Luke was going to be careful.

"You look like you could use some help, friend," he called.

"I need . . . water," the old-timer rasped in a tortured

voice. "I don't want to die . . . with such . . . a dry throat." His vest had fallen open to reveal an irregular dark brown stain low on the shirt's right side.

That was dried blood, Luke realized. "You're not going to die," he said, although he couldn't be sure of that until he checked the man's wound. "I have plenty of water. Before we go any further, though . . . is anybody else around here?"

"Not that I . . . know of. I give them 'Paches . . . the slip . . . a ways back."

Luke tensed and repeated, "Apaches?"

"Yeah. Band of . . . about a dozen of 'em . . . jumped me this mornin'. Must've run off . . . from the reservation. One of the . . . damn bucks . . . shot me with an old Spencer . . . he probably took off . . . a dead army trooper. But I led 'em . . . a merry chase . . . let me tell you. Never expected to . . . get away from 'em . . . but I was gonna make . . . the redskinned bastards . . . pay for killin' me."

The old man's story had the ring of truth to it, but Luke remained alert as he swung down from the saddle and took one of the canteens loose. He carried it by its strap as he warily approached the man on the ground. He held the rifle ready in his other hand. "Can you sit up and handle this canteen by yourself?"

"I dunno . . . Lost a heap o' blood . . . from that bullet hole."

Luke knelt beside the old-timer. He placed the Winchester on the ground, got an arm around the man's shoulders, and lifted him. With his other hand, he worked the cork loose from the canteen and tilted it to the old man's lips. The man sucked greedily at the water. Luke let him guzzle for a few seconds, then took the canteen away. The old-timer moaned.

"Not too much at once," Luke said. "You know that. It'll just come back up and be wasted."

The man's husk of a tongue scraped over his lips. "You wouldn't happen to have . . . a bottle o' somethin' . . . a mite stronger . . . would you? That might cut the dust . . . even better."

As a matter of fact, Luke did have a flask of whiskey in one of his saddlebags, but that wasn't what the old man needed. He chuckled and said, "Let's just concentrate on getting some water in you and keeping it down."

The old-timer nodded weakly. He was mostly bald, with only a few strands of lank gray hair plastered over his liver-spotted scalp. Luke let him have another drink, waited, then gave him more water as a bit of color creeped back into the man's leathery face.

"I figured I was dead for sure." His voice was slightly stronger. "I didn't want to die with the sun in my eyes . . . and I sure as hell didn't want to watch the buzzards comin' for me. That's why I put my bandanna over my face. I was just waitin' . . . for the end . . ."

"What's your name?" Luke asked.

"O . . . O'Donnell. Folks call me . . . Badger."

"I'm Luke." He left it at that, didn't give his last name. He didn't know who Badger O'Donnell was or what the old-timer was doing in those rugged hills, but he also didn't see any point in announcing that he was Luke Jensen. Too many people might recognize that name and know he was a bounty hunter.

"I'm mighty pleased to meet you, son. Now, about that whiskey . . ."

"Later," Luke said. "Right now, it might be a good idea to try to get you out of the sun. What happened to your horse?"

"Didn't have no horse. Was ridin' . . . a mule. And after I passed out and fell off . . . I got no idea what might've happened to him."

"What about your gun?"

"Reckon it must've dropped outta the holster . . . when I took that tumble. I never noticed it was gone until I'd crawled a ways . . . and I wasn't gonna go back and look for it." A rusty laugh came from the old-timer's throat. "A little later, I wished I had. If I'd had my gun . . . you never woulda found me alive, Luke. I'd have ended it . . . as soon as I saw them buzzards circlin' around up there."

"Losing it was a stroke of good luck, then. Come on."

Luke corked the canteen, slung it around his neck, and then helped Badger O'Donnell to his feet. The old man was pretty shaky, but he was able to walk with Luke's arm around his waist to support him.

They made it to Luke's horse. He put Badger's left foot in the stirrup on that side, then boosted the old-timer into the saddle. Badger grabbed the saddle horn and swayed back and forth, and Luke steadied him. When Badger seemed fairly stable, Luke said, "Hang on. I'll take it slow."

"I'm sure obliged to you, boy."

Luke grinned. "It's been a long time since anyone called me a boy. I'll take it as a compliment."

"Hell, I'm so old Methuselah's a boy compared to me," Badger said.

Luke didn't think Badger was quite that old—in his sixties, more than likely—but it was obvious by looking at him that he had spent most of his life outdoors and had lived a rugged existence. There wasn't much to him except rawhide and bone. He hung on to the horn and rocked back and forth in the saddle as Luke led the horse along the trail.

After a while they came to some scrubby cottonwoods and Luke helped Badger dismount and sit in the welcome shade with his back propped against a tree trunk.

"All right, I'd better take a look at that wound now," Luke suggested.

Badger made a face. "I had a feelin' you was gonna say that. Reckon that shirt's stuck to it 'cause of the dried blood. Gonna hurt like hell when you pull it loose." He licked his lips. "This'd be a good time for somethin' stronger to drink than water, not that I ain't obliged to you for sharin' your canteen."

"All right," Luke said with a chuckle. "Wait there."

"I ain't likely to go scamperin' off."

Luke returned to the horse, which had started grazing. He dug out the flask and took it over to the tree where Badger sat. He would have gulped down all the whiskey if Luke had let him.

After one gulp of the fiery stuff, he pried the flask out of Badger's stubborn grip. "More later," he promised.

"I'll hold you to that." Badger closed his eyes, leaned his head back against the tree trunk, and gritted his teeth. "Do your worst, son."

Luke pulled the vest aside, unbuttoned the shirt, and eased it back. As Badger had predicted, the dried blood caused the fabric of the shirt and the long underwear beneath it to stick to the wound. Badger grunted in pain as Luke probed at it.

He used water from the canteen to soak the cloth

and loosen it. He hated to do that when he didn't know where the next waterhole was, but he wanted to keep the wound from bleeding heavily. Badger might not be able to afford to lose much more of the precious fluid.

Working slowly and carefully, Luke cut away part of the long underwear and gradually uncovered the deep gash in Badger's side. Finally, he revealed the injury and the red, swollen flesh around it. Looking at the wound, he frowned. "The Apaches jumped you this morning, you said?"

"Yeah, that's right."

Luke shook his head. "I think you must be mixed up, Badger. This wound looks older than just a few hours. I'd say it happened yesterday morning, at the latest."

"Yesterday . . . Well, I don't know. Maybe. To tell you the truth, I was outta my head a lot of the time since it happened, on account of losin' so much blood, I reckon. I suppose I coulda laid up somewhere, out cold, for a long spell."

"I think that's what must have happened."

"How bad does it look? Am I shot to pieces? You think I'm gonna pull through?"

"It appears that the bullet just plowed a furrow in your side. I'm sure it hurt like hell, and you bled a lot, but by itself, I don't think it's a life-threatening wound."

Badger peered intently at Luke. "For somebody who's deliverin' good news, you don't hardly look too pleased. Tell me the rest of it."

"The wound is inflamed. Infection is trying to set in. If we don't stop it, that could kill you."

"What do you need to do?"

"Open the wound up more and clean it good."

"Oh, Lord," Badger groaned. "That'll take the rest o' the whiskey, won't it?"

"Probably."

Pale and shaken-looking, Badger managed to nod. "Do what you got to do. It's gonna hurt like blazes, ain't it?"

"I'll see if I can find a piece of wood for you to bite on."

"I'll be obliged."

Luke found a piece of broken branch about the right size and cleaned the bark off it. He gathered more wood and built a small fire. If renegade Apaches really were loose somewhere in those hills, the smoke from a fire could lead them right to them, but Luke didn't see any other option. He kept the blaze as small as possible, just big enough for him to hold his knife in the flames and make sure the blade was clean.

He let it cool for a couple of minutes, then eased the old man down on his side and went to work on the wound, enlarging it. Fresh blood flowed, along with foul-smelling corruption that told Luke he had reached the source of infection. Badger moaned as his teeth clamped down hard on the piece of wood in his mouth.

Luke poured whiskey directly into the wound, and that made Badger whimper. He used a rag to clean the blood off the blade, then heated it in the fire again.

"Bite down," he warned Badger just before he pressed the knife against the gash. Badger arched his back in pain as juices sizzled and the smell of cooking flesh rose in the air. A second later, Badger slumped loosely, having passed out. That was a blessing for the old-timer, Luke thought.

He wished he had some moss with which to pack the wound, but none seemed to grow in the mostly arid landscape. He settled for making a pad of clean cloth and tying it in place. Badger breathed noisily but didn't wake up. Luke sat back and thumbed his hat to the back of his head, drained by the effort to save the old-timer's life.

All they could do was wait to see whether that effort had been successful.

CHAPTER 12

By evening, Badger still hadn't regained consciousness. Luke had allowed the fire to burn down, so he stirred it to life again, added more twigs, and put coffee on to boil. He shaved some strips of bacon from the chunk he had wrapped up, and fried them. The combined smells of coffee and food must have had some medicinal effect, because Badger raised his head a little and said, "Uhhh?"

"I'm glad to see you've returned to the land of the living," Luke said from where he hunkered beside the fire. "Do you think you're up to trying some coffee and bacon?"

"Just . . . lemme . . . at it," Badger said as he slowly sat up. He winced. "Damn, son. It feels like . . . you carved half my side off." He added hopefully, "Is there . . . any o' that whiskey left?"

"I may have saved a drop or two for you," Luke said dryly. "When I was finished saving your life, that is."

"And I'm obliged to you. But I'll be more obliged for a drink."

"Supper first."

Badger seemed too weak to argue even though he might have liked to.

Luke got tin cups from his gear and filled them, then put bacon on a tin plate and carried it and one of the cups over to Badger. "Need help?"

"No, I think I can manage. Lemme try, anyway." Badger used both hands to hold the cup and took a sip. He was a little shaky but didn't spill any. He started nibbling a piece of bacon but after a moment gobbled it down. "Didn't realize I was hungry until I started eatin'," he said as he reached for another piece. "You might want to cook up some more."

"You must be feeling better."

"I ain't gonna be gettin' up and dancin' a jig any time soon, but I reckon I might live."

Two cups of coffee and a pile of bacon later, the old-timer leaned back against the tree and sighed in obvious satisfaction. "I ain't sayin' that's the best meal I ever et, but it was right up there," he declared. "I'm sure mighty obliged to you, Luke. If there's ever anythin' I can do to pay you back . . ."

"You can start by telling me what you were doing out here. There's not much reason for anybody to be roaming around these hills."

"That shows how much you know! There's the best reason of all . . . Gold."

Luke frowned across the fire at the old-timer. "You're a prospector? I never heard of any gold strikes around here. They've all been in other parts of the territory."

"And there was a time there hadn't been any gold strikes in those places, wasn't there? Nobody knows where gold is until somebody finds it the first time."

Luke couldn't argue with that logic. "Do you have a claim somewhere around here?"

"No, but I'm still lookin'. I been all over these hills from one end to the other more 'n once, and I know it's here. I can feel it in my bones. It's just a matter of time 'fore I find it."

That was interesting. Luke wasn't convinced that any gold deposits lurked in the area, but if Badger was telling the truth, he was very familiar with the stretch of rugged hills. Luke took another sip of coffee and said, "Maybe you could help me find something *I'm* looking for."

"What might that be?"

"Do you know of a place called the Black Castle?"

Badger's eyes, deep set and surrounded by wrinkles, widened in surprise and what might have been fear. "The Black Castle," he repeated in a croaking voice. "I never heard of it."

His reaction made it plain that he was lying. Clearly, he did know the name. And that made Luke believe maybe there was some truth to the legend of the outlaw haven.

"I think you have heard of it, Badger, and if you're as grateful to me as you claim, you'll tell me how to find it."

Badger groaned. "Oh, hell. You're an owlhoot. When I first seen you, I thought you must be, as big and ugly and all dressed in black like you are. But then you talked so good, and you saved my life, and I figured I must be wrong. But I ain't, am I? You want to go there 'cause you're an outlaw. A wanted man. The law's after you, ain't it?" Badger looked around wildly. "Is there a posse closin' in on us right now?"

"Take it easy," Luke told him. "I don't know of any

posse around here. Can't somebody want to go to the Black Castle without being an outlaw?"

"I never heard tell of anybody who did! A man 'd be a damn fool to try if he wasn't one o' that breed." Badger shook his head. "Don't ask me to take you there, son. It'd be worth your life iffen I did."

"That's a risk I have to take. Now, fate allowed me to spot those buzzards, and they led me to you, Badger. I saved your life. Doesn't that tell you that fate intends for me to find what I'm looking for?"

"Fate's one thing, and bein' a plumb idjit's another." A sly look came over the whiskery old face. "Anyway, just 'cause I heard of the place don't mean I know how to find it."

"I'll bet you can point me in the right direction."

Badger scowled. "Might've been better if you'd just let the damn buzzards have me."

"It could still be arranged," Luke said.

"And now you're threatenin' me!"

Luke shook his head. "No, you're right. I wouldn't do that. Why don't we just wait until tomorrow morning and see how you're doing then? I want to make sure that wound is healing properly, after all the trouble I went to in order to keep it from killing you. We can discuss the Black Castle again then."

Badger muttered and blew out his breath and scowled, but he didn't argue anymore. After a while he said, "I'm tired. Reckon I'll get some sleep."

Luke got one of his spare blankets and rolled it up for the old man to use as a pillow. He spread the other blanket over Badger, knowing that the air could get chilly at night, even during the summer. It wasn't long before the old-timer was snoring. The rest would help his injured body heal.

Luke slept only lightly, counting on his keen senses and those of his horse to alert him if anyone came around. The possibility that Apaches might be lurking in the area didn't make for a very restful night.

And neither did the persistent, nagging feeling he had that someone was watching him.

Luke came awake to the faint jingle of bit chains. Soundlessly, he opened his eyes and closed his hand around the butt of a Remington. He had coiled up the gunbelt around the holstered revolvers and placed them close beside him before he dozed off.

The sun wasn't up, but enough gray light filled the sky for him to see the whip-thin figure getting his horse ready to ride. Luke pushed his blanket aside and stood up, then in his stocking feet he closed in from behind without making any noise. The man cinching up the saddle didn't have any idea he was there until Luke thumbed back the Remington's hammer. That ominous sound made the man freeze.

"Going somewhere, Badger?"

The old-timer heaved a sigh. "Go ahead and pull the trigger. I got it comin', no mistake about that. It takes a mighty sorry varmint to try to steal the horse o' the man who saved his life."

"I'm not going to shoot you," Luke said as he carefully lowered the hammer. "I do want to know what you thought you were doing, though."

"What does it look like? I was gonna steal your horse and leave you here for the 'Paches! Go ahead and shoot me, damn it!"

"Is this because of what I said about the Black

Castle? You'd rather steal from me than help me find it?"

"I don't want to go back there," Badger mumbled.

"So you *do* know where it is."

"Yeah. Can I turn around?"

Luke stepped back. He didn't believe that Badger would try any tricks . . . but he hadn't expected the old man to try to steal his horse, either.

"Yes, you can turn around," Luke told him as he held the gun down at his side.

Badger did so and sighed again. "What do you know about the Black Castle?"

"Just that it's supposed to be a place where men on the dodge can go and hide out for a while. Like the Hole in the Wall up north."

"That's part of it. I can tell you the rest, iffen you're bound and determined to hear it."

"That's exactly what I want," Luke said, "but first let's take a look at that wound and see how it's doing."

The reddish-gold arc of light from the approaching sunrise was bright enough for Luke to examine the bullet gash in Badger's side. He saw at first glance that the wound was better. The redness around it had receded, and it didn't start bleeding again when he changed the dressing.

"I still make no guarantees, but I think you're going to live," he told the old-timer.

"Don't be so sure o' that. Not if you make me tell you about the Black Castle . . . and the Black Knight."

"The Black Knight!" That exclamation was startled out of Luke. "That sounds like something out of Howard Pyle's book about Robin Hood."

"It ain't from no book. I never learned how to read.

I laid eyes on the fella myself, and I'd just as soon never do that again."

"The Black Castle belongs to this man you're talking about?" Luke guessed.

"As much as it can belong to anybody, I reckon it does."

"You're not going to tell me that he wears a suit of armor and jousts with other knights."

"I never heard of no jousts, whatever that is," Badger snapped. "Do you want to hear the story or not?"

"I do."

"Best put on a pot of coffee, then, and maybe cook up some more o' that bacon. And I never did get that drop o' whiskey last night like you promised. Might use it to sweeten that coffee and get my throat lubricated so's I can talk good."

CHAPTER 13

Luke made biscuits to go with the bacon. The sun was up by the time he and Badger were eating breakfast and drinking coffee. Only a few drops of whiskey were left in the flask, but he added them to Badger's cup as promised. It was enough to brace up the old-timer.

"Here's the story as best I know it. I only heard rumors and gossip, so I could be wrong about some of it, but it starts with a fella name of Henry Stockbridge. He's from England, one o' those . . . what do you call 'em, when you're the little brother and your big brother inherits all the family money and the title and such that goes with it, and you get shipped off to America and paid to stay outta the way?"

"Someone like that is called a remittance man," Luke said. "I've run into a few over the years."

With a nod, Badger said, "Yeah, that. Stockbridge's brother is a duke or a count or some such nonsense, but he was just a nobody. Reckon that's one of the things that made him so all-fired proddy. Wasn't his fault he was born second. He just got the sorry end o' the deal."

"So this Stockbridge fellow came to America."

"Yep. After a while he come west, and when he got out here, he fell in with some . . . well, let's call 'em *shady characters*. Turns out he had a knack for bein' on the wrong side of the law. He took so well to bein' an owlhoot, in fact, that he wound up leadin' the gang."

"What does this have to do with the Black Castle?" Luke asked.

"I'm gettin' there, I'm gettin' there. Just hold your hosses. Came a time when Stockbridge was ridin' hell-bent for leather through these very hills with a posse on his heels. The fellas he'd been runnin' with all got their selves killed or took prisoner when the posse jumped 'em, so Stockbridge was the only one left and he was carryin' a law dog's bullet in him. He didn't have a chance in hell of gettin' away . . . but then he seen it."

"The Black Castle," Luke said.

"That's right. Now, understand, it weren't a real castle. It was this kinda jagged-edged rock formation with stone towers that stuck up on the corners. It looked enough like a castle that it reminded Stockbridge of the real thing like he'd seen back in England, like the one where his no-good brother the duke or the count or whatever he was lived. Stockbridge climbed up there and forted up and the way it turned out, he wasn't just able to hold off that posse. He killed ever' durn one o' them star packers before it was all over, so he figured that was a sign he ought to make the place his home. He got another gang together, pulled some jobs that got him a lot of loot, and poured all that money into building a big stone house in the middle o' that rock formation. He coulda called hisself a duke if he'd wanted to, or even a king, since he was the boss o' the whole place, but he decided to call himself the Black Knight instead. I reckon he thinks it sounds sorta spooky."

The old-timer was a good storyteller. Luke had been able to visualize the tale as Badger spun it. The whole thing seemed rather far-fetched to him, but he had to admit it wasn't beyond the realm of possibility. A man would have to have a mighty fanciful imagination to build a western version of an old English castle, declare himself to be the Black Knight, and set up an outlaw empire with the castle as its centerpiece . . . but it could have happened that way.

"When did all this happen?"

Badger dug a finger into his whiskers and scratched. "Best I can tell, it was about ten years ago when Henry Stockbridge come out here. Maybe eight since he run across the Black Castle. But that's just a guess."

"I suppose after a while he stopped venturing out and pulling robberies himself, preferring to stay there and live as the lord of the manor, taking a cut from those to whom he provided sanctuary?"

"That's it, all right. Now he just swaggers around like he's the boss of all creation. And as long as he stays in these hills, I reckon he pretty much is."

Luke had finished his breakfast. He drained the last of the coffee in his cup and sat back to digest not only the meal but also the story Badger had told him.

"Since you know all this, I suppose that means you've spent some time at the Black Castle yourself."

Badger scowled. "Don't go thinkin' that makes me an outlaw. Sure enough, I've done some things in my life I ain't all that proud of, but I ain't never been what you'd call an out-an'-out desperado. I might've, uh, let some folks think I was, though, from time to time."

"So you could visit the Black Castle."

"Prospectin' can be a mighty lonely life," Badger protested. "It was good to see other folks now and then, drink some good liquor, hear a woman laugh—"

"Stockbridge has women there?"

"Yep. He makes sure the fellas who stop over there get their money's worth. I hear tell he pays pretty well, and nobody dares treat the gals rough. For soiled doves, it ain't a bad life, I suppose, except . . ."

"Except what?" Luke asked when the old-timer's voice trailed off.

"I've heard that nobody who works at the Black Castle ever leaves the place. Stockbridge must be afraid they'll sell out to the law and tell them where it is. I don't know what happens to 'em."

"Well, that certainly sounds sinister," Luke said.

Badger shrugged. "I'm just tellin' you what I've heard. I don't know none of it for a fact, based on what I seen with my own two eyes."

"We'll assume for now that you're telling the truth."

"I am, as far as I know," Badger insisted. "Are you still gonna make me take you there?"

"I'd like to see the place for myself. It sounds quite impressive."

"It ain't safe," Badger said as he shuddered. "It's full of killers and owlhoots and men who'd carve you from gizzard to gullet without even thinkin' twice about it."

"I'm surprised that Stockbridge doesn't have rules about no violence while anyone is within the confines of his domain."

"Oh, he's got rules, and you'd best follow 'em. But

that just means if you've got a problem with some fella, you and him got to fight a duel. The Black Knight's big on duelin'." Something occurred to Badger. "Say, is that like that joustin' you was talkin' about earlier?"

"They're related, I suppose," Luke said. "They spring from the same codes of honor and chivalry."

"I don't know about that, but hombres die there all the time. As long as it happens accordin' to the rules Stockbridge lays out, nobody gets in trouble for it."

"Did you get in trouble the last time you were there, Badger?" Luke asked. "Is that why you don't want to go back?"

"Me?" Badger's bushy gray eyebrows rose. "Hell, no. I'm the quiet sort. Nobody even knows I'm around most o' the time. I just don't believe in pushin' my luck, that's all."

"Show me where it is, and maybe you won't have to go inside. If we can find your mule, we can go our separate ways once we get there."

"I'm low on supplies," Badger said with a frown.

"I can probably spare a few. And I have an extra Colt you can have . . . if you take me where I want to go."

"Well . . . you *did* save my life. I ain't overfond o' the idea, 'cause I think you're liable to wind up gettin' yourself killed . . . but if you're dead set on it, I'll take you close enough to point out the place. You'll have to find your own way from there."

"That's a deal," Luke said.

A short time later, Luke saddled his horse, swung up, and then helped Badger climb on behind him.

"Be careful," he told the old-timer. "You don't want to start that wound bleeding again."

"I sure don't. I already lost so much blood I feel like I'll be runnin' low the rest o' my borned days."

Badger had no idea where he had fallen off his mule or in which direction the animal might have wandered off. The whole experience was fuzzy in his head, so Luke decided they might as well head north. They stood just as good a chance of finding the mule that way as any other.

"Why do you have your head set on goin' to the Black Castle, anyway?" Badger asked as they rode along at a deliberate easy pace.

"Maybe I'm just curious," Luke said.

"There's an old sayin' about curiosity and cats."

He actually was curious. The tale Badger had told was bizarre enough that Luke wanted to know if there was any truth to it. But also, he hoped that he would be able to get a lead on Three-fingered Jack McKinney's whereabouts.

That prompted him to ask the old-timer, "Do you happen to know a fellow named Jack McKinney?"

"Is he an outlaw?"

"So I've been told."

"I don't run with outlaws, and the only times I've been to the Black Castle, I've minded my own business and kept my head down. Now, havin' said that, if this Jack hombre rides the dark trails and operates in these parts, there's a good chance he's been there. Are you lookin' for him?"

"I might be," Luke answered noncommittally. "Sometimes he's called Three-fingered Jack."

"How come?"

Luke laughed. "Actually, I don't know. I've never met the man myself, and no one ever explained that to me. But I imagine he has only three fingers on one hand, whatever the reason."

"Well, that name don't ring no bells, neither. And you'd best be careful askin' questions. There ain't no quicker way to get killed in that place."

"I'll bear that in mind," Luke promised.

Since the horse was carrying double—even though Badger didn't weigh much—they stopped fairly often to let the animal rest. Around the middle of the morning, they came to a spring surrounded by towering canyon walls. The spring formed a small pool before disappearing underground again. Luke gave Badger a hand slipping down from the horse's back.

"Better smell that water first before drinking it," Luke advised.

Badger snorted. "I told you, I been prospectin' in these hills for years. I know about makin' sure water's fit to drink 'fore I start guzzlin' it down."

He dropped to his knees beside the pool, cupped his hand, and brought water to his mouth. After a quick sniff, he drank and nodded in satisfaction. "Tastes good. Cool and clear. Won't find any better in these parts."

Luke swung down from the saddle and said, "I'm glad to hear that. I'll fill both canteens." He unwrapped the strap of one canteen from the saddle, turned toward the pool, and felt a heavy impact against the canteen. He took a quick step back to brace himself and looked down at the canteen in his hand.

And saw the arrow sticking out from it where the arrowhead had lodged.

If Luke had been a second slower turning around, that arrow would be buried in his back.

CHAPTER 14

Luke dropped the canteen and palmed out one of the Remingtons as he called, "Badger, look out!"

Badger dropped flat just as an arrow cut through the space where he'd been a heartbeat earlier. The shaft splashed into the pool.

Luke spotted movement on the canyon wall to his left, twisted in that direction, and saw a bronzed figure in high-topped moccasins, breechcloth, and blue shirt holding a bow pulled back, aiming an arrow at him. Luke fired an instant before the Apache loosed the arrow.

The bullet slammed into the man and slewed him around enough to make the arrow sail off harmlessly down the canyon. The Apache stumbled, lost his balance, and pitched forward headfirst off the rim. He fell the thirty feet to the canyon floor and landed in a sprawled heap signifying death.

He hadn't been alone. Another warrior let out a shrill cry as he stood up on the rimrock and loosed an arrow at Luke. The flint head barely missed Luke's right ear. The shaft struck his shoulder and ricocheted off without doing any damage. Luke fired a second shot, but the Apache had already ducked back down.

More war cries echoed in the canyon. Luke couldn't tell how many attackers there were, maybe the whole dozen Badger claimed to have gotten away from. They were on both sides of the canyon, Luke realized as more arrows whipped around him. He pulled the other Remington and fired left and right as he hurried toward the horse.

"Come on!" he called to Badger. "Let's hunt some cover!"

Badger had scrambled up and reached the horse. He yanked Luke's Winchester from its scabbard and swung it to his shoulder. The old-timer began firing, tracking the rifle's barrel along one side of the canyon and peppering the rimrock with .44-40 slugs. Luke didn't think Badger hit any of the Apaches, but the volley made them keep their heads down for a few seconds, anyway, and that respite was more than welcome.

Luke made it into the saddle with a lithe bound, then holstered one of the revolvers and held out his hand as he shouted to Badger, "Come on!"

The old prospector reached up and clasped wrists with him. It was a good thing Badger didn't weigh much. Luke hauled him behind the saddle as he kicked the horse into a run.

"Hang on!"

At least a few of the Indians were armed with rifles, as Badger had indicated earlier. Luke heard shots popping, saw geysers of dirt as the bullets plowed into the ground around them. An arrow flew past his eyes, only inches away.

"You hit?" he called to Badger.

"Not yet," the old man replied, "but some o' them shots are comin' too damn close!"

Luke couldn't argue with that. He kept the horse moving fast and pounded away from the spring. They had only one canteen now, since he had dropped the other one, but that one had a hole in it anyway from the arrow, he reminded himself. And it had probably saved his life, so he supposed that was a good trade . . . as long as he didn't wind up dying of thirst.

The canyon petered out and the trail sloped up in front of them. Luke called on his mount for as much speed as the horse could muster and galloped up the rise as more war cries came from behind them.

Badger said, "Oh, hell, they're comin' after us!"

Luke looked back and saw that the old-timer was right. Most of the time, an Apache would rather eat a horse than ride one and could run tirelessly all day. Sometimes, though, the stubborn warriors used tough little ponies as mounts. That was the case today as eight Apaches gave chase on horseback.

At least it wasn't the whole dozen of them, Luke thought grimly.

He faced front again and searched for a place where he and Badger could fort up. Spying some boulders ahead of them at the base of another ridge, Luke headed for those rocks.

They were almost there when a warrior with a bright crimson headband around his raven hair stood up from behind a boulder and aimed a Springfield rifle at them. Luke realized they were racing right into the jaws of a trap.

Before the Apache could pull the trigger, a shot blasted from the top of the ridge behind the boulders. The warrior jerked forward and dropped his rifle. He sprawled over the top of the boulder that had concealed him and didn't move.

More shots slammed through the hot air. Another Apache toppled from his hiding place in the rocks. Two more appeared, turning to fire up at whoever was sniping at them from the ridge. That gave Luke clear shots at them from behind. As he reached the boulders and hauled back on the reins with his left hand, he used the Remington in his right hand to plant a slug in a warrior's back. The man flung his arms in the air, loosing his grip on the rifle he held. He stumbled a couple of steps and then plowed the dirt with his face.

The remaining Apache, realizing he was caught between two enemies, screeched in hate and swung around. Luke was closer, so the warrior must have figured he had a better shot at him.

A bullet from the ridge shattered the Apache's right shoulder before he could bring his rifle to bear. A split second later, Luke drilled a bullet through the man's head and dropped him like a puppet with its strings cut. That cleared the clump of boulders of hostiles.

"Hang on to the horse!" Luke called to Badger as he leaped to the ground. He pouched the iron he held as he added, "Give me that Winchester!"

Badger slid down from the horse's back and tossed the rifle to Luke, who caught it deftly. He ran to one of the boulders and knelt behind it. The eight mounted Apaches were still attacking. Arrows rattled among the rocks, and bullets ricocheted from them with ear-piercing whines.

Luke sprayed rifle rounds among them. One warrior went backward off his pony as if a giant hand had swept him aside. A pony fell in a welter of dust and flailing legs, throwing its rider. Just as the Apache scrambled to his feet, Luke shot him in the chest and put him down again.

The other six men veered apart, scattering so they wouldn't be bunched up anymore. They wheeled and headed back the way they had come. Luke sent a couple of rounds after them but didn't tally any more hits. The next time he squeezed the trigger, the hammer landed on an empty chamber.

He always had extra cartridges in his pockets. He fished out a handful of them and thumbed them through the Winchester's loading gate, then cranked the lever and knelt there, waiting to see what the Apaches were going to do.

Badger said excitedly, "Somebody's comin' down that hill behind us!"

Luke already knew someone had been up there. Their unknown benefactor had ruined the Apaches' trap and killed several of them. The numbers didn't quite add up, he thought. The Apache war party had been slightly larger than Badger's estimate of their numbers.

Luke looked over his shoulder and saw a figure mounted on a rangy mule coming down the slope toward them. Rocks slid under the mule's hooves, but the animal was sure-footed and the rider gave him his head. Luke thought he recognized the mule, and by the time they reached the bottom, he definitely recognized the person who'd come to their rescue.

Aaron McKinney hauled back on the mule's reins and slid off the animal's back, clutching the old Henry rifle. The youngster was wide-eyed, and his freckles stood out against the pale skin of his face, which showed the strain he was experiencing. There was a good chance it was the first gun battle the boy had ever been mixed up in . . . and likely, those Apaches were the first men he had killed.

"Normally, Aaron, I'd want to know what in blazes you're doing here," Luke greeted him, "but right now I'll just say that we're obliged to you for saving our bacon."

"You know this younker?" Badger asked.

"I do," Luke said. "Both of you had better stay low. Those Apaches who are left might pull back a ways and try taking some potshots at us."

Badger wrapped the reins around a good-sized rock to keep Luke's horse from bolting. Aaron did the same with his mule's reins.

When both animals were crouched in relative safety behind boulders, Luke went on. "Badger, this young man is Aaron McKinney. Aaron, that old pelican is Badger O'Donnell."

"What's he doing here?" Aaron asked. "Is he a bounty hunter, too? He doesn't look like one."

Luke winced as Badger exclaimed, "Bounty hunter! You told me you was an owlhoot!"

"Actually, I never did. You just assumed that, since I wanted to go to the Black Castle."

Aaron said, "What's the Black Castle? What's going on here?"

Luke ignored the questions for the moment. His intent gaze scanned the landscape for any sign of Apaches other than the dead ones who lay scattered among the rocks and on the flats in front of the boulders. The others had ridden out of sight, but he didn't believe for a second that they'd abandoned the fight and wouldn't be back. They still outnumbered him and his companions by a two-to-one margin.

Badger said, "If you're a bounty hunter and you still figure on goin' to the Black Castle, you must really want to die."

"Blast it, somebody talk to me!" Aaron said.

It was a good chance to finish reloading the Winchester, Luke decided. While he was doing that, he said, "The Black Castle is a hideout where outlaws can go and be safe, in return for a cut of their loot to the man who runs the place."

"You think you might find my father there."

"There's a chance I might, or at least get an idea of where to look for him."

"McKinney," Badger said slowly. "Earlier you was askin' me about some hombre called Three-fingered Jack McKinney. What relation is he to this boy?"

"He's my father," Aaron said with a bitter edge in his voice. "I want somebody to track him down and bring him to justice. That's why I put a reward out for him."

Badger stared in amazement. "You put a reward on your own pa?"

"A dollar and forty-two cents," Luke said, "and a harmonica."

"It's nearly new," Aaron said. "Plays real good. I saved up for it." A hangdog look came over his face. "Then I felt really bad about spendin' the money for it when Ma and me didn't have hardly anything. I figured maybe it'd help me find somebody willing to track down my pa and see that he gets what's comin' to him."

Badger shook his head. "Boy, you can't tell me you believed that would actually work."

"You mean that somebody would go after Pa just for a bounty like that? Of course not! I'm not stupid, Mr. O'Donnell. But Pa's got other rewards on his head. I was just trying to get somebody interested enough to see what it was about, and then maybe they'd go after him for the real reward." Aaron looked at Luke. "And it worked, didn't it, Mr. Jensen? You're here."

"I'm here," Luke admitted with a wry smile. "Although so far, it doesn't seem to be working out too well. What I want to know now is why *you're* here, Aaron."

"You best save that," Badger said as he peered over the boulder in front of him. "Here come them durned Apaches again!"

CHAPTER 15

It was a frontal attack, with mounted warriors charging directly at the rocks as they shouted and fired their weapons.

As Luke squinted over the Winchester's barrel, he noticed right away that only three of the Apaches had joined the assault. "Hold your fire," he called to Aaron, who had rested the Henry's barrel on the rock in front of him and was trying to draw a bead on one of the attackers. "This is just a diversion. They're trying to keep our attention on them while the others get up on the ridge behind us."

"You sure about that?" Badger asked.

"I'm confident," Luke said. "Wait a minute and see what they do."

Sure enough, before the Apaches came within effective rifle range, they peeled off again.

As they galloped back toward the canyon where the spring was located, Badger said, "You was right, Luke. What do we do now?"

"How are your eyes, Badger?"

"Sharp as an eagle's!"

Luke doubted that, but maybe the old-timer's eyes

were good enough for the task at hand. "You keep watch on our left and see if they try to flank us that way. I'll watch to the right."

"How about me?" Aaron asked.

"Catch your breath. There'll be plenty for you to do, soon enough."

With a grim look on his face, Aaron nodded, then asked, "Are we going to get out of this alive?"

"Why, sure we are!" Badger responded immediately. "That's just a handful of Apaches out there. They're pesky as hell, but they ain't no match for us."

Aaron didn't look like the old man's bravado convinced him, but he didn't say anything else.

As Luke kept an eye on the landscape to their right, he asked, "How's that wound in your side, Badger? All that running around and jumping on horseback didn't make it open up again?"

"It hurts like blazes, but it don't seem to be bleedin' much, if any. Under the circumstances, I'm gonna call it good."

"What happened to you?" Aaron asked.

"One o' those 'Paches creased me with a rifle bullet a day or two ago. That was when they jumped me the first time. But I got away from 'em, I durned sure did! That's why I said you didn't have to worry about 'em. They couldn't even handle one old pelican like me!" Badger slapped his thigh and brayed in laughter.

Again, it didn't sound a hundred percent genuine, but Luke appreciated that he was trying to keep their spirits up.

"Have you been following me ever since I left your mother's spread?" he asked Aaron.

"Yeah," the boy answered with sullen defiance in

his voice. "I wanted to see what happened when my pa's past finally caught up to him. I wanted to see the look on his face. I still do."

Badger said, "Youngster, you got some powerful hate in you. You best be careful. Feelin's like that'll just plumb eat you up inside."

"You don't know what my father put us through," Aaron snapped.

"And you didn't think about what a bad situation you were leaving your mother in," Luke said with a note of anger in his voice. "She was barely keeping the place going with your help. How do you think she's doing all by herself?"

"She can get somebody to help her," Aaron muttered. "That dang ol' sheriff would, if she'd just go to bed with him."

"Boy!" Badger exclaimed. "You hush your mouth about things like that! That's your own ma you're talkin' about, dang it."

"Maybe so, but I know the way things work, and I've seen the way Sheriff Collins looks at her. Shoot, she could just marry him and move into town and forget all about that hardscrabble ranch."

"Is that what you want?" Luke asked. "Do you think it would be better if your father was dead and your mother was married to the sheriff?"

"I don't know *what* I want . . . except for my father to be punished for running off the way he did."

Luke let the conversation settle for a minute or two, then asked, "How did you come to be ahead of us that way? Did you know the Apaches were trying to spring a trap on us?"

Aaron shook his head. "No, that was pure dumb luck. I lost your trail, and I guess I must've circled past you somehow. I climbed up on top of that ridge to take a better look around, and that's when I heard gunshots back to the south. I saw you come riding out of that canyon, and then I spotted those Indians hiding in the rocks . . . these rocks where we are now." The youngster swallowed hard. "I couldn't just let them shoot you. So I started shooting at them."

"You told me you were good with that Henry," Luke said. "That's true, and Badger and I are probably alive because of it."

"We're obliged to you, boy," the old-timer said.

"I guess out here . . . a man's got to learn how to kill sooner or later," Aaron said.

"Some don't," Luke told him. "Some men are lucky and never encounter any real violence in their lives. But not many, here on the frontier. You're right about that, too."

"Speakin' o' that," Badger said, "I think I just saw somethin' movin' in that direction, 'bout half a mile over yonderways."

Luke turned to look but couldn't see anything. "Some of the Apaches circling around us?"

"That'd be my guess. Like you said, they've probably split up and some of the red devils are tryin' to get behind us."

"Why don't we just go up the ridge and get away from them?" Aaron asked.

Luke took his hat off, put it on the end of the Winchester's barrel, and slowly raised it up above the level of the rocks. A rifle cracked somewhere out on the flats, and the hat spun off the rifle barrel.

"One of them crawled up within rifle range." He shook his head at the sight of his hat, which now had a bullet hole in it. "He's a good shot, too. That was another reason for the distraction earlier, so we wouldn't notice him getting into position. It's hard enough to see an Apache when he doesn't want to be seen, even under the best of circumstances. The slope is steep enough that we wouldn't be able to move very fast if we tried climbing it. He'd pick off at least two of us and probably all three before we ever got to the top."

"So they got us pinned down here," Badger said. "And we can't stop 'em from flankin' us."

"That's about the size of it," Luke said.

"So what do we do?" Aaron asked nervously.

"Wait until it gets dark. Then they'll come at us from both directions at once. Do you have any fight left in you, Aaron?"

"I don't have much choice about it, do I?"

"There's always a choice," Luke said. "You can give up and die."

Aaron shook his head. "No, sir. Not without a fight."

Badger grinned and said, "I may not understand ever'thing about you, boy, but I reckon you'll do to ride the river with."

"That's my impression, as well," Luke added.

Aaron swallowed again and nodded. Luke thought it was a damned shame that a boy only twelve years old was put in the position of having to fight for his life, but Aaron wasn't the first youngster whom life had backed into a corner where it was kill or be killed. He almost certainly wouldn't be the last one, either.

* * *

The rocks provided protection from bullets and arrows but not much in the way of shade. The burning sun crawled across the sky during that long afternoon. Sweat soaked the shirts worn by Luke, Aaron, and Badger.

Aaron had an almost full canteen, so they didn't go thirsty, although at Luke's suggestion they limited how much they drank. In all likelihood, the standoff would be over once the sun went down, and they would either be dead or free to move on and find water elsewhere, possibly even back at that spring-fed pool. There was a slim chance they would survive the night and still be pinned down, so they needed to make the water on hand last as long as possible.

Aaron sat with his back against the boulder where he had taken cover. After a while, his head drooped forward so his hat brim shielded his face.

Badger nodded toward him and said quietly, "The boy's gone to sleep."

"You can, too, if you want to," Luke said. "I'll keep watch."

Badger shook his head. "When a fella gets to be my age, he don't sleep all that good to start with. Too many aches and pains . . . and memories. No, if I only got a few hours left, I'd just as soon spend 'em awake." The old-timer paused. "Damn shame about the lad, though. He ain't hardly had a chance to live yet."

"Don't go giving up. We have plenty of ammunition."

"Yeah, but them devils outnumber us two to one. And what I told the boy about 'Paches not bein' good fighters was just bull. You know that."

"Maybe, but believe it or not, I've been in worse scrapes than this and came out with a whole hide, Badger."

"I reckon in your line o' work, that's probably true." Badger shook his head. "A bounty hunter. I wouldn'ta guessed it. I suppose I should be glad I don't have no ree-ward dodgers out on me. Leastways, not that I know of."

Luke grinned. "You don't think I'd turn you in for money, do you?"

"I wouldn't want to predict what a bounty hunter might do, no more than I would a diamondback rattler or an Apache buck."

"Are you comparing me to those two things?"

"You're all natural-born killers, ain't you?"

Luke didn't have any answer for that.

Time dragged because of the heat and misery, but as the day went on, the sun seemed to dip faster and faster toward the horizon, as if something were making it speed up. That something was the impending Indian attack, Luke knew. Their lives were on a deadline now, a deadline of darkness, and it was racing toward them.

Aaron woke up and complained of a crick in his neck because of sleeping with his head hanging forward that way. Then he said, "I don't reckon it'll bother me much longer, will it?"

"You'll forget about it once the excitement starts," Badger told him, "and then when it's over you'll be so excited that we come through all right, you won't care about no little pain in the neck."

Aaron looked over at Luke. "Mr. Jensen, if you get

out of here alive and . . . and I don't . . . will you see to it that my ma knows what happened to me? Tell her I didn't back down, that I stepped up and did my part. Will you do that? I'd ask you to see that she's took care of, but that's not in any way your responsibility—"

"You can tell her about all of this yourself, if you want to," Luke interrupted him. "You might not want to. It might upset her. But that'll be up to you."

"Damn it, if I don't make it and one of you two fellas do, you've got to go back and talk to her—"

Quietly, Luke said, "Aaron, if it comes down to that, I *will* see to it that she's taken care of, and I don't mean she'll have to marry Sheriff Collins. Don't worry. Just concentrate on what we're facing here."

"And it ain't gonna be much longer now," Badger said. "The sun just set, and in these parts, when night falls, it comes down mighty hard and fast."

CHAPTER 16

Luke gave Badger the extra revolver from his saddlebags, along with a box of cartridges for it.

"Wish I still had the ol' Sharps I used to have," the old-timer said. "If I did, I'd pick them red devils off long before they got anywhere close to us."

"I don't doubt it," Luke said, although in truth he had no idea what sort of shot Badger was. "How are you at close work?"

"I can handle it," Badger said with a grim nod.

"You're responsible for covering our rear, then. Aaron and I will handle the front."

"Sounds fine to me," Badger agreed. "You boys have got long guns. 'Course, they ain't gonna do you much good once it gets dark, because you won't be able to see those heathens creepin' up on us."

"That's why we have to be ready to act fast when the time comes. Aaron, you've got a round chambered in that Henry?"

"Yes, sir, I do," the boy replied solemnly. "One in the chamber and fifteen more in the magazine."

Luke grinned in the rapidly gathering dusk. "People used to say you could load a Henry on Sunday and shoot it all week. I doubt if it'll take you that long to empty it this evening, though. Just don't rush your shots. Chances are, you won't have time to reload, so those sixteen rounds are probably all you get in this fight."

"Yes, sir. I'll remember that."

Luke heard a tiny quaver of fear in the youngster's voice. Aaron was trying to put up a brave front, but he had to be terrified. Luke was more than a mite uneasy himself. Knowing half a dozen Apaches lurked out there in the deepening darkness was enough to spook any man, no matter how much courage he had. It didn't help matters that the bodies of the Apaches they had killed earlier still lay close by, constant reminders of death.

"Get ready, boys," Badger whispered suddenly. "I just heard a rock move a little, up on the slope—"

The old-timer didn't get any more words out before a bloodthirsty screech tore the night apart.

Luke brought the Winchester to his shoulder, thinking that the remaining Apaches in the war party must be young bucks who lacked the patience to wait until the sky was completely dark. He spotted movement, a shifting of gray and black shadows, as one of the renegades leaped up from where he had crawled close to the rocks.

Orange flame spurted from the muzzle of Luke's rifle as he fired. He thought he saw the shape he was aiming at lurch backward, but it was difficult to be sure in the poor light. He jacked another round into the chamber and fired again in the same general area, then swung the Winchester to the right, toward a charging figure who loomed up out of the darkness no more than ten feet away.

To Luke's left, Aaron's Henry cracked twice, fast. The heavier booms of the Colt Badger was using came from behind them. Luke and the Apache rushing at him fired at the same time. The hot breath of a bullet brushed past Luke's cheek, then the slug spanged off a rock somewhere behind him. The man in front of him grunted and stumbled. Luke worked the Winchester's lever, fired another round, and the bullet flung the renegade backward.

"Yee-owww!" Badger yelled.

Luke spun around, saw the old-timer grappling with an Apache. The Colt roared twice more, but the reports were muffled, both the sounds and the flash, and Luke knew Badger had rammed the muzzle against the Apache's body as he pulled the trigger. They both went down.

Another figure leaped toward Aaron from behind as the boy continued to fire out into the flat in front of the boulders. Luke had the Winchester at his hip, and there was no time to raise it to his shoulder. He triggered anyway, but the Apache kept coming. Luke dived forward and rammed his shoulder into the man, knocking him away from Aaron.

The collision sent Luke sprawling to the ground, as well as jolting the rifle out of his hands. He rolled over, saw the Apache scrambling back to his feet close by, and kicked out with both feet. His boot heels caught the man in the chest and drove him backward against one of the boulders. Luke heard the solid thump as the back of the man's head hit the rock.

The Apache rebounded and started to pitch forward, probably stunned. Luke rose to meet him, the bowie knife in his left hand. He brought it up and the razor-sharp blade went into the Apache's belly.

Luke twisted the knife and ripped it to the side. The hot rush of blood and entrails over his hand seemed scalding. His face was close to the enemy's face as the Apache grunted and died.

Luke yanked the knife free and shoved the collapsing body aside, then realized the old-timer and the boy weren't shooting anymore. "Badger! Aaron! Are you all right?"

"Y-yeah, I . . . I think so," Aaron said.

Luke saw him leaning against the boulder, still holding the Henry.

A groan came from Badger, who lay on the ground beside the dark shape of the Apache he had shot.

Luke looked around, didn't see anything else moving in the shadows, and told Aaron, "Straighten up and stay alert."

"Y-yes, sir." Aaron swallowed so hard Luke heard the gulp as he dropped to one knee beside Badger.

"How bad is it?" he asked.

"I don't . . . I don't think the varmint stabbed me . . . or nothin' like that. He just . . . ran into me and walloped that bullet wound . . . in my side. Feels like . . . it's bleedin' again . . . and it hurts like hell."

"We can take care of that," Luke assured him.

"Does that mean . . . you got some more whiskey . . . squirreled away somewheres?" Badger asked with a hopeful note in his voice.

"No, but we can clean up that wound and stop the bleeding as soon as we're sure the fight is actually over."

"Oh." Badger sounded disappointed.

Luke turned his head toward the boy. "See or hear anything, Aaron?"

"No, sir. Did . . . did we kill all of them?"

"Too soon to say. But we did for some of them, anyway, and maybe the others took off for the tall and uncut. Get your mule and my horse. You're going to lead them while I help Badger. We're going up to the top of this ridge. I don't hanker to spend the rest of the night here, surrounded by corpses, and we'll have higher ground that way, too."

He got an arm around Badger and carefully lifted the older man to his feet. Badger groaned again but seemed fairly steady. Climbing the slope in the dark while keeping Badger from falling wasn't easy, but Luke managed the task. Horseshoes rang against the rocks as Aaron led the two mounts up behind them. If any of the Apaches were still around, they would hear that and know their intended victims were on the move, but nothing could be done about that.

No one else attacked them as they ascended the ridge. When they reached the top, Luke found a stand of small but hardy pines and lowered Badger to the ground so that he was able to lean back against one of the trees. Aaron tied the reins to a small pine as Luke moved back to the edge and scanned the nighttime landscape around them. All seemed peaceful and quiet. Of course, he knew how deceptive that could be.

"All right. Aaron, you're standing guard while I tend to Badger," he said when he returned to the others. He knelt beside the old-timer and pulled up Badger's vest and shirt. The dressing tied against the wound was wet with blood. Luke had to work by feel as he got one of his spare shirts from his saddlebags, tore cloth from it to make another pad, and bound it into place. It would have been easier if he could have kindled even a small fire, but he didn't want to risk it.

They had survived the battle against the Apaches, but it wouldn't pay to push their luck.

Luke gave Badger some water to keep him from getting too dried out because of the blood he'd lost, then the old man dozed off. Luke walked to the edge of the trees where Aaron was standing and said, "Anything?"

"Nope. I think maybe we killed all of them, Mr. Jensen."

"Be a good thing if we did. That way no one would be left to go back to the rest of the bunch and get help."

Aaron turned his head to stare at Luke. "You think there are more of them?"

"Hard to say. Most of the Apaches have gone to live on the reservations, but there are still plenty of holdouts in isolated areas like these hills. This war party may have branched off from a larger group, or it could be that was all of them. There's only one way to find out—wait and see what happens."

Aaron sighed and said, "I'm not sure but what waiting is almost as hard as fighting."

"That's a lesson a lot of men have learned from war."

The long night was finally over. Aaron had slept a little, Luke not at all. Badger had been restless during the night, and when Luke rested his hand against the old man's forehead as gray streaks began to appear in the eastern sky, he could tell how warm Badger was. The old-timer was running a fever. He needed better medical attention than Luke could provide for him out in the middle of nowhere.

The sort of medical attention he might be able to get at the Black Castle. Luke was confident that someone at Henry Stockbridge's stronghold would be experienced in patching up bullet wounds.

Luke needed Badger to tell him how to find the Black Castle, though, and for that, the old man needed to be conscious. Luke woke up Aaron and told him, "Keep an eye on Badger. Give him some water if he wakes up."

"What are you going to do, Mr. Jensen?"

"Go down there and take a look around," Luke said with a nod toward the boulders where the previous night's desperate battle had taken place.

With his fully loaded Winchester held ready, he walked and slid down the slope. The bodies of two more Apache warriors had been added to the four already scattered around the clump of rocks, and as the light grew stronger, Luke counted five corpses sprawled on the flats near the rocks. He had killed two Indians back in the canyon where the spring was. That made thirteen. Badger had figured the members of the war party at a dozen, but Luke had already realized that Badger's count was slightly off. The question was, had there been thirteen renegades, all of whom were now dead . . . or was there another Apache or two out there somewhere, a potential source of more danger for them?

Luke didn't know, and it would have taken quite a bit of searching for hoofprints to find out. For now, he thought it would be safe to build a fire, get some coffee and food inside Badger, and then try to locate the Black Castle.

"What did you find?" Aaron asked when he got back to the top of the ridge.

"Just a bunch of dead Apaches," Luke said. "I reckon you did for at least two more of them."

"I wish I hadn't."

"Then they likely would have killed us," Luke pointed out as he started gathering small, broken branches for a fire.

"Well, then, I wish I hadn't been forced to kill them."

"Like I said, there are always choices. As far as I'm concerned, you made the right one. Here, finish building this fire while I dig out my coffeepot."

CHAPTER 17

Coffee and bacon perked Badger up some, but he was still weaker and more disoriented than he had been before the battle the night before. If Luke had had any more whiskey, he would have gladly given it to the old man as a bracer.

"We're going to have to take you to the Black Castle, Badger," Luke told him after they had finished eating. "Do you think you can ride?"

"Yeah, I reckon so, but we never did find my mule. Or did we? I disremember. Oh, Lord, I hope the 'Paches didn't get him. He was a good ol' mule. I hate to think about him goin' in some filthy squaw's stewpot."

"I'm sure he got away," Luke said, even though he was sure of no such thing.

"You can ride with me, Mr. O'Donnell," Aaron offered without hesitation. "Neither of us weigh all that much, and my mule Titus, he's plenty strong. He can carry both of us without any problem."

Luke had been about to suggest the same thing. He was glad that Aaron had thought of it himself. Showed that the boy's mind was working. He wasn't dwelling any longer on what had happened before but was looking to the future instead.

Luke had loosened the cinches on his horse and Aaron's mule after they climbed up atop the ridge but hadn't removed the saddles. He retightened the cinches and got Badger on his feet. With Luke on one side of the old man and Aaron on the other, they boosted him into the saddle on the mule's back. Aaron climbed on behind.

Luke began to caution the boy. "He's pretty weak—"

"Don't worry," Aaron said. "I won't let him fall off."

"No, I don't believe you will," Luke said, and then he swung up into his own saddle.

The sun was halfway above the eastern horizon to their right as they started off in a generally northerly direction.

Aaron rode with one arm around Badger to steady him and the other hand holding the reins. Luke took the lead and looked back over his shoulder to say, "If you spot a familiar landmark, Badger, sing out. We're looking for the Black Castle, remember?"

"I 'member," Badger mumbled. "Lookin' for . . . Black Cass . . . Black Castle."

Luke wasn't sure how things were going to turn out with Badger in such bad shape, but pushing on was the best option they had. He didn't think he stood a very good chance of saving the old-timer's life on his own.

After a while they stumbled upon either the same rough trail Luke had been following earlier or another one like it. It led in the right direction, so he followed it. An hour later they came to a tiny creek that flowed from west to east along a rocky bed between two high walls of stone. The trail led down to a ford. The creek itself wasn't big enough to present any obstacle to crossing, but getting to it anywhere else would be difficult because of the steep banks.

Luke called a halt to let the horse and the mule drink. "Stay on the mule with Badger," he told Aaron. "The shape he's in, he doesn't need to be climbing in and out of the saddle if it's not necessary."

"Sure, Mr. Jensen," the youngster said. He sat straight and his head turned from side to side as he scanned their surroundings. "I'll keep an eye out for trouble."

"That's a good idea." Luke He took the canteens and stepped upstream to fill them while he had the chance. He hunkered down next to the stream and began filling one of the canteens.

The skin on the back of his neck prickled again as if someone were painting a target on him. He lifted his head sharply and looked around.

Aaron noticed the reaction and asked, "What's wrong?"

"I just got a feeling that somebody is watching me," Luke replied. "Somebody who's probably not a friend."

"I don't see or hear anything out of the ordinary. There's a lizard sunning himself on a rock over here. Nobody's come along to spook him lately."

"The last time I got this feeling, it was you following me."

"I'm sorry," Aaron said. "I guess I should have told you I wanted to come along, but if I had, you wouldn't have let me, would you?"

"Probably not." Luke corked the full canteen and set it aside to fill the other one.

Suddenly, Badger said, "I know this place." His voice was a little stronger than it had been earlier and sounded fairly coherent. Luke glanced up from what he was doing to see that Badger was looking around. The old-timer craned his skinny neck to peer both ways, up and down the narrow cut where the creek ran.

"You've been here before, Badger?" Luke asked.

"Yeah, I . . . I remember this creek and the way it runs through here. This ford."

"Are we getting close to the Black Castle?"

"I . . . I dunno." Badger raised a hand and massaged his forehead with his fingertips. "I'm tryin' to think, but it's kinda hard . . ."

"Take your time," Luke told him. The second canteen was full. He corked it and stood, carried the canteens over to the mounts, and handed one to Aaron.

"What we need to do . . . what we need to do is follow this creek," Badger declared with a decisive nod. "I remember now. We got to follow the creek."

"How can we do that?" Aaron asked. "There's no trail on either side, just the creek."

"We got to ride in it." Badger waved a gnarled hand toward the west. "That way. Upstream."

Luke frowned at the creek bed and decided it was just wide enough for him and Aaron to ride single file along it. But they wouldn't be able to turn their mounts around, so if the passage became too narrow for them to proceed, they would be in quite a fix. They would have to back the horse and the mule all the way out.

"Are you sure about this, Badger?" he asked.

"I'm plumb certain," the old-timer insisted. "I recollect doin' it before."

"Is this the way to the Black Castle?" Luke guessed. That seemed to make sense. An outlaw sanctuary would need to be hard to find and difficult to get in and out of.

Badger looked confused, though. "I-I dunno," he stammered. "I think so, but I ain't sure. Why else would I have—" His words stopped short as his eyes suddenly rolled in their sockets and he slumped to the side.

"Catch him!" Luke barked at Aaron, who tightened his grip and prevented the old man from toppling off the mule's back.

"What's wrong with him?" Aaron asked anxiously as he held on to Badger. "Is he dead?"

"No, I think he just passed out. Let's get him down from there, carefully."

Aaron eased Badger down into Luke's arms. Luke laid him on a small stretch of gravel next to the creek and wadded up Badger's shapeless old hat to serve as a pillow. Badger's narrow chest rose and fell in an erratic pattern, but at least he was still breathing. His face was deathly pale under the permanent tan.

Luke checked the wound, found that the dressing he had put on there before they rode out that morning had quite a bit of blood on it. "He can't afford to keep losing blood like this. If the Black Castle isn't up this creek, he may be a goner."

"We've got to save his life, Mr. Jensen."

"We're going to try our best," Luke promised. "Let me get a fresh bandage on here."

When that was done, Luke lifted Badger, still unconscious, onto the mule again.

"I've got him," Aaron said as he put his arm around the old-timer.

"Try not to put too much pressure on his side."

Luke went to his horse and stepped up into the saddle. He turned the animal's head upstream, nudged it into the water, and started following the narrow passage between looming rock walls.

The water in the creek was no more than a foot deep in most places, but there could be holes that were deeper. Luke kept a close watch for them, because if his horse stepped in one of them, the animal might lame himself or even break a leg, and that really would be a problem. Luckily, the water was clear enough that Luke had a pretty good view of the streambed.

However, when he was watching that, he couldn't look ahead of them, so his head kept falling and rising as he studied the stream and then lifted his gaze to peer along the canyon where the creek ran. It made for slow going, and with every minute that passed, he knew Badger was that much closer to dying from the fever and loss of blood.

The stone walls rose sheer for fifty or sixty feet on both sides. They looked like they were leaning in, trying to close up at the top, but Luke knew that was just an illusion, a trick of perspective from where he and his companions rode. Not much sunlight penetrated, so the gloom was thick around them.

"I don't cotton much to this," Aaron said over the quiet splashing of hooves in the water.

"Neither do I," Luke admitted.

"It gives me the fantods. What do we do if we come to a stone wall and can't go on?"

"I hope Titus is good at backing up."

"He don't care for it," Aaron said. "I reckon I can make him do it, though."

The creek's course twisted here and there, and those bends were more difficult to negotiate. The rock walls scraped against Luke's legs during those turns.

"I never realized until now how much I hate bein' closed in like this," Aaron said.

Luke motioned for the youngster to stay quiet. Voices echoed in the extremely narrow canyon. So did the sounds the horse and the mule made in the water, but those were more natural and less likely to be noticed if anyone was listening. Luke wasn't sure who that might be, but he hadn't been able to rule out the possibility of survivors from that Apache war party.

Also, if the Black Castle really did lie in that direction, it stood to reason Henry Stockbridge might have posted guards along the approach. That would explain why he had felt like someone was watching them earlier.

Luke estimated they had ridden for about a mile along the creek when the streambed began to widen a bit. Not much, but any relief from the looming oppressiveness was welcome. After a while the creek was wide enough that they were able to ride side by side. Luke motioned for Aaron to come on up and slowed his horse to let the boy catch up.

Badger was still unconscious but breathing, Luke saw as he looked over at the two of them. The old-timer's whiskery face was really haggard.

Luke looked ahead of them again and frowned when he saw a wall of stone blocking their path a hundred yards in front of them. The creek emerged from a small hole in the rock, flowing fast enough that it created bubbling whitecaps before it spread out and slowed down. Luke felt a twinge of disappointment that they had come to a dead end, but at least they had enough room now to turn the mounts around and go back to the ford. They had lost quite a bit of time, though, time that Badger might not be able to afford.

Then Luke looked up, tracking the wall to its top, and his heart suddenly slugged harder in his chest as he saw the battlements rising black against the sky. Luke had never been to England, had never laid eyes on a real medieval castle, but he had seen plenty of pictures of them in books and that seemed to be what he was looking at.

Aaron followed Luke's example and gazed upward. Eyes wide, he whispered, "The Black Castle."

"Yes, I think we've found—"

The unmistakable sound of someone working a Winchester's lever came from behind them, followed by a harsh voice ordering, "Get your hands up and keep 'em away from those guns, or we'll blow you out of the saddle!"

CHAPTER 18

From the corner of his eye, Luke saw Aaron start to reach for the Henry's stock where it stuck up from the scabbard. He said quickly, "Don't do it, Aaron. Hang on to Badger but put your other hand up."

"But Mr. Jensen—"

"Just do it."

Luke understood the instinct that made Aaron want to reach for his gun. He felt the same thing himself. Any time he was threatened, his first impulse was to fight back.

But he also knew the men behind them had the drop on them. So close to the Black Castle, those hombres would be outlaws standing guard over their haven, just as he expected. They wouldn't hesitate to shoot intruders. Sometimes you had to do what your brain dictated, not your heart.

Because of that, Luke slowly raised his hands to shoulder level, keeping the reins in his left, and made sure both were in plain sight.

"Take it easy, boys," he said in a calm, steady voice. "We're not looking for trouble."

"What *are* you looking for?" challenged the man who had just spoken.

"I think you know that as well as we do. We're looking for the Black Castle."

"Go ahead and shoot 'em," a second voice urged. "They don't look like anybody who'd be welcome here."

Without turning around, Luke said, "I thought anyone who can pay what Henry Stockbridge demands was welcome."

The response came quickly. "You know the Black Knight?"

"Never met the man," Luke answered honestly, "but my friend here told us about him and this place." He inclined his head toward Badger. "He's been here before. And he's hurt and badly in need of help."

"Who is that? Don't move, mister." One of the guards walked along a narrow ledge that Luke hadn't noticed.

He figured the man was trying to get a better look at Badger, and said softly to Aaron, "We're outlaws running from the law, understand? Nothing about—"

"You don't have to tell me," the boy replied, equally quiet. "I know what you mean."

The sound of the creek was enough to keep the guards from overhearing their whispers. Luke and Aaron sat silently after that while the guard stepped down from the ledge and waded through the creek to move in front of them, covering them with a Winchester the whole time.

The man was a lean, roughly dressed, beard-stubbled hardcase with a tightly rolled and creased black hat on his head. He looked up at the three newcomers and said, "Hey, I think I know that old man! His name's Badger, ain't it?"

"See, I told you he'd been here before," Luke said. "An Apache shot him in the side a few days ago. He's running a fever and needs medical attention."

The outlaw scoffed. "You think you'd find a sawbones here, mister?"

"Maybe not, but I was confident that I'd find someone with experience at patching up bullet wounds. Hell, I can do it myself as long as there's some hot water and whiskey and an actual bed where he can rest. I'm sure those things are available, aren't they? For the right price?"

The other guard stepped into view on the ledge and pointed his rifle at the riders. He was a tall, burly man with a blond beard. "What's your name?" he demanded.

"Luke. The boy is Aaron. And as your friend already said, the old pelican is Badger."

Luke didn't offer any other names. One name was enough for most riders of the dark trails. They tended not to be inquisitive because they didn't want anybody poking into their background, either.

"Don't reckon I've ever seen anybody bring a kid here," the dark-haired owlhoot commented.

"He didn't *bring* me," Aaron snapped. "We ride together, that's all."

The two guards exchanged quick grins.

"Proddy, ain't he?" the blond-bearded one said. "All right, I reckon we don't have enough reason to go ahead and kill you, so it'll be up to somebody else to decide what to do with you. Ride on ahead, but I'll be over here keepin' an eye on you, and if you get a hand too close to your guns or try anything else that looks funny, I will shoot you. Got it?"

"We've got it." Luke lowered his hands, but only part of the way, and used his knees to nudge the horse into motion. Aaron had to bang his heels against the mule's flanks to start it walking along the creek bed again.

As they approached the towering stone wall, Luke saw some things that hadn't been visible from farther away. The wall had a deep crack in it that, because of the angle at which it slanted into the stone, was almost invisible except from certain angles. He thought that the two guards probably had been concealed in a similar fissure back up the canyon.

A ledge slanted up the cliff face as well, then doubled back on itself and continued that zigzagging pattern as it climbed toward the top. Luke frowned as he studied the path. It didn't look natural to him. Someone had hewn it out of the rock, going to a lot of trouble and expense. Henry Stockbridge? Luke didn't see who else could have done it.

He wondered if Stockbridge had climbed that stone wall to escape the posse pursuing him. It would have been a harrowing ascent, but desperate men were capable of desperate things. Later, when Stockbridge had decided to establish his stronghold there, he could have brought in laborers to cut that trail, as well as to build the great stone house that was supposed to be up there.

Once the work was done, had Stockbridge murdered the laborers so they could never reveal his secrets, as the Egyptian pharaohs had done with the slaves who built the pyramids? Luke didn't know, but he had a hunch he shouldn't put it past the man.

Until he met Henry Stockbridge, he had no way of guessing what he might be capable of.

Three more heavily armed hardcases stepped out of the crack in the rock near the creek's origin and the bottom of the trail. One of them called to the blond-bearded guard, "Who's that, Hannigan?"

"Says his name's Luke," Hannigan replied. "The boy's Aaron, and the old man is Badger."

"Badger O'Donnell? Hell, I remember him!"

"You do?" Hannigan said. "I never heard of him."

"That's because you've only been in these parts for a couple of years. O'Donnell and his gang robbed banks and held up trains all the way from Texas to California!"

Luke and Aaron looked at each other for a second. It seemed like Badger hadn't been entirely forthcoming about his history. He wasn't just some old desert rat of a prospector after all.

But he had fought side by side with them against the Apaches, so whatever Badger had done in the past didn't matter all that much. Luke still wanted to save the old-timer's life if he could.

"He's hurt, ain't he?" continued the man who had heard of Badger.

"That's right," Luke said. "An Apache war party jumped him a few days ago and a bullet left a deep crease in his side. He's lost a lot of blood, and now he's got a fever, to boot. He said this was the closest place to get help, and since the boy and I were headed here anyway, we were glad to bring him along."

"Why were you coming here?"

"Now, why do you think?" Luke asked with a note of impatience in his voice. "We need to lie low for a while, until some folks who are trying to find us give up and go home."

"You tryin' to tell us you got a posse on your trail?" another man said. "Hell, that fella with you is just a kid!"

Aaron bristled. "I may be young, mister, but that don't mean I can't use a gun when I need to. If you want to find out—"

"That's enough," Luke said sharply. He looked at Hannigan and the other guards and added, "I wouldn't push too hard if I were you. Like he said, he's young, but he's also a little loco. You don't mind if I say that, do you, kid?"

Aaron played along and grinned. "Hell, no. Nobody else better call me crazy, though."

Hannigan said, "He looks like a farm boy, but Billy Bonney didn't look like all that much, either. Listen, boys, if this old man really is an outlaw who's been here before, I reckon we ought to let 'em go on up. If Stockbridge don't like it, he can kill 'em once they're inside the castle."

"If he gets riled up because we let 'em in, he's liable to kill *us*," one of the other men argued.

Luke looked at Badger's gray, haggard face and said, "To hell with all this wrangling. Come on, Aaron. We're going to get Badger the help he needs."

"Wait just a damn minute!" a guard yelped. "You can't ride past without our say-so."

Luke fixed a cold, hard stare on him. "Well then, give it or reach for that gun on your hip, mister, because I'm damned if I'll sit here and let my friend die while you flap your jaw." He heeled his horse ahead, toward the ledge.

"Aw, hell. Get outta their way," Hannigan said. "I believe him, and I don't want to tangle with him."

The other guards glared, but they moved aside reluctantly and allowed Luke and Aaron to ride onto the ledge and start up toward the top of the cliff. The muscles of Luke's back tightened, but no shots roared out. The guards were willing to push the decisions on to someone else, as long as they believed they could get away with it.

The ledge, like the creek bed for most of the way they had followed it, was just wide enough for one rider. That made it a one-way trail. If anyone started down while they were going up, it might mean trouble. Luke didn't hear any hoofbeats above them, however, so maybe their luck would hold.

Luck or no luck, he wasn't turning back until he got Badger the help that the old-timer needed.

Turning his head to look over his shoulder, he told Aaron, "You did good back there. For a minute, I almost thought you really were loco."

"I was so scared I was half-crazy. Does that count?"

Luke chuckled. "It should. Men do strange things sometimes when they're frightened. An unpredictable man is almost always a dangerous man."

"Are you calling me a man, Mr. Jensen?"

"Right now we're partners. That's the main thing. And call me Luke, blast it. Forget that other name."

"Sorry, M—I mean, Luke. I'll try to remember."

"Be a good thing if you did. All our lives might depend on it."

Luke had already given some thought to the chance that somebody he had captured and turned over to the law in the past might be at the Black

Castle. That was certainly possible. It was a risk he had to run, though.

The ledge turned back on itself half a dozen times before it reached the top. Now that he had gotten a better look at it, Luke was more sure than ever that the trail was man-made. So was the opening at the end of it. Arched on top, it reminded him of the mouth of a railroad tunnel. Someone must have used dynamite to blast through the cliff, all the way to the high plateau on the other side. The stone walls that surrounded it, carved by the elements into the battlements he had seen from below, provided protection that even an artillery barrage might not be able to breach. No army on foot would be able to get in there very easily, either. The way the place was built, a small force could hold off a horde of attackers.

At the moment, the tunnel-like entrance seemed to be undefended. Luke figured there were guards, just none that he could see. He, Aaron, and Badger rode through it for about fifty yards, and when they emerged, Luke and Aaron laid eyes on the Black Castle for the first time.

CHAPTER 19

It was enough to take a man's breath away. A massive pile of stone with two stories and guard towers on the corners, it looked even more like a real castle than the jagged ridges surrounding the plateau. The place was built of huge blocks that must have taken a score of men to maneuver into place with pullies and derricks and mules. Comparing the Black Castle to the Egyptian pyramids, as Luke had done mentally a short time earlier, wasn't that much of a stretch.

"Lord have mercy," Aaron murmured when they reined in. "It's like something out of a storybook."

"Yes," Luke agreed. "There should be pennants and banners flying from the battlements, and it needs a moat, a drawbridge, and a portcullis. But other than that . . ."

Instead of the things Luke had named, the castle's entrance had two huge wooden doors. Even though they weren't open at the moment, he guessed they were thick enough to stop anything short of a cannonball . . . and they might stop that, too.

To the right was a long, low building made of logs,

also sturdy-looking although nothing compared to the castle. Luke guessed that was a barracks of sorts. He didn't know if any men lived there permanently or if Stockbridge drew his guards from the outlaws who showed up looking for sanctuary and that force was always changing. There were probably different levels of accommodation for those who sought to lie low for a while. Those who couldn't afford to stay in the castle most likely bunked out in the barracks.

Looking around, Luke also saw a barn, corrals, a blacksmith shop, a smokehouse, and a couple of other buildings that were probably used for storage. The place appeared to be self-sustaining for the most part, although he didn't see any gardens nor did he know what sort of water supply they had. He wondered if Stockbridge had managed to tap into that underground stream somehow. That seemed like something a man would do if he was ambitious enough to have built such a place. Supplies could be packed in on mules, and plenty of game—deer, antelope, mountain goats—roamed the hills to provide fresh meat.

A man could arrive there and never leave. Evidently, that was just what Henry Stockbridge had done.

Half a dozen men on horseback emerged from the barn and rode toward the newcomers.

Luke said, "Let's just sit here and wait for them to come to us."

"Look at that fella in the lead, Luke. He's mighty big."

That was true. Even on horseback, Luke could see how tall and broad-shouldered the man was. He rode in front of the others on a huge black stallion. He was hatless, and his long black hair blew in the wind. A thick black beard curled on his jaws and chin. He was dressed in black as well.

"This is just a wild guess," Luke said dryly, "but I suspect that must be the Black Knight."

"You'd best not joke with him," Aaron warned. "He don't look like the sort of hombre who'd take kindly to it."

"Don't worry. I'll treat this occasion with the solemn dignity it deserves."

"You recognize any of those other fellas?"

Luke was already studying the big man's companions. They were all hardcases dressed in trail clothes, the sort of gunmen and killers who could be found in hundreds of places west of the Mississippi. He knew their breed, but he didn't see any familiar faces.

When he said as much, Aaron responded, "Good. If you don't know any of them, that means they don't know you."

"That's right," Luke said, continuing to be impressed by the sharpness of the boy's mind. "We should be safe . . . for now."

The black-bearded man brought the stallion to a halt when he was twenty feet away from Luke, Aaron, and Badger. Without any greeting, he rumbled in a deep voice, "I know that old man. He's Badger O'Donnell."

"That's right," Luke said. "We ran into him a couple of days ago, after he tangled with some Apaches. He's wounded and needs medical attention."

"And who might you be?" the man asked.

Luke heard vestiges of a British accent in his voice, but Stockbridge's time in the United States had erased most of it. "They call me Luke, and this is Aaron. If you need to know any more than that, you're out of luck."

Laughter boomed out of Stockbridge's barrel chest. "From my perspective, it's you who would be out of luck, my friend, since you're quite outnumbered and outgunned. If I were to say the word, you'd be dead in a matter of seconds, but as it happens, I respect a man's desire for privacy. I never insist that my visitors give me their full names, or their true names, as far as that goes. So Luke and Aaron it is. Now, tell me, what made you believe you could simply ride in here and demand help for your friend?"

"We're not demanding anything," Luke said. "Badger fought beside us when that Apache war party attacked again. I'm not going to stand by and let a comrade in arms die if there's something I can do to save him. He said to bring him here, so that's what the boy and I did. We've fulfilled our obligation."

Stockbridge cocked his head to the side and regarded Luke with curiosity. "You sound like an educated man."

"Self-educated, mostly. I got enough schooling when I was a boy to learn how to read, and I took the responsibility from there."

"Whereas I learned my lessons on the playing fields of Eton, as they say. Regardless of the differences in our backgrounds, I believe we could have an interesting conversation, Luke. For that reason, and because I'm fond of that old reprobate, I'm not going to kill you." Stockbridge lifted the reins and started to turn the stallion around. "Bring him along. There's a doctor here."

"An actual doctor?" Luke asked as he kneed his horse into motion.

"That's right. As you Westerners call them, a sawbones."

The men who had accompanied Stockbridge split apart so Luke and Aaron could ride between them, then fell in behind them and Stockbridge.

The black-bearded man looked over at Luke and went on. "I'm not sure we've ever had a child visit us here at the Black Castle before."

"I may look like a kid, mister," Aaron said, "but I've had to grow up fast."

Stockbridge laughed again. "An excellent response, lad. I like a boy with confidence."

"I got plenty of confidence . . . and a Henry rifle I know how to use."

"You shouldn't have to demonstrate that skill while you're here. The Black Castle is a haven of peace . . . most of the time."

Someone must have been watching from inside. The doors swung open before the riders got there. Stockbridge reined in and swung down from the stallion's back. Luke followed suit and reached up to take Badger from Aaron.

A middle-aged Mexican woman came out of the castle. She was striking looking, with white streaks in her long, raven hair.

Stockbridge said to her, "Send someone to fetch Dr. Mitchell, and show our visitors to one of the empty rooms on the first floor."

"*Sí*, Sir Henry," the woman said.

"Sir Henry?" Luke repeated as the servant stepped back to usher them into the castle.

"Self-dubbed, in the absence of the queen, I'm afraid. But since I'm the closest thing to a knight in these parts . . ."

Luke shook his head and said, "It's no business of mine, one way or the other."

Badger was unconscious. Luke carried the frail bundle of rawhide and bone that was the old man's body and followed the woman into a vast foyer paved with flagstones. Aaron came behind them, looking around warily as he held the Henry. Stockbridge strode along beside Luke. Their footsteps echoed from the high ceiling.

The woman led them down a hallway with walls covered by colorful tapestries of hunting scenes and pastoral landscapes. Luke figured that as a member of British aristocracy, Stockbridge must have ridden to the hounds as a young man, and those tapestries must remind him of home.

They went into a room furnished with a comfortable-looking four-poster bed. She hurried to take a blanket out of a chest of drawers and spread it on the bed to protect the comforter from getting bloody. Luke lowered Badger into that welcoming softness. The woman shooed Luke aside and moved in to start removing Badger's clothes.

Aaron stood just inside the room and asked, "They're gonna take good care of him, aren't they?"

"We will," Stockbridge answered from the hallway. "Mr. O'Donnell was welcome here as a guest in the past and has done nothing to disabuse himself of our hospitality. Everything possible will be done for him." He paused. "In fact, here comes the doctor now."

Stockbridge stepped aside so a short, stocky man with thinning, curly gray hair could bustle into the room. The man wore a gray tweed suit that had seen better days and carried a black leather bag. Luke caught a whiff of whiskey coming from him, but the medico was clear-eyed and didn't appear to be drunk.

"I'm told there's an injured man here." he said.

Stockbridge waved a hand toward the bed. "There lies your patient, Doctor."

The man's eyes widened in surprise as he looked at the scrawny figure stretched out on the blanket. "That's old Badger. I haven't seen him around here for months. What happened to him?"

"A deep bullet crease in his right side," Luke said. "It didn't penetrate and do any damage to his internal organs, but he lost a lot of blood and now he's developed a fever."

The doctor grunted. "Infection has set in. This may be touch and go."

"I tried to clean the wound with whiskey when I first found him and thought I had gotten it patched up well enough. But we ran into more trouble after that and he got banged around some. Since then we've never been able to keep the bleeding stopped consistently, and he's gotten weaker and weaker."

"I'll clean the wound with carbolic and explore to see if there's a source of internal bleeding. Other than that, all we can do is keep him comfortable. I'm Doctor Hiram Mitchell, by the way."

"Luke's my name. Do your best for him, Doc."

"Of course," Mitchell replied, sounding somewhat offended by the thought that he might do any less. "Now, you've done your part, so you can go on. If I need assistance, Paloma is here."

The Mexican woman nodded gravely.

"Come to the main hall," Stockbridge invited Luke and Aaron. "I'll have coffee and food brought."

"We'll be much obliged to you," Luke said. "You and I haven't made any kind of financial arrangements yet, though, and from what I've heard about this place, I got the idea that's pretty important to you."

Stockbridge dismissed the idea with a wave. "We can discuss that later. Right now, I feel a certain obligation, a debt of honor, if you will, because you helped a former guest of mine. You should take advantage of my largesse."

"We will," Luke said. "Won't we, Aaron?"

"Sure, I guess," the boy said. "I don't know what that fancy word means."

"It means you're now my guests, too, for the time being," Stockbridge said. "If you don't cause any trouble, that may last for a while."

"Sounds good to me. I'm not lookin' for trouble."

Stockbridge smiled. "How seldom we look, but how often it finds us anyway."

"Shakespeare?" Luke asked.

"No. A bit of philosophy of my own." Stockbridge gestured for them to join him. "Please."

He led them along the echoing corridor and then down another and through an arched entrance into a large hall dominated by a huge table that had been polished to a high sheen. Heavy chairs sat along both sides and at each end.

"I'm a little surprised the table's not round," Luke said.

"A clever reference," Stockbridge said. "But despite the fact that I've read *Le Morte d'Arthur* numerous times, I've no wish to emulate the man. He came to a tragic end, you know, and I have no intention of doing so."

Four men came into the hall through another door then, and Luke glanced over at them. They were more of the same sort of hardcases he had seen outside. Except for one, who was as roughly dressed as the others and packing an iron on his hip like them, but he hadn't been able to grow much of a beard because of his age. The way his sandy-colored stubble stuck out in a few bristly, scattered patches testified as to how young he was.

Aaron saw the young man at the same time Luke did, and his response was instantaneous. He stared and exclaimed, "Thad!"

CHAPTER 20

Everyone in the room stopped short. Thaddeus McKinney looked just as shocked as his younger brother was. His mouth opened and closed a couple of times before he was able to get any words out.

Finally he spoke. "Aaron? Aaron, what the hell are you . . . Is it really you?"

Aaron handed the Henry to Luke and rushed across the big hall to throw his arms around his brother. "I was afraid I'd never see you again," he said in a voice choked with emotion. "I figured you'd gone off and got yourself killed!"

"No, I . . . I'm fine," Thad said as he awkwardly returned the hug and patted Aaron on the back. "But I still don't understand what you're doin' here."

Aaron stepped back, and his face flushed with anger. Without any more warning than that, he hauled off and punched Thad in the stomach. Thad was bigger, but Aaron put all the power he packed in his lean body into the blow. The punch took Thad by surprise, and as Aaron's fist sunk into his belly, he gasped and doubled forward. His eyes got big and his face turned red, but in his case it was because he couldn't catch his breath.

"You . . . you little bastard!" he forced out.

"Don't you say things like that!" Aaron cried. "You're insultin' Ma when you do!" He swung again and landed a blow on Thad's jaw.

Thad staggered to the side but caught himself. Then with a bellow of rage, he grabbed Aaron around the waist and lifted him off the stone floor. "You crazy fool!" he yelled.

Aaron tried to kick and hit him, but he was too close to put much into the blows.

"Stop it!" Thad said. "Stop it, or I'll have to hurt you!"

Beside Luke, Henry Stockbridge chuckled. "Should we put a stop to this? One of them might do some actual damage to the other."

"I don't think so," Luke said. "They're brothers."

"So I gathered. But it's been my experience that sometimes the battles between brothers can be the most vicious of all."

Luke had never known that sort of fraternal conflict in his life. He got along very well with his brother Smoke and their adopted brother Matt. Of course, he had gone years after the war without ever seeing Smoke, and he hadn't even been aware of Matt's existence until a few years earlier. When he and Smoke—Kirby—had been kids, they had squabbled some, of course, like all youngsters, but never anything serious.

Aaron had some deep-seated anger to express against Thad, so Luke decided Stockbridge might be right. It might be a good idea to intervene in their fight.

However, before he could do that, one of the men who had come into the room with Thad stepped up and grabbed Aaron from behind. He was taller than Thad, so Aaron's feet were a good eighteen inches off the floor as the man wrapped arms the size of young tree trunks around his chest.

"Settle down," the man warned in a gravelly voice, "or I'll squeeze you and bust ever' bone in your body, kid."

Luke moved in, poked the Henry's barrel into the man's back, and said, "I don't think so. Now let him go."

The man looked over his shoulder at Luke. His face was lumpy and misshapen, and his ears stuck out at right angles to his head. He sneered defiantly. "I don't know who you are, mister, but you just made one hell of a mistake."

"I'm that boy's friend," Luke snapped, "and you're not going to hurt him."

"I might hurt *you.*"

"You're welcome to try, any time you want." Luke pushed harder with the Henry's barrel.

The man's craggy face twisted even more with hatred, but he loosened his grip on Aaron. The boy dropped to the floor, lost his balance, and fell to his knees.

Thad had caught his breath, glared at his brother, and demanded, "What the hell did you think you were doin'? Why'd you start hittin' me that way?"

"Because you've got it comin'!" Aaron raged back at him, fighting to hold back sniffles. "You never should've run off and left Ma and me in the lurch like you did."

"You don't know nothin' about it. You don't know what I was goin' through."

"The hell I don't! I was right there, too, remember?" Aaron struggled to his feet. "What about Pa? Is he here?"

Stockbridge nodded toward Aaron and said to Luke, "This boy is Three-fingered Jack's son as well?"

Luke nodded but didn't take his eyes off the man whose back he had poked with the rifle. He still had the Henry pointed in that hombre's direction. "That's right."

"And are you a member of the family? An uncle, perhaps?"

"Just a friend," Luke said. "I was headed in this direction anyway, so when the kid asked me if he could come along, I told him all right."

"And now Ma's there alone," Thad said accusingly.

"You abandoned us first," Aaron shot back at him.

Thad ignored that and frowned at Luke. "You're no friend of the family, mister. I never laid eyes on you before."

"That's because you've been gone for a while." Aaron jerked a thumb toward Luke and went on. "Him and Ma, well, they've been courtin' lately." He was just making that up off the top of his head, Luke knew, but he supposed the story was believable enough. Amelia McKinney was certainly still an attractive woman. Luke wouldn't have minded getting to know her better, under different circumstances, even though he had no interest in settling down at that point in his life.

If there had ever been such a point, he reflected, it had surely come and gone. Maybe all the way back in the spring of '61, when he might have married the schoolteacher Lettie Margrabe if the Yankees hadn't embarked on the War of Northern Aggression.

Luke pushed those fleeting memories out of his mind. He needed to concentrate on what was happening in the here and now in the Black Castle. If Thad McKinney was there, it was a good chance that Three-fingered Jack was, too.

"I don't believe it," Thad said in response to the bit of fiction Aaron had just come up with. "Ma's still married to Pa. She would never take up with some other man."

"Why not? For all she knows, Pa is dead, and you are, too!"

"I don't care. It just wouldn't be right!"

The jug-eared man ignored the McKinney brothers and pointed a blunt finger at Luke. "You and me got a score to settle, mister. I'm callin' you out."

"A gunfight?" Luke asked.

Stockbridge said, "Actually, since you were the one challenged just now, Luke, the choice of weapons in this duel is yours."

"I don't want to fight any damned duel. I didn't come here for that."

Stockbridge's face hardened. "Unfortunately, you have no choice. There are rules here, you see, and the main one is that any offense to a man's honor has to be settled."

Luke let out a humorless grunt of laughter. "Maybe we should joust, then."

"Don't make fun of my heritage," Stockbridge said. His voice was dangerous.

"My apologies," Luke said immediately. "I should take this seriously."

"Indeed you should."

"So if the choice of weapons is mine . . . I choose bare hands."

A grin spread across his opponent's face. "I'll break you in half, mister, and I'll enjoy every second of it."

"We'll see." Luke had thought about declaring that guns or knives were his weapon of choice, but he didn't necessarily want to kill this man. Whipping him in a hand-to-hand battle might be enough to settle things.

At the same time, he didn't expect his opponent to hold back any. The man intended to kill him . . . and he just might do it.

"I still want to know if Pa's here," Aaron said.

"I can answer that," a new voice spoke up from elsewhere in the room.

Luke turned to look. The man who had spoken had come into the hall through the same door Luke, Aaron, and Stockbridge had used earlier. He was an inch or so under medium height, slender, and had a close-cropped brown beard. At first glance he wasn't very impressive to look at, but then Luke noticed the piercing, deep-set eyes surrounded by lines of experience that hard years had put there. This man had plenty of drive and leadership lurking within him despite his rather mild-looking exterior, and Luke was sure that under the right circumstances, his true personality would come out like a brilliant flame burning through a flimsy barrier.

Luke wasn't a bit surprised when Aaron cried, "Pa!"

For one thing, he had noted that the little finger and ring finger of the newcomer's left hand were missing.

It probably took a lot to shake Jack McKinney's

calm demeanor, but he was upset at the sight of his younger son. As he walked closer, he said, "Aaron, is that really you? I . . . I can't believe it."

Aaron's face was a study in mixed emotions. Obviously, he wanted to run to his long-lost father and embrace him. At the same time, anger had driven him to come on this quest, and that same anger, currently directed at his father, still blazed inside him. He recovered from his initial shock at seeing McKinney and said, "I'm surprised you still remember me, Pa. You've been gone a long time, and I was just a little kid when you ran off and abandoned us."

McKinney stopped short and looked like he'd been slapped, which was probably just what Aaron intended.

From behind, Thad cuffed his little brother on the side of the head. "Don't talk like that to him. You don't know a damn thing. He's your old man. Show him some respect."

Aaron turned fiercely toward Thad, hands clenching into fists. "I'll show you—"

"Boys." McKinney's voice wasn't loud, but it was sharp enough to stop Aaron from swinging a punch. "Both of you stop it." He walked toward them again and came to a stop where he could look Aaron up and down. "You've grown a lot. Look like a mighty fine boy."

"No thanks to you," Aaron snapped.

McKinney smiled sadly. "Yeah, you hate me, don't you? You think you've got good cause to, and you know what? Maybe you do."

"No, Pa," Thad said quickly. "He's just a dumb kid—"

McKinney held up his maimed left hand to stop his older son. "Aaron's got a right to feel whatever he wants to, just like you did when you decided to come looking for me. I never wanted you to do that, remember? That was all your idea."

"It's best we're together again," Thad argued. "Family belongs together."

"Well, now I'm here, too," Aaron said, "and by God, if the two of you are gonna be outlaws, then so am I!"

CHAPTER 21

Jack McKinney stared at his younger son for a couple of seconds before he started shaking his head. "That's loco. You're just a boy."

Aaron pointed at Thad and said, "I'm only four years younger than him. If he's old enough, so am I."

"Absolutely not—"

"This family discussion will have to wait, Jack," Henry Stockbridge interrupted. "I promised our new arrivals food and coffee. Why don't you join us?"

McKinney looked warily at Aaron and then nodded. "Yeah. Yeah, I'll do that. But we've got a lot to talk about." He glanced over at Luke. "Such as who this hombre is."

Thad said, "Aaron claims he's Ma's new beau."

Well, that impulsive move on Aaron's part had just backfired nicely, Luke thought. McKinney looked at him with a mixture of anger and regret. "Is that true?"

Since the fiction was established, Luke decided it would be best to play along with it for now. "A man who would ride off and leave such a woman behind doesn't have any right to complain when someone else appreciates her, my friend."

"We're not friends," McKinney said coldly. "If you've been looking out for my boy, I'm obliged to you for that, but you never should've brought him here and you shouldn't go sniffing around other men's wives."

"Don't insult her by talking about her in such a degrading fashion."

Stockbridge held up his hands and said impatiently, "Gentlemen! I've already told you that you can talk about all these domestic matters later."

The massive, jug-eared man pointed at Luke and asked, "What about him and me settlin' our grudge?"

"You can join us for dinner, Creager, if you'd like, and we'll determine the particulars of that matter. If you promise to behave in a decent manner."

"I'll behave," Creager rumbled, but he didn't sound enthusiastic about the idea.

It was going to be a mighty uncomfortable meal, Luke mused. A jealous husband, a vicious outlaw, and a mad Englishman who fancied himself a knight for dinner companions . . .

He supposed he had been in worse situations, but he couldn't remember when.

Three attractive young women served dinner— one Mexican, one Chinese, and a cool, slender blonde who, when she spoke, sounded like she came from back east somewhere. Philadelphia, maybe, Luke thought. How she came to be at the outlaw stronghold in the Arizona Territory badlands was quite a mystery, one Luke wouldn't have minded solving, but he had more urgent matters on which to concentrate.

Stockbridge sat at the head of the long table.

Three-fingered Jack McKinney was to his right, the burly Creager to his left. Thad was next to his father, and Aaron sat next to him. Luke would have taken a seat on that side of the table, but Stockbridge smiled and waved him into the chair beside Creager. The outlaw looked at him like a wolf casually regarding a lamb that he would get around to slaughtering later.

The food was decent—venison steaks, beans, potatoes, biscuits. The coffee was excellent, hot and strong the way Luke liked it.

As they ate, Stockbridge said to McKinney, "You remember old Badger O'Donnell, don't you, Jack?"

"Sure," McKinney replied. "What about him?"

Stockbridge pointed to Luke with the fork he held, a piece of fine silver that might have come from England. "Our new friend brought him in a short time ago. Badger was wounded in a fight with some Apache renegades. Dr. Mitchell is tending to him right now."

McKinney frowned and said to Luke, "You did that?"

"Badger has become a friend in the short time I've known him. We fought side by side against the Apaches. If I could save his life, I was going to."

"Well . . . I appreciate that. Everybody likes old Badger. We never pulled any jobs together, but we crossed trails now and then, usually here at the castle."

Stockbridge smiled. "Everyone in these parts comes to the Black Castle sooner or later."

Luke could believe that. He wondered for a second just how much all the reward money the place represented would add up to. Then he pushed the thought away. It would take an army of bounty hunters to capture the Black Castle and its inhabitants, and he wasn't sure it would be possible even then.

Right now he was only interested in Jack McKinney. Somehow, he had to get McKinney away from the castle.

Without any apparent prompting except his own maliciousness, Creager leaned toward Luke and said, "I'm gonna rip your arms off and beat you to death with 'em, you son of a—"

"That's not polite dinner conversation," Stockbridge broke in. "Try not to be a complete brute, Creager."

"You said we could talk about it. I want to know when I can kill this hombre."

"You two can settle your differences this evening. Say, in the courtyard as the sun goes behind the western cliffs?"

"That's hours from now," Creager objected. "I want to tear him apart right now."

"Postponed pleasures are often the sweetest." Stockbridge's voice hardened as if to signal that he wouldn't tolerate any more disagreement. "Sundown it is."

Creager grimaced but nodded in acceptance of that decree. He would have to wait for his bloody fun. The cruel grin he directed toward Luke made it clear that he was looking forward to it.

Dr. Mitchell came into the hall as they were finishing the meal. "I was told you fellows were in here and thought you'd like to know how Badger is doing."

"Doing well, I hope," Luke said.

Mitchell nodded. "Actually, yes. I was able to clean out the wound and found some blood vessels that hadn't been cauterized, so I tied them off and that took care of the bleeding. Now we have to wait for the infection to clear up and the fever to break, but I'm guardedly optimistic that he'll make a full recovery. He's resting fairly peacefully now."

"That's excellent news, Doctor. Thank you." Stockbridge waved toward the food still on the table. "There's plenty if you'd care to join us."

"Thank you, Sir Henry, but I'm a bit weary. I thought I'd go back to my quarters for a while."

Remembering the smell of whiskey on the medico earlier, Luke suspected that Mitchell wanted a drink more than rest, but it didn't matter. He was grateful for the man's efforts and said, "You have my thanks as well, Doctor."

"You didn't do a bad job treating the injury. I think if you hadn't run into more trouble, there's a good chance Badger would have been all right."

"That's kind of you to say, but I'm not a professional."

"Not at medicine, maybe," Mitchell said, "but I'll bet you provide a lot of work for doctors . . . and undertakers."

Creager said, "He'll be needin' the services of a gravedigger when I get through with him, that's for damn sure."

"That's enough, Creager," Stockbridge said. "Your bluster has worn out its welcome."

McKinney said, "Creager rides with me, Sir Henry. Does that mean I'm not welcome here anymore?"

Stockbridge shook his head. "I didn't say anyone was no longer welcome here. I just think Creager should go somewhere else until the time for his appointment with Luke." He scraped back his chair. "And I should leave you and your sons alone as well, since you have a great deal to talk about."

"Thank you." McKinney looked over at Luke. "You stay put. You're part of this, too."

"Not really," Luke said.

"You brought Aaron here. You know my wife. I want you to stay."

Luke wasn't sure where else he would go. If he wandered around the Black Castle, Creager might lurk somewhere and wait for him, hoping to speed up their confrontation. Luke wasn't afraid of the outlaw, but he didn't see any point in hurrying things along. He shrugged and said, "All right."

Stockbridge ushered Creager out of the hall. The outlaw cast a hate-filled look over his shoulder at Luke as he left the room. The servants topped off everyone's coffee, and then they withdrew, as well.

McKinney lifted his cup and peered intently over the top of it at Luke. "I want the truth."

"About?"

"You and my wife."

Luke's response was truthful, although open to interpretation in some respects. "Mrs. McKinney is a fine woman. I admire her and would like to get to know her better, if circumstances ever permitted such a thing."

"Does that mean that the two of you haven't . . ." McKinney's question trailed off as he glanced at his sons, both of whom looked uncomfortable at the course the conversation was taking.

"I try to conduct myself as a gentleman," Luke

snapped, "for what that's worth. It seems to me that the one you should be talking to is your wife. But you'd have to go home in order to do that. What do you think, McKinney? Is it time to give up the outlaw trail?"

"You know I can't do that," he replied in a voice tinged with regret. Luke was a little surprised to see regret on the man's face and in his eyes. Almost as if McKinney hadn't *wanted* to abandon his home and family and take up an owlhoot's life.

That was an intriguing thought, but one that Luke didn't have time for. He said, "I'm not going to gossip, McKinney. You might as well accept that."

McKinney turned to look at Aaron. "What about you? Do you have anything to say?"

"About Luke and Ma?" Aaron crossed his arms over his chest and glared stubbornly. "You'd do better worryin' about the sheriff, Pa."

"Collins?" Thad said. "Is he still mooning around?"

"You didn't think he'd stop just because you ran off, did you?" Aaron asked. "Hell, he probably thought that'd just make Ma more likely to take him up on whatever he suggested."

Distractedly, McKinney said, "Watch your language, boy. So Sheriff Collins has his eye on your ma, does he? I never liked that fella, badge or no badge." He shook his head. "We'll put that behind us for now. What in the world made you decide to try to find me, Aaron? Was it because Thad did?"

Thad said, "Don't blame me for whatever this loco little kid did, Pa."

Aaron started up out of his chair. "I'm not loco!"

"Don't you start tryin' to hit me again!"

Both boys were on their feet, facing each other angrily. McKinney got up, too, and stepped between them.

"Both of you stop it," he ordered. He glanced at Luke. "You have any kids?"

"Not that I know of," Luke drawled.

"They're a blessing, but they can be a sore trial, too," the outlaw said. "You boys sit down. Aaron, you didn't answer my question."

"About why I came lookin' for you?" Aaron dropped his gaze to the table. "I don't really know. I guess . . . I guess I just wanted to see you again."

Luke was reminded again that the boy was quick-witted. Aaron didn't say anything about the homemade wanted posters or the desire he had expressed to see his father "get what was coming to him." Stuck in the outlaw stronghold as they were for the time being, that wouldn't have been a very smart thing to do.

Slowly, McKinney nodded. "I wish you hadn't done it. But it's a good thing in a way, I guess. Now that you're here, I want you and your brother to go home. Both of you."

"Wait a minute, Pa!" Thad exclaimed. "You said I could ride with you. I even held the horses for the gang on that last job, and you told me I did just fine."

"That's over," McKinney said. "I never thought it was a good idea, and now that Aaron's here, I know it wasn't. You're gonna go home and forget you ever saw me."

"I can't do that," Thad said miserably. "I can't go back to workin' my fingers to the bone on that spread, all for nothing."

"Helping your ma isn't nothing. Neither of you is cut out for this life, and you know it. You're going home, and that's my final word on the deal."

Luke said, "I don't want to intrude on a family decision, but there's something you'd better consider, McKinney."

"Oh? What's that?"

"We've already had one brush with Apache renegades, and it's uncertain whether we wiped out that war party. There could be more of them roaming around. You send these boys back through the hills alone, they might not make it."

"I wasn't counting on them going alone," McKinney said as he looked squarely at Luke. "I thought maybe you could take them."

CHAPTER 22

For a moment, Luke didn't respond. Then he asked, "Why would I do that?"

"You said you'd like to get to know my wife better. This is your chance."

"She strikes me as the sort of woman who's unlikely to forget that she has a husband."

"So she won't have a husband anymore," McKinney said. "Get these boys back to her, safe and sound, and you can tell her I'm dead." His mouth twisted. "I might as well be. She'll believe you, especially if these two back up your story." He nodded toward Aaron and Thad.

"Pa, that's crazy," Thad objected. "I'm not goin' home, and even if I did, I wouldn't lie to Ma and tell her that you're dead. That just wouldn't be right."

"No, it wouldn't," Aaron said. "I agree with Thad this time."

Luke said, "I don't like the idea of lying to Mrs. McKinney, either. She deserves the truth."

"What truth? That her husband's a no-good outlaw who steals from innocent folks and guns down anybody who gets in his way?" McKinney laughed humorlessly. "What makes you think that's gonna make her feel any better about things?"

Luke supposed the man was right about that. He was torn about what he should do next. He had ridden into these hills for a couple of reasons. He wanted the bounty on Three-fingered Jack McKinney, and he had promised Amelia that he would bring Thad back safely to her if he could. McKinney was offering him the chance to accomplish one of those goals.

There was one more thing he was after, he realized— an answer to the question why Jack McKinney had abandoned his family for the life of an owlhoot in the first place. He didn't have that, and if he accepted McKinney's proposition, he likely never would.

"We're getting ahead of ourselves here," he said. "You're forgetting, McKinney, that I have an appointment with your friend Creager. I may not be around after sundown, if he has his way, so talking about me taking the boys home is a bit premature, wouldn't you say?"

McKinney shook his head. "I'll tell Creager to forget it, that he's not going to fight you. He's not my friend, but he *is* part of my gang. He'll do what I tell him, or he'll have to deal with me."

Creager was twice McKinney's size, but the calm, confident way the outlaw made the statement told Luke that if it came to a showdown between McKinney and Creager, McKinney wouldn't be using his fists . . . which meant he was probably pretty quick with the gun on his hip.

"I don't run from trouble," Luke said deliberately. "Creager made his challenge, I took him up on it, and that's the end of it. We'll settle matters between us without any interference from you, McKinney.

Besides, I'm not sure Sir Henry would allow it to be called off now. He seems rather adamant about having his rules followed."

McKinney grimaced. "I can talk sense to Stockbridge."

"A man who built a castle in the middle of the Arizona badlands?" Luke asked. "He doesn't seem like a good candidate for a reasonable approach."

He hoped none of the servants were eavesdropping and would tell Stockbridge what he had just said. The Englishman might take offense, and for the time being, at least, Luke needed him to remain neutral.

With obvious reluctance, McKinney said, "All right. You settle things with Creager. But after that's over . . . if you're still here . . . we'll talk more about this."

"Fine," Luke said. "I intend to survive."

"You know," McKinney said, "despite everything I've heard, I almost hope you do."

Luke could tell that McKinney wanted to talk to his sons alone, so he got up and left the big hall, keeping an eye out for Creager.

There was no sign of the brutal, jug-eared outlaw, but as soon as Luke stepped out into the castle's foyer, a woman stood up from the chair where she had been sitting and, evidently, waiting for him. He recognized her as the attractive blonde who had helped serve dinner.

"Good afternoon, Luke," she greeted him. With a smile, she added, "I'm sorry to be so informal, but that's the only name we know for you, isn't it?"

"It's enough. What's your name?"

"Adele," she said. "Is *that* enough?"

"Plenty. What can I do for you?"

"Actually, Sir Henry asked me to wait out here for

you and show you around after you finished talking to Mr. McKinney and his sons."

"That's very kind of you," Luke said. "I'd enjoy that. I have to admit, I'm curious about this place. It's not the sort of thing you run across every day on the frontier."

Adele laughed, a pleasant, musical sound that Luke enjoyed. "No, I suppose not. But then, Sir Henry isn't a typical frontiersman, at least not from what I've seen of them . . . and him."

Luke wondered just how close the relationship was between the Englishman and this obviously well-bred young woman. It was none of his business, he knew, but he wondered anyway.

He was also curious if she had overheard any of the conversation between him and the McKinneys, but if she had, she gave no sign of it. She seemed pleasant and friendly, but of course that could be an act.

As they walked along the tapestry-lined hallway, he asked, "Are you going to be showing me the room where I'll be staying, as well? Or will I be bunking in one of the other buildings I saw when we rode in?"

Her smile didn't waver, but she said, "About that . . . Sir Henry feels that it would be best to wait until later to decide about your accommodations."

"Ah. Until after we've all seen whether I'm going to survive my appointment at sundown with Creager, eh?"

"You have to admit, it could be a moot point."

"Will you be disappointed if I don't? Survive, that is."

"As a matter of fact, I will," Adele said. "To be honest, there aren't that many men around here who can carry on an intelligent conversation. Sir Henry is just about the only one. But I think I'd enjoy talking to you, Luke."

"Better than Creager?"

Her calm, smiling mask slipped a little for the first time as she shuddered slightly. "Creager is an animal. I'm sorry that you have to deal with him." A note of viciousness came into her voice as she added, "Since you had the choice of weapons, you should have chosen firearms. He's fairly fast on the draw, but I believe you could have beaten him."

"I'd just as soon not have to kill anybody on my first day at the Black Castle."

"You wouldn't be the only man who's done so. But it *is* rare, I'll admit."

The great hall where Luke had been earlier was used for feasting, but in addition, adjoining it was a small dining room, also with a highly polished table and ornately carved chairs. Portraits of stern-looking men and pale women hung on the walls.

Luke nodded toward them and asked, "Sir Henry's ancestors?"

"I don't really know, but I doubt it. When he came here from England, he didn't bring much with him, according to what he's told me about those days."

"That's right. He was a remittance man, wasn't he?"

Adele frowned. "I'd suggest that you don't use that term around him. He doesn't care for it. And it's no longer true, actually. He cut off any contact with his family long ago. He doesn't take any money from them and hasn't for a long time. As far as he's concerned, he has no family anymore."

"The system over there *does* seem unfair at times," Luke said. "Everything depends on an accident of birth. Of course, that could be said of a lot of things in this country, as well."

"Let's go look at the courtyard, shall we?" Adele suggested in a murmur.

"That's where Creager and I are supposed to meet," Luke said as she took him along another hallway to a heavy wooden door with iron straps nailed on it. It looked more like the entrance to a dungeon than a courtyard.

When she swung it open, though, making a little noise from the effort, he saw that the castle was built around an open central area not visible from outside. There were gardens with flowers and plants that were especially lush for Arizona, and a fountain where water bubbled.

"Stockbridge sunk a well to that underground stream." Luke was impressed by what he saw. "I wondered if he might not be using it as a water supply, but I didn't expect that he'd created a little oasis here."

"It's beautiful, isn't it?" Adele gestured with a slender hand toward a bench near the fountain. A cottonwood tree provided shade over it. "Why don't we sit down?"

As they sat on the bench, Luke said, "Your real job is just to keep me occupied until it's time for my showdown with Creager, isn't it? Sir Henry doesn't want me trying to get away."

"You couldn't if you tried. There are too many guards. You'd never get down the trail without being cleared from up here."

"Stockbridge must have some way of communicating with the men down below. Signal flags? A system of bells with ropes running to them?"

Adele smiled faintly and shook her head. "Visitors don't really need to know about things like that."

"There must be a back door to this place. I can't

imagine anyone as intelligent as Sir Henry would build it so there was only one way in and out."

"Again . . ."

"I don't need to know that," Luke finished for her. He chuckled. "I understand. I suppose Sir Henry might grow to trust me enough to share some of this information with me . . . provided I live long enough."

"There's only one way to find out," Adele said coolly.

"Well, then, why don't we talk about something more pleasant? Tell me about yourself. You're originally from Philadelphia, aren't you?"

Her blue eyes widened in surprise. "How in the world did you know that?"

"The accent. It's not that strong, but I can hear it. I've known some upper-class ladies from the Main Line."

"My, you're just full of surprises, aren't you? Are you sure you're not from back east yourself?"

He grinned. "Nope. Raised on a farm in Missouri, up in the Ozarks. But I've traveled in a lot of different circles since then."

"I'd say so. I know that Sir Henry is impressed with you."

"The feeling is mutual." Luke paused. "So, you were going to tell me about yourself . . ."

She laughed and shook her head. "There's not that much to tell. My father was a wealthy man, with the emphasis on the word *was*. He got involved with some rather . . . shall we say shady . . . associates and lost all his money. Desperation gave him the idea of going west. After all, that's what Horace Greeley said to do, and despite not being a young man, my father decided to take that advice. He packed us up and we all headed west." Adele's voice hardened as she went on. "We made it as far as Kansas City before he was robbed and murdered in an alley. That left my mother and me to fend for ourselves. She died six months later from drinking too much laudanum. An accident, I'm sure."

Adele's tone made it clear she didn't believe her mother's death was an accident at all. Luke didn't say anything. He had heard similar stories many times before and was willing to allow his companion to disclose as much, or as little, as she wanted.

"Since then, I've been here and there and done this and that," Adele continued. "No need to rehash all of it. Then I came to the Black Castle and met Sir Henry. It's not a bad life. I'll stay here as long as he wants me to." She smiled again. "Tell me about you. How did that farm boy from Missouri transform into a worldly gentleman?"

By being betrayed and almost killed in the war, Luke thought. *By spending decades riding lonely trails and risking my life to bring in bad men.* But he said, "It's not an interesting story. Like you, I've been here and there, done this and that."

"Most of it involving gunplay, I imagine."

Luke just shrugged.

Adele changed the subject. "Why don't we talk about more pleasant things? Have you actually been to Philadelphia?"

"I have. I haven't spent much time there, but I've visited a couple of times. It's a beautiful city, full of history."

They spent the next couple of hours talking about Philadelphia and all the history and culture to be found there. Adele was a good conversationalist and a charming companion, and Luke enjoyed the respite from the grit and danger of his normal life. He was aware, though, that the sun was dipping steadily toward the battlement-like cliffs on the western edge of the cup that contained the Black Castle.

The respite came to an end when the big man called Creager stalked into the courtyard from the castle, followed by Sir Henry Stockbridge—the self-styled Black Knight—as well as Three-fingered Jack McKinney, Aaron, Thad, and a dozen more hardcases.

Creager stomped up, planted himself in front of Luke, and growled. "All right, mister. It's high time for you to die."

CHAPTER 23

From the corner of his eye, Luke saw Adele cringe a little. Clearly, she was frightened of the big outlaw. He wondered if Creager had made advances toward her in the past . . . and if he did, had he gotten what he wanted? Were Adele and the other women who worked here essentially prostitutes, expected to go along with any of the men who approached them?

Luke pushed those thoughts away as Stockbridge said, "Time to settle the differences between the two of you, Luke." He nodded toward the cliffs. "The sun will be setting in just a few minutes. Are you ready?"

Luke stood up from the bench and nodded. "I am," he said as he took off his hat and handed it to Adele. "If you'd be so kind as to hang on to that for me, my dear . . ."

"Of course," she murmured.

Stockbridge smiled. "I see that the two of you have been getting along. I hoped that you would."

"Adele is beautiful and charming. I'm obliged to you for suggesting that she show me around and spend the afternoon with me."

Creager's mouth twisted in a snarl. "Can we get on

with this, damn it? I'm tired of waiting to kill this son of a bitch."

Luke unbuckled his gunbelt and motioned Aaron over to him. "Would you mind holding this?"

"Me?" Aaron said as he stared up at him. "Sure, Luke, I'd be honored to."

Luke pointed to the Colt Creager wore and said, "I believe you should disarm, too." He unbuttoned the sleeves of his black shirt and rolled them up over muscular forearms.

Creager sneered at him, and for a second his hand hovered over the revolver as if he were thinking about snatching it from the holster and blasting away at Luke.

Stockbridge noticed the same thing and said in a sharp tone, "I'll have that gun, Creager. Now."

Creager growled deep in his throat, but he unbuckled the gunbelt and handed it to Stockbridge. He took off his hat and sailed it away, unmindful of where it landed on the paving stones near the fountain. He stripped off his vest and shirt, revealing a pale, almost hairless torso covered with thick slabs of muscle. His hands clenched into fists. Knobs of bone stuck out at his knuckles. "I can't decide whether to beat you to death or just tear you apart."

Luke didn't respond to that, saying to Stockbridge, "You'll call it?"

"I will," Stockbridge answered. "Adele, come here and stand with me."

She followed his command but kept her eyes on the ground and Luke thought she looked like she wished she were somewhere else. Stockbridge didn't give her leave to go and so she stayed, standing next to his tall, broad-shouldered form.

"All right, gentlemen," Stockbridge said after another tense minute had gone by. "Commence."

Creager didn't wait. He sprang forward with surprising grace and speed for such a big man and whipped a left at Luke's head.

That blow might have ended the fight then and there . . . if it had connected. Luke swayed back and the huge fist missed him by several inches. Instantly, with Creager's left side turned toward him and open, Luke leaned in and hooked a right into the man's ribs. Creager grunted and swung the left in a backhand that Luke avoided as well. Creager's belly was defenseless for a split second. Luke twisted at the waist and hooked his left into it, a short punch but one that packed considerable power.

He moved back quickly as Creager roared and lunged at him again, swinging his arms like a maddened bear. Luke got out of the way of that charge. As Creager went past him, Luke hammered a punch into his left kidney. Creager caught his balance and turned to throw a long, looping punch that Luke ducked under easily.

Too late, Luke realized that Creager's blow was a feint. The outlaw hadn't allowed blind rage to overwhelm him as Luke had thought. Creager's right foot came up fast. The toe of his boot sank into Luke's belly, causing him to stagger back. The kick had driven the breath from his lungs and he gasped for air. Creager came at him in a flying tackle.

Luke knew that if Creager got him down on the ground, pinned him there with his greater weight, that would be the end for him. He couldn't avoid the attack completely, but he moved aside enough that he was able to writhe out from under as they went down. He smashed his left elbow into the side of Creager's head to slow him down, then rolled away.

Creager caught hold of Luke's ankle and upended him again as Luke tried to make it to his feet.

He landed on his belly and barely scrambled aside before Creager dove on top of him. Luke managed to stand up before the outlaw could grab him.

Creager was still down and Luke had no compunction about kicking him while he was on the ground, but Creager rolled onto his butt and scuttled backward, out of reach. Luke could have gone after him, but he had a hunch that was what Creager wanted him to do. Luke stood back instead, waiting, grateful for the chance to catch his breath.

While Creager clambered to his feet, Luke looked past the big outlaw to where Stockbridge stood with Adele, McKinney, Aaron, and Thad. Aaron looked worried, and Adele was pale and clearly concerned. McKinney just watched coolly but with keen interest, as did Stockbridge.

"More of a challenge than you expected, Creager?" Stockbridge asked.

The amusement in his voice made Creager growl in anger again. He spat several curses, then spoke to Luke. "Why don't you stand and fight me? Man to man! Fist against fist, without all the dancin' around!"

"Stand still and let you hammer me senseless?" Luke said, trying not to pant and let Creager see how much the fight was taking out of him. "I don't think so."

"I'll do more 'n knock you senseless. I'll hit you until your head busts wide open like a gourd!"

Luke managed to smile. He raised both fists,

planted his feet, and stood there in a pugilist's stance, seemingly daring Creager to come at him.

Creager took up the challenge. He spewed more curses and barreled in with both fists swinging.

Luke weaved back and forth, barely avoiding the blows that would have done terrible damage to him if they had landed. He snapped punches of his own into Creager's face, peppering the outlaw with hard jabs that caused Creager's already lumpy features to swell. Blood welled from Creager's nose and sprayed from his lips when he shook his head to clear his brain. He bellowed an incoherent shout and drove in harder than ever.

Luke could tell that he was tiring, though. Creager's punches had begun to slow. They didn't have the same sizzle on them.

Creager backed off after Luke landed several sharp blows, then charged again, holding his arms up in front of him to protect his head and face instead of throwing punches. Luke knew Creager was trying to barrel into him and bowl him over. His own reactions were slowing down, too, but he summoned up enough speed to dart aside. As Creager stumbled past him, Luke clasped both hands together and clubbed them into the back of Creager's neck with all the force he could muster.

Creager went down hard, too out of control to even attempt to catch himself, and his face crunched into one of the paving stones. He tried to heave himself up as blood flowed from his now misshapen nose, but he didn't have the strength. His muscles gave up the effort and he slumped back down and didn't move. His head was turned to the side so he was able to breathe. Air rasped and bubbled in his nose and throat.

Stockbridge pulled Creager's Colt from the holster he held and extended it toward Luke. "Here. You can end it with his own gun."

Luke stood there with his chest heaving. After a moment, he shook his head. "It's already ended. Creager doesn't have any fight left in him." He looked at Stockbridge. "There's not some rule that says I *have* to finish him off, is there?"

Stockbridge regarded Luke with narrowed eyes and then shoved the Colt back into leather. "No, there's no such rule. The decision is up to you. But you have to be aware that Creager wouldn't have extended any mercy to you if the situation had been reversed."

"I know," Luke said. "That's why I made sure that it wasn't."

Stockbridge had to laugh at that. McKinney smiled faintly in admiration. Aaron gazed at Luke as if he had suddenly grown several feet taller.

Adele just looked relieved.

Luke went to her and took his hat from her, then reclaimed his gunbelt from Aaron. As he buckled it on, he said to Stockbridge, "This affair is over as far as I'm concerned. I'd appreciate it if you'd see to it that Creager understands as much."

Stockbridge nodded. "I can make it clear that no more trouble between the two of you will be permitted here at the Black Castle . . . but I can't control how he feels, or what might happen outside of this place."

"Fair enough," Luke said.

McKinney said, "There are still things Luke and I need to talk about. Things to settle."

"Later," Stockbridge decreed. "I'm sure that after that altercation, Luke would like to clean up and rest a bit. Adele, please show our visitor to his quarters."

"I'm not staying in the bunkhouse?" Luke asked. "I don't have enough money for anything fancy."

"That's not necessary. After putting on an exhibition like that, you're an honored guest, Luke. If you'll follow Adele . . ."

Luke was willing to do that.

She took him to a room on the second floor that was large enough for a comfortable-looking bed, a table with a washbasin on it, a ladderback chair, and not much else.

Luke said, "I'd like to get my saddlebags and Winchester."

"They'll be brought to you later," she promised.

Luke would have rather fetched his gear himself, but he knew it wouldn't do any good to argue. Before he had ever set out to find the Black Castle, he had burned all the reward posters he usually carried with him. He'd known that he might be heading into an outlaw stronghold, and having those dodgers would have marked him as a bounty hunter or a lawman. Either way, they would have served as death warrants for him.

There was nothing else in the saddlebags that might cause a problem for him. Supplies and a few books, that was all. Stockbridge might be interested in the books, but they wouldn't give him any reason to have Luke killed.

"There'll be a light supper later. Would you like for me to come and get you when it's ready?"

"That would be fine. Thank you."

"Is there anything else you need?" She was standing close to him as she asked the question.

Luke could have reached out and taken her into his arms without any trouble. He had a pretty strong hunch that she wouldn't object if he did. But after the battle with Creager, not to mention the strains and perils of the past few days, he was worn out. He smiled and said, "Not right now. But . . . perhaps another time."

"Opportunities should be seized," she said with a slight husky tone creeping into her voice. "A person never knows when they might not come again."

"True. But all of life is decisions, and we just have to live with the ones we make."

She looked intently at him for a moment, then smiled and shook her head. "You go from carving up Creager like a Christmas goose to dispensing bits of philosophy and wisdom. You're an unusual man, Luke."

"I've been accused of a lot worse."

She lifted a hand and put it on his arm. Squeezing for a second, she promised, "I'll be back when it's time for supper."

"I'm looking forward to it," Luke said, and meant it.

As soon as she was gone, he peeled off his shirt, took the rag from the table, wet it in the basin, and scrubbed off the sweat from the battle. Then he stretched out on the bed, still half-dressed, closed his eyes, and was instantly asleep.

CHAPTER 24

A knock on the door roused Luke from slumber an unknowable time later. He slid one of the Remingtons from the coiled gunbelt he'd earlier set on the chair beside the bed. Holding his thumb hooked over the hammer, ready to draw it back, he went to the door. "Who's there?"

He stepped quickly to the right. The door seemed thick enough to stop a bullet, even a close-range shotgun blast, but it didn't hurt to be careful.

"I have your gear, señor," a man answered. "Your saddlebags and rifle. Señorita Adele said that you wanted them."

Keeping the revolver ready, Luke lowered it to his side and opened the door with his other hand. A middle-aged Mexican man with drooping mustaches came in carrying the saddlebags and Winchester.

"Just put them on the bed," Luke told him.

The man did so, then said, "I am Tomás. I work in the stables. I will be caring for your horse and the boy's mule."

"Thank you, Tomás." Luke reached into his pocket,

slid out a half-dollar, and handed it to the man. "I know you'll take good care of them."

"Even without this, señor, because Señor Stockbridge says it is to be so . . . but *muchas gracias.*"

The hostler left, but it was only a minute later when another knock sounded on the door, this one softer. Luke again asked who was there and wasn't surprised when he heard the answer.

"Adele."

He still had the gun in his hand when he opened the door. She raised her eyebrows at the sight of it and said, "You're not going to need that. We're just going to supper."

"I'll feel better with it, unless Stockbridge objects. Is Creager going to be joining us for this meal, as well?"

She shook her head. "He's going to have difficulty with solid food for a while, I'm afraid. I believe the only ones who are going to be there are you and me, Sir Henry, of course . . . and Jack McKinney."

"Three-fingered Jack, eh? Do you know how he lost those two fingers?"

"I've never asked, and he's never volunteered the information. Do *you* know?"

"I'm afraid not," Luke said. "He used to be a rancher, though, and men who work with cattle often lose fingers. Get one caught just wrong in a loop of rope, and that'll pop it right off."

A dainty little shudder went through Adele. "I'm glad I wasn't raised on a ranch, then. I have better things to do with my fingers." She smiled, and he couldn't tell if she was trying to imply something with that comment or whether it was innocent.

Here in the Black Castle, he thought, it was probably best not to assume innocence of any kind.

Stockbridge and McKinney were already seated in the small dining room, Stockbridge at the head of the table, McKinney to his left. The food was on the table, and glasses of wine stood next to the place settings. Luke held the chair opposite Stockbridge for Adele, then sat to her left.

"Are you refreshed now after the earlier unpleasantness?" Stockbridge asked as he picked up his wineglass.

"I'm fine," Luke answered. "A bit sore, maybe, but nothing to worry about. I've been in fights before."

"Yes, I can tell that," Stockbridge said with a chuckle. "Your nose has been broken more than once, hasn't it?"

McKinney said, "Not as badly as Creager's is. Doc Mitchell set it for him, but breathing's going to hurt for a while."

"I didn't seek out that fight," Luke said.

Stockbridge said, "And no one would have objected if you'd put a bullet in his head. You'd earned that right by accepting his challenge and then defeating him. So I don't think our friend Creager really has a great deal to complain about."

"That won't stop him from complaining," McKinney said. "And I don't reckon he regards any of us as his friends right now."

Adele sipped her wine and said, "Couldn't we talk about something more pleasant?"

"Of course." Stockbridge waved a hand magnanimously. "And while we're at it, dig in, gentlemen"— he raised his glass to Adele—"and lady."

The food was good, strips of steak, peppers,

onions, tortillas, stew, and beans, south of the border fare as tasty and well-prepared as any that Luke had had in Mexico.

While they were eating, McKinney looked across the table at Luke and said, "We have some unfinished business."

"You don't want to fight a duel, too, do you?" Luke asked.

McKinney laughed. "Not hardly. Despite certain . . . circumstances . . . I don't believe you and I need to be enemies, Luke."

"If you're talking about your wife, let me ease your mind. I admire the lady, but that's all. Despite what Aaron said, there's nothing between us."

McKinney nodded solemnly. "I appreciate you saying that. If you actually do admire her, maybe you'll agree to what I asked you to do earlier."

"Take your boys back to her, you mean?" Luke drank some of the wine, then shook his head. "I don't think I can do that, Jack. At least not now. It wouldn't be . . . healthy . . . for me to head back in that direction."

McKinney's face tightened as he said, "The law is after you, you mean."

"I'm not the only man is this place who finds himself in that situation, I'm sure."

Stockbridge said, "You're certainly not. That's why the Black Castle exists, after all, as a safe haven for men in our line of work."

"What in blazes am I going to *do* with them, then?" McKinney asked with what sounded like a genuine note of dismay in his voice. "I planned on leaving here tomorrow."

Luke said, "I have a suggestion. Take them with you. And me, too."

McKinney stared across the table at him, and even Stockbridge and Adele looked a little surprised.

"Thad's already been riding with you," Luke went on. "Aaron's a smart boy and doesn't back down from anything."

An angry flush began spreading across McKinney's face. "You think I want my sons to be outlaws?" he demanded.

"It's been good enough for you," Luke pointed out.

McKinney's open hand came down on the table with a sharp crack. "You don't know a damn thing about it, mister. I have reasons for everything I've done, but they're *my* reasons and none of your business." His eyes suddenly narrowed in suspicion. "It sounds to me like you're just trying to worm your way into my gang."

"I admit that I wouldn't mind having some partners to ride with, at least for a while," Luke said. "This life is hard for a man alone, with no one to watch his back. Also, I understand your concern for your sons. I don't know Thad, but I've grown fond of Aaron, and we've faced trouble together. I don't want to see anything bad happen to him. That's why I thought I could go along and sort of help you keep an eye on both of them. Look out for them and make sure nothing happens to them."

"Mighty generous of you," McKinney snapped.

Luke shook his head. "No, not at all. I'm looking out for myself, too. But answer this for me, Jack . . .

Whatever you're planning next, don't you think you could use another good man to help you carry it out?"

Stockbridge gestured with the wineglass he held, waving it toward Luke. "He has a point, Jack. Even in the short time he's been here, Luke has demonstrated his abilities. When you consider that he also saved old Badger and fought off Apaches to get here, you have to give him credit."

With a surly glare, McKinney said, "That doesn't mean I'm going to just welcome him into the gang with open arms. And what about Creager? How do you think he would take it if he found out the man who busted his nose was going to be riding with us?"

"It's your gang," Luke pointed out. "If Creager wants to be part of it, I suppose he'll do whatever you say."

In the tense silence that followed that statement, Adele said, "You men always have to wind up talking about business, don't you? It's never enough to simply enjoy a good meal and some good company."

Stockbridge said, "I'm sorry, my dear. But these things are important and need to be settled."

"Of course, Sir Henry," she responded instantly, even though there hadn't been even a hint of a rebuke in his tone.

McKinney still didn't look happy, but he said, "I know good and well that if I send those boys home, they won't go. And it'd be dangerous if they did. I hate to say it, but they might be better off with me for now. Sooner or later, though, they've got to go back to their mother."

"We can figure something out," Luke said. "Maybe after things have had time to cool off some, I could circle back in that direction and take them with me."

"I don't like it," McKinney said, "but that may be the best way to go for the time being." He pointed across the table at Luke. "I want your word that you'll do your best to keep them safe, though."

"Of course. You have it. I don't want to see any harm come to them."

"As for Creager . . . he doesn't call the shots in my bunch. I do. You'd be smart to keep an eye on him, though."

"Believe me," Luke said, "I intend to."

McKinney sat back in his chair and frowned. "I guess it's settled, then. You and the boys will come with us when we ride out in the morning."

"Where are you heading?" Luke asked.

McKinney shook his head and said, "You'll find out about that when you need to, and not before."

"Fair enough."

Stockbridge leaned forward. "You *will* be sure that my percentage comes my way, Jack?"

"Of course," McKinney replied. "I want to know this place will be here when we need it."

Stockbridge smiled and lifted his glass. "A pleasure doing business with you, as always. Now we can continue with our supper."

The meal had lost some of its appeal for Luke, but he put up as good a façade as he could. He had known that he stood no chance of capturing Jack McKinney as long as the outlaw was in the Black Castle. Getting him out of the stronghold and away from his gang was the best way to bring him to justice. Cutting him out of the herd like that, so to speak, wouldn't be easy. In some ways, Luke was putting himself in an even more dangerous position, and he knew it.

There was also the question of whether Aaron McKinney still wanted his father brought in and turned over to the law. If he didn't . . . if he had decided to forgive McKinney . . . that would complicate things even more. Luke might have to give up on capturing the outlaw and figure out a way to get Aaron and Thad back safely to their mother.

He could always go after Three-fingered Jack McKinney later, he told himself grimly.

CHAPTER 25

Although the atmosphere was still rather strained, the rest of the late supper went smoothly enough. Adele steered the conversation to art and music, and then after the meal was over, Stockbridge suggested that they have brandy in a parlor where Adele could play the piano for them.

"I appreciate the offer, Sir Henry," McKinney said, "but I'm a mite tired and tomorrow will be a busy day, so I reckon I'd better turn in."

"All right," Stockbridge said. "How about you, Luke?"

"Other than some slick-haired opium addict with no talent pounding the keys in a saloon, I haven't heard any piano music in quite some time," Luke replied. "So I won't pass up this opportunity."

Stockbridge smiled. "You won't regret it. Adele is an excellent musician."

"Stop it, Sir Henry," she said. "You're embarrassing me." Her smile told Luke that she enjoyed the compliment, however.

McKinney said good night, then the other three went to the parlor where Paloma brought snifters of brandy to them. Adele sipped from hers, then set it on a small table next to the piano. She sat down on a bench and let her fingers trail over the keys with seemingly effortless ease, coaxing a tuneless but appealing medley of notes from them.

Luke and Stockbridge sat in armchairs next to a massive fireplace that was cold at that time of year. The stone mantel above it was quite impressive.

Stockbridge crossed his legs and asked, "Cigar?"

"Don't mind if I do," Luke replied.

The Black Knight took two fat cheroots from his vest pocket and handed one of them to Luke. They trimmed the cigars, then Stockbridge snapped a match to life and lit both smokes.

As they sat back to puff on the cheroots and sip brandy, Luke said, "I almost feel like I'm in some fancy club back in Philadelphia or Boston."

"Or London," Stockbridge said as he regarded the glowing coal at the end of his cigar. "I'm British, you know."

"I recognized the accent. You don't have much of one, anymore, but it's still there for someone who's familiar with such things."

"You've known Englishmen before?"

"Quite a few, in fact." Luke smiled. "Even without the accent, I think I'd have a hunch that only an Englishman would build a place like this and call himself a knight."

Stockbridge laughed, a booming sound that for a second drowned out the song that Adele had begun to play on the piano.

"Yes, it is rather obvious, isn't it? And a bit bizarre, too. As you said, we might as well be taking our ease in a gentleman's club, and yet just outside these walls lies the wilderness of Arizona Territory, filled with snakes and scorpions and bloody-handed Apaches. The men who come here as my guests are outlaws— bank robbers and killers—as far from being gentlemen as anyone could ever imagine. We're surrounded by the untamed American frontier, yet here in the Black Castle lies a refuge from all that."

"An oasis," Luke murmured. "I saw the garden and fountain in your courtyard earlier this afternoon, remember. Another contrast, all that beauty surrounding the spot where two brutes tried to beat each other to death."

"That description fits Creager well enough, but you're hardly a brute, Luke," Stockbridge objected.

Luke blew a smoke ring and said, "All men can be brutes, under the right circumstances."

"I suppose that's true." The Englishman's voice hardened slightly as he went on. "My brother, for example, is an aristocrat and highly respected, and yet he's also a vicious boor. If he'd had his way, instead of sending me to America the family simply would have locked me up in a tower somewhere and let me rot."

"A long-standing tradition," Luke drawled.

"Ah, yes, Richard III. You know the story from the play or the histories?"

"Both."

"Well, I'm no defenseless prince. And someday, when I have enough money and power, my brother Cecil will rue the day when he—" Stockbridge stopped short, shook his head, and waved the hand holding the snifter. "Never mind all that. Let's just enjoy the music, shall we?"

Luke did enjoy Adele's playing. She ran through a number of classical and light operatic compositions.

He knew some of them, while others were new to him. She was skilled, no doubt about that. She must have had lessons back in Philadelphia, before her father lost most of his money, he thought.

When Luke and Stockbridge had finished their cigars and brandy, and Adele brought another piece of music to a close, Stockbridge stood up. "This was a very pleasant evening, but I think it's time to say good night. I hope you sleep well, Luke." He smiled. "Are you ever going to tell me your last name?"

"Maybe," Luke said. "When I come back here." He *was* going to come back one of these days, he told himself.

A fortune was waiting inside those walls for the bounty hunter who could figure out how to capture the Black Castle. It seemed like an impossible task, but Luke thought there must be a way. He would need help to do it, though. One man couldn't, and neither could an army . . . but the right *group* of men . . .

He put that intriguing thought out of his mind and took Adele's hand when she left the piano and went over to them. He lifted her hand and pressed his lips to the back of it, then said, "Thank you for all your kind attention today, and for the beautiful music this evening."

"Perhaps I can play for you again sometime."

"I'm looking forward to it."

Stockbridge linked his arm with Adele's and said to Luke, "Paloma will show you back to your room."

"I'm sure I can find it—"

"It's no trouble for her."

Luke understood that the man didn't want him wandering around the castle by himself. Since he planned to ride out the next day with McKinney's gang, he didn't see any point in pressing the matter, so he just smiled and nodded.

"Good night, Luke," Adele said over her shoulder as Stockbridge led her from the room.

"Good night," he told her. Their eyes met for a moment, and he thought he saw something there, a wish that she was going with him and not Stockbridge. Or maybe he just imagined the whole thing, he told himself as the servant woman appeared in the doorway to escort him back to his room.

It didn't really matter anyway.

Nothing happened to disturb Luke's sleep that night. Other than being a little stiff and sore from the battle with Creager, he felt pretty good as he got dressed and went downstairs.

The smells of coffee and bacon led him to the great hall where a number of roughly dressed men were having breakfast at the long table. Stockbridge wasn't there, but Jack McKinney was, as well as Creager. Luke assumed the men were McKinney's gang having one more meal before riding out of the Black Castle.

He was very happy to see Badger O'Donnell sitting at the table, looking pale and gaunt but sitting up under his own power as he ate. A bulge under his flannel shirt marked the location of the bandages wrapped around his midsection. He grinned and started to stand up when he saw Luke, but Luke waved the old-timer back into his chair.

"I'm mighty happy to see you looking better, Badger, but don't push yourself too hard," Luke said as he came up behind Badger's chair.

The old outlaw turned and reached up to clasp Luke's hand. "I'm tolerable better, and it's all thanks to you, son. I'd never have made it here if it hadn't been for you. When Doc Mitchell told me you was ridin' out today, I knew I had to see you again so I could thank you."

Luke smiled. "It was my pleasure. I've enjoyed getting to know you."

Badger looked a little rueful as he went on. "I reckon I owe you an apology for sorta misleadin' you about me bein' a prospector and all. Truth is, I *have* done a mite o' prospectin' in my time—"

"Don't worry about that," Luke broke in. "I didn't exactly fill you in about all the details of *my* life, either. We've become friends, and that's all that matters."

"Durned straight it is." Badger squeezed Luke's arm.

Stockbridge walked in. He cleared his throat, prompting Luke to pat Badger on the shoulder and then walked toward the head of the table, passing along behind some of the members of McKinney's gang.

Creager was on the other side of the table, so Luke got a good look at him. The big man had a strip of plaster over his nose to stabilize the cartilage that Doctor Mitchell had worked back into place. Huge bruises surrounded both hate-filled eyes as he glared at Luke. He didn't say anything, though, and turned his gaze back to his plate. It seemed likely that McKinney had had a talk with him and warned him not to cause any more trouble.

Even if Creager had agreed to that, Luke didn't expect it to last. The venom would continue to fester under the surface until sooner or later it would erupt again. Luke intended to be ready when that happened.

McKinney stood up and gestured toward an empty chair at the table, beside the place where Aaron sat. Thad was next to his father, then the younger brother.

As Luke walked toward the empty chair, McKinney said, "Some of you fellas have already seen him, but for those who don't know, this is Luke. He's going to be riding with us for a while."

One of the men spoke up, saying, "Luke? That's all? Just a front handle?"

"Make the back one Jones," Luke said. "That'll do as good as any."

Several of the men nodded in acceptance. A lot of hombres who called themselves Jones or Smith rode the owlhoot trail. As a matter of fact, for a number of years Luke actually had gone by the name Luke Smith, when he was still trying to conceal his true identity as a Jensen.

As Luke sat down next to Aaron, the youngster said, "My pa says you're coming with us. Is that right?"

Luke looked over at Aaron and tried to read the boy's expression. He had a good poker face for his age. Not for a second had Luke forgotten that Aaron was the only one who knew he was really a bounty hunter. Aaron could point a finger at him any time and seal his fate. Luke was too outnumbered to survive if it came down to a gunfight. The best he could do would be to take some of the varmints with him. But so far, Aaron had held his silence.

All Luke could do was hope that would continue. "That's right. I thought I'd ride with your pa and the rest of the bunch for a while. Is that all right with you?"

Aaron grunted. "Why wouldn't it be?" He turned his attention back to the plate of food in front of him, shoveling in flapjacks, eggs, and bacon with the appetite of youth.

Maybe that was a signal that he didn't intend to betray Luke. Luke hoped so, but he thought it would be a good idea to have a heart-to-heart talk with Aaron anyway, as soon as he found a chance to speak to the boy privately.

Breakfast was good. After Luke washed down the food with a couple of cups of strong coffee, he felt better. One by one, as the outlaws finished, they got up and left the room. Luke supposed they were going to get their horses ready to ride. Since apparently he was the last one to arrive for breakfast, he was also the last to finish, although Jack McKinney and his sons lingered in the hall with him, taking their time finishing their coffee.

When Luke was done, too, McKinney said, "I told Creager I didn't want any more trouble between the two of you. He agreed."

"But you don't really believe him," Luke guessed.

McKinney shrugged. "I think he means it . . . right now. He's still a little addled. But he hasn't forgotten that he hates you, and I don't reckon he ever will. How are you at having eyes in the back of your head?"

"I've lived this long, haven't I?"

McKinney chuckled. "Good point." He drained the last of his coffee from the cup. "Let's go."

The boys got to their feet as Luke stood and said, "I have to get my saddlebags and rifle."

"They've already been brought down and put on your horse. Sir Henry runs an efficient operation here."

Luke didn't like the idea of other people handling his gear again, but he supposed there was no point in complaining about it. After saying good-bye to Badger, who would continue to recuperate there, and shaking hands with him, Luke walked out of the castle with McKinney, Thad, and Aaron.

The rest of the gang had assembled in front of the huge structure. Most were already mounted. Several pack animals were loaded with supplies, as well. He spotted his horse, saddled and waiting for him, and walked over to it.

Before he could mount up, Stockbridge walked out of the castle and came over to shake hands with him. "Your visit was brief but entertaining, Luke. I hope you'll come back sometime in the future."

"I'm planning on it." It was a completely honest answer.

Stockbridge turned to McKinney and shook with him, too. "Good luck to you in your next endeavor, Jack. I'm sure we'll be seeing you again, as well."

"More than likely," McKinney agreed. "Although one of these days I plan to get out of this business."

"Most men who ride the dark trails and hear the owl hoot feel the same way," Stockbridge said with a smile. "In reality, though, few of them ever leave this way of life behind."

"You did."

Stockbridge said, "No, I just found a slightly different path to ill-gotten gains." He let out one of his booming laughs. "At heart, I'm still just as much of a brigand as ever!" He stepped back and lifted a hand. "Farewell, gentlemen! *Vaya con Dios*, as our friends from below the border say."

Luke had swung up into the saddle. He lifted his reins and waited for McKinney to take the lead. With Aaron and Thad riding right behind him, McKinney led the way. Luke hung back to blend in with the others, and he also wanted Creager in front of him, not behind him. Creager gave him a baleful look, then nudged his horse into motion.

As Luke fell in alongside some of the outlaws, he glanced back at the castle. He had thought he might see Adele again this morning, but she hadn't been at breakfast and she wasn't with Stockbridge as the gang pulled out. Maybe she was watching from one of the windows in the castle, but Luke couldn't tell about that.

Reluctantly, he put her out of his mind. She had made her own choices, and while he wished her the best, that was all he could do. He was surrounded by men who would have happily killed him in an instant if they knew he made his living by hunting their kind. *That* was what needed to occupy his attention, not some cool, attractive blonde from Philadelphia.

With Three-fingered Jack McKinney at their head and Luke in the middle of the bunch, the gang rode through the tunnel, out of the stronghold, followed the zigzag trail down to the creek, and single file, headed up the narrow canyon into the Arizona badlands.

CHAPTER 26

The trip along the canyon past the guards was uneventful. They emerged from the canyon where the creek ran and turned west, riding through the hills toward higher elevations.

Luke felt the eyes of Stockbridge's men on him. Much of the time since setting out on his journey, Luke had felt he was being watched, and as it turned out, that sensation had been absolutely accurate. First Aaron had followed him, keeping an eye on him, and so had the Apaches. Then, as he and his companions rode toward the Black Castle, Stockbridge's guards had looked on.

While inside the castle, Luke had often felt like he was under observation, as well, and no doubt he had been. He had a hunch that the servant woman, Paloma, had been ordered to keep an eye on him.

Out in the open again didn't mean he was out of danger. Creager wanted him dead, for sure, and so would every one of the other outlaws if they ever discovered the truth about him.

With that on his mind, Luke walked up casually to Aaron when the gang stopped around midmorning to rest their horses for a spell. He was wiping sweat from his mule's flanks with a rag.

Luke said quietly, "You and I need to have a talk."

"About what?"

"I reckon if you stop and think about that, you'll have a pretty good idea."

Aaron glanced over at him for a second, then turned his attention back to what he was doing. Without looking at Luke, he said, "Nothing's changed . . . yet. If it does, I'll let you know in time for you to do something about it."

Luke took that to mean Aaron still wanted his father brought to justice. If the youngster decided differently, he would warn Luke, so that the bounty hunter could slip away without having his true identity revealed.

Whether or not Luke would actually do that if such a situation arose . . . well, he wasn't sure about that. He supposed he would have to wait until the time came. But at least he was more confident now that Aaron wouldn't betray him without warning. He'd had a hunch that was the case. Confirmation was welcome, though.

"All right. I'm glad to hear that."

"Glad to hear what?" a voice asked behind them. Luke looked over his shoulder and saw Jack McKinney standing there. The boss outlaw was light on his feet.

"Luke was talkin' about my mule," Aaron answered without any hesitation. "I was afraid he was going lame, but now I don't reckon he is. I think he just had a little pebble in his shoe, and it must've got shook out while we were riding."

McKinney nodded. "When we make camp tonight,

you'd better check it closer. A man can't afford to take any chances with his mount. Isn't that right, Luke?"

"It sure is," Luke agreed. He clapped a hand on Aaron's shoulder and added, "Keep an eye on that jughead, kid." Turning to McKinney, he went on. "When do you think you'll tell us where we're headed?"

"When the right time comes," McKinney responded with a faint edge to his voice. "You'll know."

"Good enough." Luke nodded and strolled back to his horse, aware that Creager was watching him from about ten yards away. The big man's lumpy face was impassive, as emotionless as the chunk of rock it resembled, but that didn't fool Luke. He knew that he still needed to be wary. That would never change until there was another showdown between them.

A short time later, the men mounted up and rode on. When Luke tried to fall in farther back and behind Creager, the outlaw reined his horse to a halt and let several of the other men ride past him. Luke had no choice but to heel his horse into motion.

Creager fell in alongside him, riding about ten feet away. "If you think I'm going to let you behind me again, you're loco," the big outlaw rumbled. "I felt all mornin' like I had a target painted on my back, and now I know why. You were thinking about how you're going to kill me, weren't you?"

"The thought never crossed my mind," Luke said.

Creager snorted in obvious disbelief.

"It's true. We settled things between us. As far as I'm concerned, it's over."

"The hell it is. I'm starting to think clearer now. You must have pulled some sort of trick I haven't figured out yet. That's the only way you'd ever beat me."

Creager hawked and spit in Luke's direction. The gob of spittle landed on the ground between their horses. "You should've killed me while you had the chance. You won't ever get another one."

"I'm not looking for one," Luke said, but he knew Creager would never accept that. "But I won't get careless and let anybody bushwhack me, either."

Creager laughed, coldly, humorlessly. "When I kill you, you'll know it's me doing it. Never you worry about that."

Neither man said anything else. The tense silence hung between them as they rode.

The outlaws halted from time to time to rest the horses but didn't stop at midday for a meal. They made do with jerky and biscuits brought from the Black Castle, eaten in the saddle as they rode and washed down with water from their canteens. Although some, Creager included, also took nips from flasks they brought out from their saddlebags. Luke was a little surprised that McKinney allowed them to drink whiskey while they were on the trail, heading for a new job, but he supposed McKinney knew his men and had a pretty good idea how strict he could be with them.

In the afternoon, McKinney turned south before they reached the mountains and led the gang in that direction. Off to the right several miles, Luke saw a dark line meandering across the landscape from north to south and knew it marked the thicker vegetation along the course of the Colorado River. Settlements were scattered along the river, founded to serve the needs of the mines in the mountains beyond. Evidently, one of those settlements was the gang's destination.

That theory made sense to him. Some of those towns had banks. Others had express offices with safes where gold shipments from the mines were locked up until they could be shipped downstream to reach the railroad in Yuma. Any of those could provide a lucrative target for a bunch of desperadoes.

They made camp that night at the edge of an arroyo. A couple of men went down into the arroyo to build a fire, cook some supper, and boil a pot of coffee. The sky was clear and it was safe enough to venture down there. They could have hot food and coffee without risking the flames of a campfire being spotted by Apaches or anybody else who might be hostile toward them. But . . . nobody with any sense actually made camp in an arroyo, even when it wasn't during Arizona's brief rainy season. The danger of flash floods was too great.

After everyone had eaten, Jack McKinney stood up and said, "I reckon it's time we talked about what we're going to do. About fifteen miles south of here, right on the river, is a town called Stanton. It doesn't amount to much, but it has a bank. A trail right on the other side of the river leads up to several mines. A riverboat's due to dock there day after tomorrow and take on gold shipments from those mines. So the vault will be full of ingots tomorrow night . . . ingots that we're going to relieve it of."

"You know all this for a fact?" Creager asked.

"I do," McKinney snapped, as if he didn't like having his information questioned. "I got word about the boat's schedule a while back from a fella who works in the bank and promised to tip me off in exchange for a part-share. I'll get to him later, so nobody will suspect him of being part of the holdup. I knew we had to wait a while before pulling the job, so I figured that was a good time for us to pay a visit to Stockbridge's place. We've been on the move so much the past couple of years, it was good to stop and rest and relax for a spell, wasn't it?"

Several men called out agreement to that.

McKinney slipped his hands into the hip pockets of his jeans and went on. "Here's how we're going to do it. I said there wasn't much to Stanton, but there *is* a saloon, and some of you will be in there starting a ruckus as a distraction at the same time as the rest of us are breaking into the bank. We'll dynamite the vault door, load as much gold as we can onto a wagon, and light a shuck out of there. The rest of you take off, too. We'll rendezvous in the hills, split up the ingots among the pack mules and our horses, and head back deeper into the badlands for a while. Any questions?"

"Where do we get the wagon?" an outlaw asked.

"There's a freight outfit in town, too. We'll take one of theirs."

Creager said, "What if there *aren't* any there right when we need one? Seems like that's an awful lot riding on what's really nothing more than a matter of luck."

Thad got to his feet and snapped at Creager, "If my pa says there'll be a wagon there, there'll be a wagon there."

"Don't take that tone with me, boy," Creager rumbled.

McKinney held up a hand. "The fella who tipped me off swore he'd never seen the wagonyard when it didn't have at least one wagon in it. Maybe it *is* luck to count on that, but it's a calculated risk."

"Something else," Creager said. "Gold's heavy. We can't put a whole vault full of it in one wagon and hope to make any time with it. Chances are that'd kill the mules within a mile. We need more than one wagon."

McKinney shook his head. "That won't work. Once we split the ingots up among us, we can carry only so many of them anyway. So we take only what we can get away with."

"You mean to leave gold in the vault?" Creager sounded like he couldn't comprehend that.

"We won't have any choice. If we got enough wagons to empty it, we'd have to keep using them to haul all that gold instead of divvying it up. And I don't know about you, Creager, but I don't particularly want to get away from a posse while traveling with three or four heavily loaded wagons. Especially not through rough country like we'll be in."

The moon and stars provided enough silvery illumination for Luke to see the angry glare on Creager's face as the big outlaw growled before finally accepting McKinney's answers. "All right, damn it. You don't have to talk to me like I'm some wet-behind-the-ears kid." He gestured curtly toward Thad and Aaron and added, "We've got two of *them* along already."

"I can carry my weight, mister. Don't you worry about that," Thad responded hotly.

"And so can I," Aaron added as he jumped to his feet.

Creager laughed harshly. "Yeah, but you're both little pissants, so *your weight* don't amount to much, does it?"

"That's enough," McKinney said. He looked at his sons. "I mean all of you. Sit down."

Grumbling, Thad and Aaron sank back down to the ground where they had been sitting.

"Anybody else want to argue with my plan?" McKinney asked, his tone making it clear that he wouldn't take kindly to it if anyone answered in the affirmative. After a moment, he went on. "All right, then. We'll post some guards, and everybody else can get some sleep. Probably won't be any sleeping tomorrow night, so take advantage of the chance while you've got it."

McKinney didn't pick Luke to take one of the guard shifts, which wasn't surprising because he was a new man. The outlaws would have to trust him before they would willingly place their lives in his hands.

That wasn't likely to happen, Luke thought as he rolled up in his blankets against the chill that descended quickly in the dry air. He wouldn't gain the gang's trust because he wasn't going to be with them long enough for that. He needed to think of a way to ruin the plan for robbing the bank in Stanton, and at the same time cut Three-fingered Jack out of the herd and get him away from the other outlaws so he could be captured.

Oh, and somehow stay alive while he was doing those things, Luke reminded himself.

That was all.

CHAPTER 27

Since they had only fifteen miles to cover the next day, and they wouldn't be hitting the bank until after dark, the outlaws didn't worry about getting an early start the next morning. They lingered over bacon, flapjacks, and coffee.

The cookfire was built in the arroyo again, close against the bank so the slight overhang broke up the thin tendril of smoke that rose from the crackling flames and kept it from being noticeable. They took this precaution even though it was possible there were no hostile Apaches on the territory side of the mountains that were across the border in Mexico.

It was also possible some of the red devils were lurking within a hundred yards, watching and waiting like a pack of wolves for a chance to cut out any stragglers. The chances of any war party big enough to jump twenty heavily armed hardcases were pretty slim, but let a man or two be caught alone and that carelessness could be worth their lives.

Creager seemed to be in a surprisingly good mood. Maybe the thought of those gold ingots had cheered him up, Luke mused over a cup of coffee as he watched the big outlaw stuffing flapjacks in his mouth.

Creager winced a little as he ate. His lips were still swollen and tender. That didn't slow him down much, though.

Three-fingered Jack McKinney ambled over to Luke and sat down beside him on the same slab of rock. "Tonight you'll ride into Stanton with half a dozen of the other boys. You'll go to the saloon, and after you've been there half an hour, you'll start a fight. I don't care who starts the ball or how, as long as it's enough of a fracas to cause a lot of racket and attract plenty of attention."

"Star packer attention, I reckon you mean," Luke said. "You seem to know a lot about this settlement, Jack. Just what *is* the law dog situation there?"

"There's a town marshal and one deputy, that's all. And they don't actually work for the town. The mine owners pay them. Their main job is to protect any gold that happens to be in Stanton. They protect the citizens and look after the rest of the town, too, but that comes after taking care of the gold."

"Then what makes you think they'll both rush down to the saloon just because a fight breaks out?"

"They won't," McKinney said with a shrug. "But chances are, one of them will, and that cuts the odds against us in half and keeps everybody else in town occupied, too. If you work it right, during that tussle you and the other boys can knock out quite a few of the townsmen. If they have to regain consciousness before they can join a posse and come after us, so much the better."

Luke nodded slowly as he considered what McKinney had said. It actually wasn't a bad plan. He wondered about something else and asked, "What about the marshal? If he stays close to the bank and sends his deputy down to the saloon, you'll still have to deal with him."

"Then that's what we'll do," McKinney said in a flat voice. "Deal with him."

Luke knew what that meant. They would kill the local lawman if he got in their way, which he was likely to do since he worked for the mine owners. "It's not really my place to say this . . . but I hope you'll keep Aaron well away from that. He's just a kid."

"You're right," McKinney said without an ounce of friendliness in his voice. "It's not your place."

"The boy and I rode the river together. Well, that creek leading to the Black Castle, anyway. I like him. Don't want to see too much happening to him, too fast."

McKinney gazed narrow-eyed at him for a moment, then nodded. "I'll give you that. I reckon you're just looking out for the boy's best interests. And I appreciate you doing that before. But it's my job now."

McKinney had a funny way of showing that, Luke thought. Letting a twelve-year-old youngster ride with a bunch of hardcase killers and thieves didn't seem like it was in his best interests. But maybe that wouldn't last much longer.

Luke drank the rest of his coffee and dashed the grounds into the dirt. He stood up and said, "I'd better get my horse saddled."

"Yeah. We'll be riding in a little while."

Intentional on Luke's part, his horse was picketed next to Aaron's mule. As he draped the saddle blanket over his mount's back and smoothed it, he sensed movement beside him and glanced over to see Aaron reaching for the mule's saddle blanket.

As the boy got the blanket in place, he said without looking at Luke, "I didn't know we'd be robbing a bank so soon after we left."

"No, there was no way to predict that," Luke said, just as quietly, "but those are the cards we've been dealt."

"We can't let them get away with it. They're liable to . . . to kill somebody."

Luke thought of what McKinney had said about Stanton's marshal. "Yes, that's certainly a possibility."

"Maybe you can get word to the law somehow. Set a trap for them."

"Someone could be killed if we did that, too." Luke paused. "Thad could be, or your father."

"When it comes to Pa, I . . . I don't care."

Luke thought Aaron's declaration didn't sound completely convincing. It was one thing to nurse a hate for someone you hadn't seen for five years. Spending time with him, though, especially when he was your own flesh and blood, might make things different.

"He deserves whatever happens." Aaron had the blanket on the mule and paused to lift the saddle and with a grunt of effort, put it in place. "Thad, though . . . I don't understand why he had to run off, too, but I don't want to see him hurt."

"Neither do I." Luke had his saddle on the horse and began tightening the cinches. "I'll do what I can to stop them and to keep Thad safe. But you need to steer well clear of any trouble, so I don't have to worry about you, too."

"All right, Mr. J . . . . Jones. I'll try."

Luke turned away. To anyone watching them, it wouldn't have appeared that he and Aaron said anything to each other except a few idle comments. No one was close enough to have heard the conversation, he judged. He pulled the picket pin, untied the reins from it, and led the horse over to the area where the gang was assembling.

Within a few more minutes, everyone was ready to ride. They set out with McKinney and his sons leading the way again.

Luke wasn't sure what made him turn his head to the left at just the right moment, but as he looked in that direction, he caught a glimpse of movement atop a ridge about half a mile away. There and then gone, vanishing much too quickly for him to pick up any sort of detail.

It might have been the flick of a deer's tail, he told himself. Maybe a mountain lion on the prowl; there were a few of the big cats around there. It might have even been a bird.

But there were other explanations, too. Some that were not so innocent.

He and Badger and Aaron had never been absolutely sure whether or not they had accounted for every single member of that Apache war party, Luke reminded himself.

A line of small, rocky, mostly barren hills that ran north and south rose about a mile from the Colorado River, and between those hills and the stream lay the settlement of Stanton. The gang used the hills as cover as they approached, laying up behind them about midafternoon to wait until night had fallen before riding into town.

After they had all dismounted, McKinney caught Luke's eye and inclined his head toward the nearest hill. "Come up there with me and help me keep an eye on the settlement."

That struck Luke as odd, McKinney asking the newest member of the bunch to accompany him, but then he thought of a possible explanation. Could be that McKinney was trying to keep him and Creager apart as much as possible because he didn't trust the brutish outlaw not to lose control.

Luke didn't want another battle with Creager complicating things, so he nodded his agreement. "Sure." He picketed his mount, then followed McKinney up the hill. McKinney was carrying a pair of field glasses.

Luke caught up to him and commented, "I'm surprised your boys didn't want to come along."

"They did," McKinney said. "I told them to stay down there with the others."

"You have a reason for that?"

"None that I feel obliged to share with you," McKinney snapped. "The sun's in the west, though, and I don't want it reflecting off anything and maybe warning folks in town that somebody is up here in the hills. They might take it for an Apache war party and start getting ready for a fight."

"You don't want that, so you don't want to risk Thad or Aaron giving us away."

McKinney shrugged. "They're young and inexperienced . . . the exact opposite of you, *Jones*." The emphasis on the name made it plain McKinney didn't believe for a second that it was real.

Before they reached the hill's crest, the two men

took off their hats and got down on their hands and knees to crawl closer. They bellied down at the top and eased their heads up to take a general look at the situation.

Stanton had one main street that formed the business district and three cross streets on which residences and smaller businesses were located. Several fairly large houses were scattered around the outer edges of the settlement. Luke wondered if they belonged to men who owned mines in the mountains on the other side of the river.

At the far end of the middle cross street was a dock extending into the Colorado. Luke lifted his gaze to the far side of the river and saw a large, sturdy-looking, flat-bottomed ferry tied up over there. On the Stanton side, another ferry was landing at the dock on the far end of the middle cross street.

"Why didn't they just build the dock for the riverboat on the far side of the river, so it could take on the gold shipments directly?" Luke asked McKinney.

"There's a big sandbar close to the western bank," the outlaw explained. "The mine owners didn't know that at first, but they figured it out pretty quick-like when three or four boats got stuck and they had a devil of a time getting them unstuck. The river's deep enough for the ferry to make it, though. At least it is most of the time, when the river's not running low. So they decided the next best thing was to put the dock on this side and let the town grow up around it on the eastern bank. They ferry the gold across, load it on wagons, and store it in the bank's vault until a riverboat picks it up."

"Seems dangerous, hauling it up and down the

street in wagons like that," Luke commented. "That's twice when a bunch like us could hit it."

"Some have tried. There are always enough guards on the wagons to keep them from being successful, though. Most of the men who made a grab for the gold wound up shot full of holes. The others are all down at Yuma now."

"The mine owners don't post guards in the bank?"

"They do, but not as many since they trust the vault. It's one of the best, supposedly. But we'll take care of the guards and dynamite will take care of the vault door." McKinney glanced up, saw that a cloud was about to drift in front of the sun, and waited until it had, then lifted the field glasses. He studied the town quickly and grunted in satisfaction. "Everything appears normal," he said as he passed the glasses to Luke. "Take a look?"

"I've never been here before. I don't know what's normal in Stanton."

"Your instincts will tell you if something's not right."

"You have a lot of confidence in my instincts," Luke said dryly.

"No, I have confidence in my own instincts. And they tell me you're a man who's been in a lot of tight situations and knows how to handle them. Am I wrong about that?"

"No, not really," Luke answered truthfully. He knew bank robbers and how they operated. He had captured—or killed—enough of them.

While the sun was still behind the clouds, he put the field glasses to his eyes and scanned the town. Stanton looked peaceful in the late afternoon. A few people were still moving around, but as the day eased on toward evening, most folks were either already in their homes or wrapping up their business for the day.

"Where's the saloon?" he asked.

"North end of town on the west side of the street. It takes up most of that block."

"I see it," Luke said. "What about the bank?"

"Southeast corner of the intersection between the main street and that middle cross street."

"Marshal's office?"

"At the far end of the block where the bank is, on the same side of the street."

"So the marshal's handy."

"Yeah. He can get from his office to the bank in less than thirty seconds, I'd say."

"And the saloon where we're going to be staging that distraction is only a little more than a block away."

With a shrug, McKinney said, "I wish there was more distance between them, but those are the cards we've been dealt. The guards in front of the bank will all be looking toward the saloon once the fight breaks out. We'll dispose of the ones in back and go in that way. The guards in front won't know anything's going on until the dynamite goes off. We'll have men waiting for them if they come rushing in. Same goes for the marshal."

Luke handed the field glasses back to McKinney. "And once those of us in the saloon hear the blast, we light a shuck out of there?"

"Yeah." McKinney waved a hand toward the area where the rest of the gang was waiting. "We'll meet back here and head east with the wagon for a ways, then stop and divvy up the gold."

Luke rubbed his chin, frowned in thought, and then asked, "Where are Thad and Aaron going to be while all this is going on?"

"They're going to wait here."

"They won't like that, especially Thad. I've got a hunch he'll want to be right in the middle of things."

McKinney shook his head. "I don't care what he wants. He'll do what I say."

"Are you sure about that? From what I've seen of Aaron, he can be pretty headstrong, and Thad probably takes after you as well."

"I don't care about that. I'm not going to let them argue with me."

"You know your boys," Luke said, but that angle worried him. Thad and Aaron were wild cards. He wished he could be certain they would be safe, but he might not have that luxury if he wanted to stop the gang from killing some of the guards and the marshal, and making off with a fortune in gold. Stopping that plan was already going to be difficult enough, although he had a glimmer of an idea that might work.

The sun dropped below the clouds and spread reddish-gold rays across the mountains and the hills to the east. In less than an hour, he estimated, it would slide behind the peaks and night would fall with the suddenness common to the region.

McKinney must have been thinking the same thing. "It won't be long now."

Luke heard a note of anticipation in the boss outlaw's voice.

McKinney was right. One way or another, it would soon be over.

CHAPTER 28

As dusk began to settle over the landscape, Luke and Three-fingered Jack McKinney went back down the hill to join the others. An air of tense anticipation hung over the temporary camp.

One of the outlaws asked, "Does everything look all right down there in the town, Jack?"

"Yeah," McKinney replied. "Nothing out of the ordinary going on. All of you know the plan. We should be able to carry it out without any trouble. Well . . . not *too* much trouble, anyway."

Creager, with his thumbs hooked in his gunbelt, rasped bitterly, "You and your new *segundo* didn't hatch a new scheme while you were up there?"

"What are you talking about, Creager?"

The brutish outlaw nodded toward Luke. "You took Jones with you to check things out. Usually that would've been me or one of the other boys. We all figure you've decided he's second-in-command now, even though he's only been part of the gang for a day."

A few displeased mutters came from the other men. Creager had been down there trying to stir up trouble, Luke realized.

"Nothing's changed," McKinney said sharply. "You can just get that idea out of your heads. I'm still the boss of this bunch, and that's all you need to know."

"That's right," Thad spoke up. "My pa's the boss, and we don't need to be questioning what he does."

A faint smile touched McKinney's lips. "I'm glad to hear you say that, son, because I've decided that you and your brother are going to stay behind on this job."

Thad swung around toward him, eyes widening in the fading light. "What? What are you talking about, Pa? I'm going with you. Sure, Aaron needs to stay behind—"

"Why?" Aaron broke in. "How come you think you get to go along and I don't?"

"Neither of you is going along," McKinney said before Thad could answer his brother's question. "You're both staying here, where we'll all meet up when the job's over. There's not going to be any arguing about it."

Thad's jaw clenched tight as he said, "That's not fair."

A harsh, humorless laugh came from Creager. "That's what happens when you bring brats along on a job for men."

All three McKinneys turned angrily toward him. Thad was about to say something, but his father waved him silent. "You sound like you don't like the way I'm running this gang, Creager," McKinney said with a dangerous note in his voice. "You feel like doing anything about that?"

"With a fortune in gold waiting for us a mile away?" Creager shook his head. "No, I don't suppose I do feel like that right now. We'll wait and see how things play out. Leave it at that."

"You'd better leave it at that from now on," McKinney

said with a curt nod. He looked around at the others. "Anybody else have anything to say?"

"Let's go get that gold," one of the outlaws responded.

Several of the others chuckled at that, and the tense mood eased slightly.

McKinney smiled and nodded. "Soon. We need to wait for it to get darker first . . . but we won't wait too long."

The men tended to their horses as shadows lengthened and then closed in. Luke was aware of Creager's hostile stare directed toward him but ignored it. However, when he had a chance he drifted over to where Jack McKinney was standing with his sons. "Creager's going with you to the bank, isn't he?"

"I'm not going to send him into the middle of a saloon brawl with you," McKinney replied. "Too easy for him to shoot you in the back or stave your head in with a table leg during all the confusion."

"That's what I was thinking. He said he wanted to settle things between us face-to-face, but I don't know that he meant it."

Thad said, "I don't trust him, Pa. He's got the idea in his head of taking over the gang."

McKinney sighed and nodded. "I know. He's going to make trouble sooner or later. But I'd like to get this job behind us first."

"You really ought to let me come with you," Thad argued. "I can keep an eye on your back and make sure Creager doesn't try to double-cross you."

"He won't do that. Not with as much loot at stake. No, the trouble will come later . . . but I don't reckon it would be a good idea to postpone it for too much longer." McKinney put a hand on his older son's shoulder. "Anyway, I need you to stay here with Aaron. You two are a hell of a lot more important to me than any gold shipment ever could be."

"Wouldn't know that by the way you went off and left us struggling on that ranch," Aaron said.

McKinney frowned at him. "You think you've got all the answers to everything, boy, but maybe you don't. You might want to keep that in mind."

Aaron just gazed back at him stubbornly. After a moment, McKinney shook his head and walked off to talk to some of the other outlaws.

Thad said to his brother, "You need to quit raggin' on Pa about that. He only did what he thought was best."

"Is that so? He ever explain it to you?"

"Well . . . no. But I know he believed he was doing the right thing."

Aaron just snorted to show how much he thought of Thad's faith in their father.

Thad stomped off, following McKinney.

When they were out of easy earshot, Luke said quietly to Aaron, "This is working out for the best. You and Thad will be safe while I deal with your father."

"In the middle of a bank robbery?" Aaron asked with a skeptical frown.

"If I'm lucky, there won't be a bank robbery. I'll try to grab your father when the rest of the gang goes stampeding out of town. When you hear them coming, you boys lie low and stay out of sight. They won't hang around to look for you. They'll go on and light a shuck out of here. You can ride into Stanton in the morning and find me if I don't find you first."

"I'll have to tell Thad who you really are."

"It'll be too late by then for him to do anything about it," Luke pointed out. "Three-fingered Jack will be in jail."

"Or dead," Aaron said bleakly.

"I'll try to see to it that doesn't happen."

"Do whatever you have to," the youngster said. "As long as he pays for runnin' off and abandoning Ma."

Luke nodded. Aaron was carrying a mighty heavy load of hate and regret, he thought. It would be a lot for a full-grown man to bear. The weight had to be crushing for a twelve-year-old boy.

The stars had begun to appear in the sky almost as soon as the sun dipped below the peaks to the west. By the time another hour had passed, they glittered in the heavens like diamonds spread out on an ebony cloth. A half-moon lay low to the eastern horizon.

McKinney circulated among the men, picking out who would start the brawl in the saloon and who would go with him to the bank. It wasn't exactly an even split. Luke and seven other men would head for the saloon. A total of eleven outlaws, including McKinney, would hit the bank.

"Remember," he told the men who would be going to the saloon, "drift in one or two at a time so you won't be noticed, and then once you're all in there, wait half an hour before you start the melee. That'll give us time to get in position at the bank."

Luke and several of the other men nodded in understanding, then swung up into their saddles and rode out.

They scattered on the other side of the hills when they could see the lights in the settlement burning in the distance. Luke rode alone, and as he did, he mused over everything that had happened so far, going all the way back to his first sight of that homemade wanted poster promising a bounty of one dollar and forty-two cents and a used harmonica. Certainly one of the strangest jobs he had even taken on, it promised to be more so before it was over.

Riding quickly because he wanted to be the first one to reach the town, Luke swung to the north and approached Stanton from that direction, as if he were following the river and had been all day. That brought him into the settlement at the end of the street where the saloon was located, so he didn't have far to go once he reached the buildings.

A glance along the street revealed to him that most of the businesses were dark and closed for the night. A couple of blocks down, the general store was still open, with a wagon parked at the high front porch that also served as a loading dock. A man wearing a canvas apron, either a clerk or the store's proprietor, loaded crates into the wagon bed.

Luke could also see the dark bulk of the bank, which appeared to be constructed out of bricks and had a second story, making it the most impressive building in Stanton. As he reined to a halt in front of the saloon, he looked closely at the front of the bank and spotted a couple of tiny orange glows in the shadows along its porch. Guards were posted there, just as McKinney had said, and two of them were smoking quirlies.

Luke turned his attention to the saloon. Also as McKinney had indicated, it was large and took up most of the street frontage on the block. At the northern end of the building was a barber shop with its traditional striped pole out front, but other than that, the saloon was the only business.

Garish yellow light spilled through the windows on either side of a broad entrance sporting batwing doors. Luke dismounted and tied his horse at a hitch rail with four other animals, then stepped up onto the boardwalk and pushed through the batwings into the saloon's smoky, raucous interior.

He had been in countless places just like it and saw immediately that the customers were split roughly evenly between miners from the shafts in the mountains across the river and cowhands from the spreads to the south and southeast. East and northeast of the settlement lay stretches of desert and badlands where vegetation was too sparse to support cattle.

Tobacco smoke and the smells of spilled liquor and unwashed human flesh filled the air, along with the tinny sounds coming from a rinky-dink player piano in one corner. A low rumble of male laughter and conversation flowed beneath the music like an underground river, counterpointed by an occasional strident laugh from one of the saloon girls, the slap of cards on green felt from the poker games, and the clicking of a roulette wheel that spun in the back of the room.

All of it was music to Luke's ears. As squalid as the place might be, that sort of saloon was as close to a home as he had.

He walked to the bar, which was on his right. Dressed in heavy canvas shirts and trousers, and thick-soled work shoes or hobnailed boots, a group of miners stood at the end of the hardwood closest to the entrance. They passed around a bottle of whiskey, filled their glasses, and then roared out one obscene toast after another.

To Luke's left, half a dozen cowboys stood hipshot,

drinking beer, their high-crowned hats thumbed back on their heads. He saw a couple of them cast narrow-eyed, disapproving glances toward the miners at the other end of the bar.

That same sort of mix extended to the tables where men sat and drank or where games of chance were going on. Everyone seemed to be having a good time, but Luke sensed an undercurrent of natural hostility between the men who made their living going down into dark, narrow holes in the ground and the others who spent their days riding the range under wide open skies. Those two extremes could never fully understand each other. An uneasy truce, an effort to tolerate each other, was the best either side could do.

As Luke rested both hands on the bar's front edge, a bartender with a white apron over a red jacket came along the hardwood and nodded pleasantly to him. "What can I do for you, mister?" The man's slicked-down brown hair was parted in the middle, and he had a prominent Adam's apple.

"I don't suppose you have any brandy."

The bartender shook his head. "Not much call for it. Not *any* call for it, come to think of it. Got beer and several kinds of whiskey, but no matter what's on the label, they'll all peel the paint off your innards, if that's what you're lookin' for."

"I'll just take a beer as long as it's cold," Luke said. "My innards need what paint they have left on them."

The bartender grinned at him and filled a mug from a barrel under the bar. As he set it in front of Luke, he said, "Coldest beer you'll find in this part of the territory, friend. That'll be two bits."

Luke picked up the mug, which had foam spilling

over the top, and used the thumb of his other hand to point at the group of miners. "Those damned stinking dirt-grubbers are going to pay for it," he told the bartender in a loud, clear voice.

The words might not have been heard in other parts of the room, but they carried to the miners just fine and interrupted their revelry. Their profane japing at each other came to an abrupt halt, and in the surprised silence that took its place some of the men slowly turned their heads to scowl at Luke.

One of them, a burly gent with a bald head and a dark, sweeping handlebar mustache, glared and demanded, "What the hell did you just say, mister?"

On the other side of the hardwood, the bartender's eyes bugged out slightly in alarm as he started shaking his head back and forth, trying to catch Luke's attention.

Luke ignored him and grinned at the bald miner. "I said you and your friends would pay for my drink. It's the least you can do for a man who works at an honest job instead of crawling around in the dirt like a squirming pack of worms."

The miner's big hands clenched into blocky fists as he took a step toward Luke. "Why, you—"

Luke stopped him by holding up a hand. "My apologies, friend. I never should have called you worms. You're not worms."

The miner's jaw jutted out like a rocky shelf as he waited to hear what Luke was going to say next.

Luke glanced around the room. He was the first of McKinney's gang to reach the saloon, just as he'd intended, and if his plan was going to work, he had to keep it that way. He couldn't afford to waste any more time. "I wasn't specific enough. You're not worms.

You're filthy, disgusting maggots, feasting on the hard work of real men."

And just in case that wasn't enough to do the trick, with a flick of his wrist he slung the entire contents of the beer mug into the bald-headed miner's face.

CHAPTER 29

For several heartbeats, the man was too stunned to do anything except stand there in front of the bar with the foamy amber liquid dripping off his face while he stared at Luke.

Then, with a deafening bellow of rage, he charged.

Luke let out a yell of his own as he set his feet and braced himself. His shout of *"Yeeehaaahhh!"* echoed from the ceiling. It was the legendary Rebel yell, the battle cry of the sons of the Confederacy who had headed west by the tens of thousands after the end of the War of Northern Aggression.

Luke had spotted a man wearing an old Confederate campaign cap with a broken black bill among the group of cowhands standing farther along the bar. Just as Luke hoped, the man let out a Rebel yell of his own and rushed along the bar to come to Luke's aid if necessary, one southern boy pitching in to help another. Luke saw that response from the corner of his eye, then had to focus all his attention on the bald-headed miner, who swung one of those sledgehammer fists in a wild, looping blow.

That punch would have ended the fight then and

there if it had landed, but Luke ducked under it. The knobby-knuckled fist still came close enough that he felt the wind of its passage. The miner's midsection was wide open, so he stepped in while the miner was slightly off balance from the missed punch and hooked a left and a right into his belly.

It was almost like punching the sandstone bank of an arroyo. The miner didn't even grunt. He just whipped a backhand at Luke's head.

Luke jerked out of the way again, and the man's hand struck his hat and sent it flying. A second later, the man grabbed the front of Luke's shirt and hauled him forward. Luke couldn't afford to let the miner wrap him up in a rib-crushing bear hug, so he stomped a boot heel down on top of the man's left foot and lowered his head and rammed the top of it into the man's face.

That two-pronged attack made the miner yell in pain and lean back as blood spurted from his flattened nose. He let go of Luke's shirt. Luke clubbed both hands together and brought them up in a smashing blow that caught the man under the chin. The miner's head rocked back from the impact. Luke slashed a side-hand blow to the exposed throat, and the miner staggered against the bar, choking and coughing.

"That son of a bitch is fightin' dirty!" another miner yelled. "Get him!"

The group swarmed forward.

As Luke got ready to meet their attack, the cowboy in the Rebel cap stood shoulder to shoulder with him and said, "Let's whip us some Yankees!"

A second later, the area in front of the bar was

filled with flying fists and the meaty sound of punches landing on flesh and bone.

The fact that one of their own was in the middle of the fracas was enough of an excuse for the Reb's friends to leap into action with enthusiastic yells. The battle spread quickly around the room, as cowboys and miners who had been playing poker in relative peace a moment earlier cursed and lunged at each other, overturning tables and sending cards, coins, and greenbacks flying. Painted saloon girls in short, spangled dresses screamed in alarm and scrambled to get out of the way of the wildly punching men. Judging by the way the bartender's mouth was working, he was yelling at the men to stop fighting, but nobody could hear him over the uproar and wouldn't care if they did.

All the while, the rinky-dink strains of the player piano continued dancing through the tumult.

As if the yelling and cursing by the combatants, combined with the crash of furniture being broken and thrown bottles shattering, wasn't enough of a commotion, several meek-looking townsmen bolted from the saloon and shouted for the marshal. The few people on the street took up the hue and cry, and as the shouts rose over the settlement, even more people poked their heads out of doors and windows and hollered demands to know what was going on. Within minutes, the ruckus had roused the entire town, except for a few very sound sleepers and those who had passed out from drinking.

Inside the saloon, Luke had no way of knowing all that, but he hoped his ploy had been successful. Jack McKinney and the men with him wouldn't be in

position to make their move on the bank yet, and if
the guards hired by the mine owners to protect the
gold had any sense, they would be on full alert,
aware that such a brawl could serve as a distraction
for an attempted robbery. McKinney's group was
large enough that they might be able to fight their
way into the bank despite that, but not without at-
tracting a great deal of attention . . . too much attention for them to have the time needed to blow the
vault open with dynamite.

With their plans ruined, their most likely reaction
would be to get out of Stanton while they had the
chance. Most outlaws were practical enough to cut
their losses and abandon a job when the odds were
against them.

What Luke had to do was find McKinney and capture him without the rest of the gang realizing what
was going on. He had to get away from the saloon
and all the chaos going on inside it.

Seeing his hat upside down on the bar where it
had landed, Luke snatched it up and clapped it on
his head, then leaned quickly to the side as a yelling
miner tried to punch him in the face. As the man
crowded against him, Luke slammed a fist into his
belly and had more luck than he'd had with the bald
hombre earlier. That man's midsection was a lot
softer. He gasped and doubled over as he turned
green and sick-looking. Luke shoved him away.

The space between Luke and the batwinged entrance was filled with men flailing away at each other.
He had no choice but to run that gauntlet. Ducking
his head, he plunged into the melee and shouldered
men out of his way. Several times, fists thudded into

his back and shoulders, but he shrugged off the impacts and kept going. Once he tripped over a fallen battler but caught his balance before he wound up on the sawdust-littered floor himself. If he had fallen, he could have been stomped senseless in a matter of moments.

Finally, he stumbled toward the batwings right in front of him. Before he could reach them, someone grabbed his shoulder from behind and hauled him around.

The bald-headed miner had hold of him. He appeared to have recovered from the throat punch, but his face was still bright red, even where it wasn't smeared with blood from his broken nose. He yelled hoarsely, "You're not goin' anywhere!" and clamped both hands around Luke's throat.

Luke felt the man's thumbs digging for his windpipe and knew he had only a few seconds to break free before the rage-filled miner did serious damage to him. He grabbed the man's wrists to brace himself and brought the toe of his boot up into the miner's groin. The vicious kick made the miner's eyes bulge almost from their sockets. Luke had learned many years earlier that when it came to battling for his life, there was no such thing as fighting dirty.

There was only winning and losing—and survival.

Wrenching hard on the man's wrists, Luke tore the hands away from his throat, hooked a foot between the man's calves, and jerked his legs out from under him. The man fell, landing so hard that Luke felt the floor shiver under his feet.

Quickly, he turned and pushed out through the batwings onto the saloon's porch.

The first thing he saw was a familiar figure reining a horse to a rearing halt in front of the saloon. The rider was one of the men who was supposed to start the brawl that had broken out early.

"What the hell happened?" he called to Luke.

"I don't know! As soon as I stepped in there, all hell broke loose!"

To Luke's left a man came flying through one of the saloon's windows, which sprayed glass everywhere as it shattered. The luckless man rolled and skidded across the porch and fell into the street. Somebody had put a lot of effort into throwing him through the window.

"You mean it's a real fight?" the outlaw asked as he fought to get his spooked horse back under control.

"Yeah! We'd better get out of here while we still can! Have you seen McKinney?"

If the outlaw thought that was an odd question under the circumstances, he gave no sign of it. He just waved a hand wildly toward the bank. "Him and the others ought to be gettin' close, but they'll have to call it off now!"

With that, he was able to wheel his horse around and kick it into a run away from the saloon. Luke didn't pay any more attention to him. He untied his horse from the hitch rack, swung up into the saddle, and trotted toward the bank.

There was a chance McKinney and the others hadn't yet reached the settlement and had turned back without ever getting there once they heard the sounds of the brawl starting prematurely. Luke realized that he might have to postpone making an attempt to capture McKinney. But he'd had to act as quickly as he did in order to prevent innocent men from being killed and the bank from being looted. He could come up with some other plan to nab Three-fingered Jack later on if he needed to.

He gave the bank a wide berth when he saw the guards clustered in front of it, bristling with rifles and shotguns. He nudged his horse into a gallop as if all he wanted to do was get away from the fight, which was spilling out of the saloon and into the street. When he glanced over his shoulder, he saw several knots of men punching away at each other.

He rode around a corner and onto one of the cross streets. A man yelled at him from one of the houses, asking him "what the hell all the commotion" was about. Luke ignored the man and hurried on, heading toward the hills east of the settlement where the members of the gang were supposed to rendezvous.

The drumming of his horse's hooves, plus the distance as the town fell behind him, made the sounds of battle fade. He hadn't heard any shooting and was glad no gunplay had erupted. In the morning, the men involved in the brawl would have sore heads, maybe even a few broken bones, but they would still be alive. The saloon's owner would have some damage to repair and broken furniture to replace, but that was better than having the bank cleaned out.

The moon was higher, casting a wash of silver light over the landscape. Luke watched for any sign of other men on horseback and had ridden perhaps a mile when he spotted movement ahead. Urging his mount to greater speed, he closed in and soon came within hailing distance of three riders.

"McKinney!" he called. "Is that you?" Even if the boss

outlaw wasn't in the bunch, maybe they could tell him where to find the man.

The riders reined in and turned to face Luke as his horse trotted toward them. The moonlight was bright enough for him to see that Three-fingered Jack McKinney wasn't among them, though they were members of the group that had gone with him to raid the bank.

"Jones!" one of them exclaimed. "What happened? We were still a quarter of a mile from town when we heard the uproar start."

Luke brought his mount to a halt beside the other men. "One thing we didn't count on. That saloon was full of miners and cowboys who hate each other's guts, and they started fighting on their own. We never got a chance to start the brawl when we wanted to!"

"Damn the luck! When we heard all that commotion going on, Jack said we had to turn back. Said the guards would be ready for trouble and we'd wind up having to shoot it out with all of them."

"I'll bet Creager wasn't happy with that," Luke said.

Another outlaw laughed harshly. "I thought they might reach for their guns and settle it then and there. Creager was all for gallopin' in and shootin' it out with the guards, and devil take the hindmost! But in the end, he went along with Jack's order to scatter and then meet up back at the rendezvous later tonight."

An all-out assault on the town like Creager wanted would have resulted in a lot of innocent blood being spilled. Luke felt some grim satisfaction that he'd been able to prevent that.

"So you don't know where McKinney is? I thought I'd better tell him what happened."

The men shook their heads.

"He headed off into the dark like the rest of us did. You can tell him about it when we get back to the rendezvous." The outlaw who spoke paused to spit, then shook his head in apparent disgust. "I sure was lookin' forward to gettin' away with a wagon full of gold."

Luke turned his horse away from the others and said, "Those people in town don't have any reason to raise a posse, since they don't know how close they came to having the bank hit, but riding in a bunch like this probably isn't too smart anyway. I'll see you fellas later."

None of them wished him luck or called farewells as he rode away. He was the new man, after all. They didn't have any real fondness for him yet and likely never would since he didn't intend to be among them for very long.

He circled through the hills, counting on instinct to guide him back to the rendezvous point. He felt the opportunity to wrap up this odd quest slipping away from him, but he couldn't do anything about it except wait and see how the hand played out.

That thought was going through his mind when he suddenly spotted a lone rider in front of him. Luke increased his mount's pace, and as he drew closer, he realized the man was the right size and build to be Three-fingered Jack McKinney.

The man stopped short with no warning and wheeled his horse around. Moonlight glinted on the gun he held. He'd heard Luke coming up behind him and didn't take any chances on being ambushed.

Luke drew back on the reins with his left hand and raised his right in the universal gesture of peace as his horse slowed. "Hold your fire, boss," he called. "It's me, Luke Jones." He was close enough that he could see the other rider's face, although the man's hat brim cast a shadow over it. Certain he had found McKinney, Luke thought maybe his luck was going to hold, after all.

McKinney lowered the iron in his hand but didn't pouch it. "Jones, what in blazes went wrong back there?"

"A bunch of proddy miners and cowboys in that saloon jumped the gun on us," Luke explained, edging his horse nearer. He wanted to get close enough to buffalo McKinney over the head with one of his Remingtons. It would help if McKinney holstered his own Colt first, though.

"You mean they just started fighting for no good reason?"

"None that I could see," Luke said.

McKinney let out a bitter curse. "That's the one thing I didn't count on, and that was enough to ruin the timing of the whole thing."

"I ran into some of the other boys. They told me Creager wanted to go ahead with the raid."

"It would have been fine with Creager if we'd stormed in there, gunned down everybody we saw, and burned the town to the ground as we left." McKinney snorted contemptuously and jammed his gun back in its holster. "That's not the way I do things, no matter what Creager wants."

Luke's hand moved inconspicuously toward the Remington on his right hip. He was ready to jerk it from leather and lay the barrel alongside McKinney's head with enough force to knock the boss outlaw cold when he heard a sudden swift rataplan of hoofbeats from behind him.

His reflexes jerked him around. A rider moving that fast on such a night didn't have anything good in mind.

A big, dark shape bulked up out of the shadows, and a gravelly voice shouted, "You! It was your fault!"

Creager!

Luke palmed out the Remington he had been reaching for, but Creager already had a gun in his hand. He fired as he charged, muzzle flame blooming in the darkness like a crimson flower. Luke felt a terrible impact slam into his head. The Remington slipped from his fingers, unfired. He knew he was falling, toppling out of the saddle, but oblivion swallowed him whole before he ever hit the ground.

CHAPTER 30

Luke had been knocked out enough times in his life to know what was going on as he began to regain consciousness. A throbbing, all-too-familiar pain originated in his head and radiated out to fill his entire being. He knew what would come next, too—more pain, a sickness deep in his belly, and dizzying disorientation when he tried to open his eyes and move. That would just make it worse.

Maybe he ought to stay still without giving any sign that he was starting to wake up, he decided. Also, the sound of voices, faint and incomprehensible at the moment, had begun to penetrate his cobwebbed brain, and he thought it might be a good idea to wait until he figured out who they belonged to and what they were saying.

One of the voices rumbled, sounding like wagon wheels on bad road. *That has to be Creager.* The sharp, angry tones that answered came from Three-fingered Jack McKinney. That were arguing about something, and Luke had a pretty good idea what it had to be.

Him.

Specifically, his life, which Creager no doubt wanted to bring to a swift and final ending.

Gradually, the fuzziness in Luke's hearing faded as the pain in his head subsided to a dull ache. He began picking out words in what McKinney was saying.

". . . no proof that . . . ruined our plans."

"Who the hell else could have done it?" Creager's deep, gravelly rumble was easier to understand. "You heard what Bolton said. He saw Jones coming out of that saloon while the fight was going on. Jones caused a ruckus early just to keep us from robbing that bank!"

Creager was smarter than he looked, Luke thought.

"Why would he do that?" McKinney asked. "Luke stood just as much to gain as any of the rest of us."

"How the hell do I know?" Creager rasped back. "All I'm sure of is that he's to blame."

A new, higher voice joined in the argument. "The only reason you think that is because you hate him to start with!"

"Stay out of it, kid," Creager said. "When we want to hear your whining, we'll ask for it. And that'll be never!"

McKinney said, "Creager's right that you need to stay out of it, Aaron. This is something for the men to decide."

"Thad and me have had to play the parts of men ever since you rode off and left us." Aaron sounded just as angry with his father as he had been with Creager.

"Don't talk to Pa like that," Thad responded. "Go over there and sit down on that rock, like he told you before."

"Go to hell," Aaron muttered. Luke heard boots scuffing the ground near him, and then he could tell by the sounds that Aaron was sitting down on the ground beside him.

While the others were talking, Luke had moved his arms and legs just enough to discover that he wasn't tied up, although not so much that anyone would notice unless they happened to be looking right at him when he moved. Even though he was still free, he knew he was in no shape to put up any sort of fight. He had to wait, bide his time, let more strength seep back into his body while bloody-handed outlaws stood around him and debated his fate.

"Well, there's nothing we can do about it now," McKinney went on. "The boat will dock in Stanton today to pick up that gold shipment and take it back downriver. We might as well move on and figure out another job somewhere else."

Creager said, "They still have to take the gold from the bank to the dock. We could hit the place then."

"Between the guards who'll come in on the riverboat and the ones already in town, those mine owners will have forty armed men on hand. I'm not going to ride right into a bear trap like that with my eyes wide open. They'd wipe us out, Creager, and you know it."

"Damn it, I thought you had more sand than that!"

"Are you calling me a coward?" McKinney asked.

"I'm just saying you never used to hesitate so much before those brats of yours joined up with us. You need to get rid of 'em. Send 'em back home bawlin' to their mama!"

"The boys aren't going anywhere," McKinney said. "It's too dangerous—"

"It's dangerous to *us* just having them around!" Creager broke in. "You can't think straight anymore because you're too busy worrying about them."

Luke heard mutters of agreement from some of the other men. He didn't like the way this confrontation was shaping up.

"You've already put this damn stranger who calls himself Jones ahead of me, just because you're grateful to him for helping your brat," Creager continued. "We've been riding together for years, McKinney. You taking his side the way you did sticks in my craw."

"I didn't take his side. I just stopped you from finishing off a man who may not have done anything wrong. I'll talk to Jones when he comes to. We'll get to the bottom of this."

"It's too late for that. You're gonna have to choose, McKinney. Me and the rest of the boys, or those kids and that double-crossing stranger!"

An uneasy silence followed Creager's ultimatum. Luke thought it was time he got a better handle on the situation. He didn't move, but he opened his eyes to narrow slits.

They were no longer in the little depression on the other side of the hills from Stanton that had served as the gang's rendezvous point. A small campfire crackled and gave off a flickering red glow that revealed mostly desert and a few rocky knobs around them. Luke guessed that the gang had headed east after regrouping and probably had gone several miles before stopping again.

Having a fire wasn't the smartest thing in the world when it came to the chance of renegade Apaches being out there somewhere in the darkness. Nobody could do anything about that, though. The fire was already burning.

The light from it illuminated a tense scene. McKinney and Thad stood on one side of the flames,

to the left of where Luke lay on the ground with
Aaron sitting beside him. Creager was on the other
side of the campfire with the rest of the gang. Luke
wondered if some of them had moved to where
Creager was when he'd started arguing with McKinney
in a show of support for the brutish outlaw.

Regardless of how it had developed, things didn't
look good. If all the men on Creager's side of the
fire were ready to back his play, McKinney and his
sons were facing overwhelming odds.

"What's it gonna be, McKinney?" Creager asked.
"Get rid of the brats and give Jones to me so I can
settle my score with him . . . or am *I* gonna be the boss
of this gang from here on out?"

McKinney's lips drew back from his teeth in a furi-
ous grimace at the challenge.

"You think I can't shade you on the draw, Creager?
McKinney's whiplike body had a crouch to it. His
hand hovered over the butt of his gun, ready to hook
and draw.

The obvious threat didn't seem to have any effect
on Creager. He stood calmly and said, "Maybe you
can, maybe you can't. Even if you put lead in me,
I'll put a bullet in *you* before I go down. You know
that, McKinney. And as soon as you kill me, the rest
of the boys will finish you off, along with Jones and
those kids!"

McKinney's eyes flicked to the other men. "You
wouldn't shoot down innocent boys," he said, but he
didn't sound completely convinced of that.

"Look, Jack, we just want things to go back to the
way they used to be," one of the men said. "You runnin'
things, plannin' jobs that netted us a lot of loot and
dodgin' the law dogs."

Another man said, "It's been a good run, Jack. You've done right by us. But a gang like this is no place for youngsters. They're muddlin' up your thinking, and you know it."

"So you're backing Creager's play?" McKinney asked bleakly. "You're going to let him take over?"

"He's got some good ideas," a third outlaw spoke up. "He knows of a bank we can hit that'll put a lot of money in our hands."

"Oh? Where's that?"

An ugly grin stretched across Creager's face as he replied, "Singletary."

Luke felt just as shocked as McKinney, Thad, and Aaron. Singletary was the county seat close to where the McKinney spread was located, where he probably still had friends, or at least people he had considered friends during his earlier life as a law-abiding rancher and farmer. Ever since returning with the gang to that part of the country, he had avoided pulling jobs in what he probably considered his hometown.

"By God, you're not going near there," McKinney said after a few seconds of stunned silence.

Luke saw movement then, a darting shape coming up behind McKinney, and he knew instantly that one of the outlaws in the back of the group had slipped away into the darkness, circled around, and was about to attack McKinney from behind. It was an effort to complete Creager's takeover of the gang without a gunfight that would probably leave several of them dead.

"McKinney, look out!" Luke shouted as he tried to push himself up off the ground, hoping his muscles would work.

The attacker was too close. The gun in his hand rose, then chopped down viciously while McKinney was still turning toward him. The revolver slammed into McKinney's head with a dull thud. McKinney's knees buckled. He had gotten his gun out of its holster, but it never came up before the outlaw hit him again and knocked him to the ground.

"You bastard!" Thad cried. He clawed at his gun.

Close beside Luke, Aaron tried to scramble to his feet and lift the heavy Henry rifle he clutched.

Luke saw guns coming up on the other side of the fire and rammed a shoulder against Aaron, knocking the boy off his feet as shots began to roar. Bullets whipped past him and sizzled through the space where Aaron had been a second earlier. Luke got a hand on the Henry's barrel and yanked it out of Aaron's grip.

"Kill 'em all!" Creager bellowed.

The man who had just knocked McKinney to the ground tried to follow that order, swinging his gun toward Luke.

Luke struck first, using the Henry like a club to knock the outlaw's gun arm aside. He grabbed the man's shirt with his other hand and slung him toward the fire. The outlaw stumbled and fell, rolling through the flames and screaming as they caught his clothes and hair on fire.

That served to scatter the burning brands and plunge the camp into deeper shadow. Muzzle flashes split that darkness as Thad triggered shots and the rest of the gang returned them.

Luke turned the rifle where he could use it and told Thad, "Grab your pa and get up the hill!" He sprayed several rounds among the outlaws as fast as he could work the Henry's lever and pull the trigger.

The gang scattered, giving them a few seconds' respite.

Luke hoped that would be enough. Looking around earlier, he had noticed some rocks up on the hillside that would serve as decent cover if he and the three McKinneys could reach them. "Aaron, go!" he snapped at the boy. "Get up the hill!"

Thankfully, Aaron had enough sense to scramble to his feet and obey the order, racing up the slope through the shadows. Barely upright, McKinney was only semiconscious, but he stumbled along as Thad held onto him and urged him up the hill.

Luke backed away, still firing to keep the outlaws' heads down. He sent some shots toward a dark mass he took to be the horses, not intending to kill any of them but figuring if he could spook the animals, that would also serve as a distraction. Shrill, frightened whinnies sounded.

A man yelled, "Don't let those horses stampede, damn it!"

Luke glanced around, saw Aaron scoot behind a rock and Thad and McKinney drop behind a good-sized boulder. Luke felt the wind-rip of a bullet passing close beside his ear as he threw himself down behind a thick slab of stone.

"Aaron, do you have any more bullets for this old Henry?" he called to the youngster.

"I've got a whole pocket full of 'em!" Aaron replied.

Luke checked his holsters. His Remingtons were still there, the loops on his shell belt were full, and he had extra rounds in his pockets, too. He smiled for a second in the darkness. "I'm going to toss the rifle back over to you. Ready?"

"I'm ready," Aaron said.

More shots blasted from below as Luke raised up to toss the Henry over to Aaron. Some of the slugs came close enough that he heard them whistle through the air, but no closer. Luke dropped down again as Aaron caught the rifle.

"Thad, how's your father?" Luke called. He could just make out Thad and McKinney on the far side of Aaron.

"He's starting to come around," Thad replied. "He's got a cut on his head that's bleeding some, but I don't think he's hurt too bad."

"How are you fixed for ammunition?"

"I've got plenty! Just let those varmints try to come up here!"

Luke wasn't sure if the young man was telling the truth or if Thad's answer was for the benefit of Creager and the other outlaws, to make them believe they faced stiffer opposition than they really did. However, at least for the time being he and the McKinneys had good cover, the high ground, and enough bullets to put up a fight. A chance, in other words, and no man could ask for much more than that.

The shooting from below died away. The outlaws could keep throwing lead up, but they would be wasting time and bullets.

A long, tense quarter of an hour ticked past, and by then McKinney had recovered enough to shout down the slope, "You boys better listen to me! It's not too late to call this off! Nobody's dead yet!"

"You think we'd ever trust you again?" Creager called back. "You made it clear where you stand, McKinney!"

"I wasn't talking to you, Creager! You're a dead man no matter what those other fellas decide to do! I'll see to that myself! But the rest of you . . . put your guns away, move out into the open away from Creager, and we'll forget this whole damn thing ever happened! Creager and I will settle this between ourselves, the way it ought to be!"

Since no shooting was going on, Luke was able to hear the buzz of conversation down below as the outlaws talked about what McKinney had said. For a moment, he hoped that maybe they would actually listen to reason.

But then one of the men shouted, "Forget it, McKinney! We're goin' with Creager to Singletary to empty out that bank!"

Yells of agreement came from several more of the outlaws.

McKinney began, "I won't let you—"

A bray of laughter from Creager interrupted him. "You can't do a damned thing to stop us! You're out in the middle of the desert, miles from anywhere, with no horses! We don't even have to kill you! The desert—or the Apaches—will do that for us!"

Luke's heart sank as he understood what Creager meant to do. Sure enough, within moments he heard men moving around and then the sound of horses. The outlaws threw a few last shots up the slope, but then hoofbeats rolled out and filled the darkness.

"They're leavin' us here!" Thad cried. He stood up and started emptying his revolver in the gang's direction as they rode away.

McKinney grabbed the back of the youngster's shirt and pulled him back down. It was a good thing he did. A few more shots blasted and one of those slugs might have found Thad by blind luck. The hoofbeats swelled up, then began to fade.

Luke, Three-fingered Jack McKinney, and his two sons were alone on the knob, set afoot with nothing around them for miles and miles except snakes, scorpions, bad water, and worse . . . Apaches.

CHAPTER 31

Quietly, Luke said to his companions, "We'd better wait a while before showing ourselves, just to make sure they're not trying to trick us. They could have left some riflemen behind to pick us off."

"I was just thinking the same thing," McKinney said. "How are you holding up, Jones? You got shot in the head a while ago, after all."

Luke lifted a hand to the side of his head and gingerly explored the painful, sticky welt he found there before saying, "Creager just grazed me with that bullet. It hurts like hell, but it seems to have stopped bleeding. And my skull is so thick that it takes a lot to dent it."

"You're lucky. An inch to the side and that slug would have gone through your brain."

"Yeah, but an inch the other way and it would have missed me entirely," Luke said dryly. "And Creager would be dead now. You can bet a hat on that."

McKinney grunted and said, "No bet."

"How about you?" Luke asked. "How's that skull of yours?"

"It hurts, but I'm pretty thickheaded, too. Thad, Aaron, are you boys all right?"

"I wasn't hit, Pa," Aaron replied. "Thanks to Luke."

"I'm fine," Thad said. "Just mad as hell. Creager's as loco as a rabid skunk."

"He's not crazy," McKinney said, "just greedy and mean. I can't blame the other boys too much for following him. They're scared of him, I reckon."

"Well, I'm not!" Thad insisted. "I'm gonna kill him the next time I see him."

Luke said, "Seeing Creager again involves getting out of this predicament first." He drew his bandanna from his pocket, rolled it into a crude bandage, and tied it around his head so that the bullet graze was covered in case it started to bleed again. He could feel the dried blood where it had trickled down the side of his face.

"I guess I'd better go down and see if any of the horses got away from them," he said as he stood up at last. "If we can get our hands on a mount or two, it'll help."

"I wouldn't get your hopes up," McKinney advised.

"Believe me, I'm not."

Luke kept one of the Remingtons in hand as he went down the slope. Some embers from the scattered fire still glowed. It hadn't been an actual camp for the outlaws; they had just stopped there to decide what to do with Luke, and Creager had turned that into a showdown over who was going to run the gang.

Luke searched, but it didn't take him long to determine that none of the horses were still around. Creager and the other men had taken all the animals with them, including the four that Luke and the McKinneys had been riding. They were well and truly set afoot.

That was one of the worst things that could happen to a man.

"Come on down," Luke called to the others. "All the horses are gone."

McKinney and the two youngsters joined him near the remains of the fire.

Aaron asked, "What are we gonna do now?"

"Do you know where we are, McKinney?" Luke asked.

"Nine or ten miles east of Stanton, I'd say," the outlaw replied with a sigh. "Once we met up at the rendezvous, we rode pretty hard for a while before we stopped. You don't remember any of that because you were out cold and tied over your saddle. Creager wanted to go ahead and finish you off as soon as he shot you off your horse while we were talking, but I wouldn't let him. I said we couldn't do anything until we'd talked it over with the whole gang."

"I'm obliged to you for that. You saved my life, McKinney. That squares any debt that was between us."

"I don't know about that. You looked after my boy Aaron and saved his life more than once. That carries a lot of weight with me."

Thad said, "We can talk about it all night, but like Aaron asked, what now?"

"Stanton's not so far away that we can't walk it," McKinney said with a frown.

When Luke realized he could *see* that frown, he knew dawn couldn't be far off. Gray light had begun to appear in the sky to the east.

"Walk nine or ten miles?" Thad said. "The sun will be up before we get there. You know how hot it gets out here as soon as the sun rises, Pa."

"We'll just have to deal with that." McKinney drew

a deep breath. "In fact, we'd better go ahead and get started while it's still cool."

It was more than just cool. The air held a definite chill, as it always did at that time of the early morning. The dry air heated up and cooled off extremely quickly, depending on whether the sun was up.

McKinney was right. Since they didn't have anything except the clothes they wore and the guns they carried, there was no reason to tarry. Luke and McKinney knew how to steer by the stars, so they didn't have any trouble knowing which way to go. They walked around the knob where they had taken cover and headed west.

"We can get horses in Stanton," McKinney said as the sky grew lighter, sounding almost as if talking to himself and trying to figure out their course of action. "It won't be easy to beat Creager to Singletary, but we have to try."

"Why?" Thad wanted to know. "Everybody there hates you or looks down on you, Pa. It's been that way ever since the newspapers started writin' about you and the gang. I understand why you want to catch up to Creager and kill him, but what does the bank in Singletary matter? Let him clean it out. Then we can take that money from him when he's dead."

"I lived close to that town for a lot of years, boy," McKinney snapped. "Bought supplies and did business there many a time. Maybe the townsfolk don't feel the same way about me anymore, but I've still got some loyalty to them. Besides, there's your mother to think about."

"What about her?" Aaron asked. "If she's out at the ranch, nothing will happen to her. It'd just be pure bad luck if she happened to be in town at the same time as Creager and the rest hit the bank."

"You don't understand—" McKinney began, then broke off with a shake of his head.

"Then make us understand," Aaron challenged. "Tell us what it is you're not tellin' us, Pa."

For a long moment, McKinney didn't answer as they trudged across the sandy ground. Then he sighed and said, "Creager knows where the ranch is. I never figured there was a reason to keep it a secret from him. But one day he saw the picture of your mother that I carry with me all the time." He touched his shirt pocket, apparently without thinking about what he was doing, and Luke took that to mean the photograph was still there. "When Creager saw it, he said some things . . . things that make me believe he might stop there before he goes on to town, especially now that he's got even more of a grudge against me."

Thad made an angry sound deep in his throat. "You should've gone ahead and killed him, Pa, right then and there."

"I know it," McKinney said. "But I passed it off like he didn't mean anything by it and figured just to be sure, I'd never let the gang get anywhere close to the place. That's one of the reasons I never came back."

Aaron said, "Wait a minute. You carry a picture of Ma around with you?"

McKinney smiled at his younger son. "Why wouldn't I?"

"Because I figured you didn't gave a damn about her," Aaron said bluntly. "Or about us, neither. If you had, you never would've run off like you did."

McKinney winced a little at the boy's words, almost as if he'd been slapped. He shook his head. "The reason I left is because I cared about her. About you and Thad, too."

"That doesn't make any sense," the youngster argued. "If you cared about us, why'd you abandon us?"

Thad said, "Leave him alone. You hectoring Pa that way isn't going to do any of us any good."

"You must know the story," Aaron flared back at him. "Probably think I'm too young to know. Just a damn little kid is how you think of me."

"Stop it," McKinney said. "Thad doesn't know any more than you do." He paused. "But maybe it's time you did."

For a moment, neither of his sons responded.

Then Thad said, "You don't owe us any explanations, Pa."

"The hell he doesn't!" Aaron said.

With a parent's habitual sharpness, McKinney said, "Watch your language, son." Then his tone softened as he went on. "I'm going to tell you boys the truth. I figure you've got it coming."

Luke understood why McKinney felt that way. The outlaw knew it was a distinct possibility they wouldn't make out of their situation alive. It was still miles to the settlement, and a lot could happen in the hours it would take to cover that distance. If they *didn't* survive, Three-fingered Jack wanted to make sure there were no more secrets between him and his sons.

"I wasn't always a horse rancher and farmer," McKinney went on. "I took that up after I met your ma and married her. Before that . . . well, let's say that I wasn't the most law-abiding fella you'd ever meet."

"You were an outlaw," Aaron said in an accusatory tone.

"Guilty as charged. Except I was never actually charged. The law never caught up to me. There were wanted posters out on me, but under another name, and the descriptions and the likenesses on them didn't really match up that well to the real thing." McKinney held up the hand missing two fingers. "And in those days, I didn't have this to be a dead giveaway to who I was. Your ma did that."

"What!" Thad exclaimed. "Ma cut off your fingers?"

"That's crazy!" Aaron added. "She'd never do that!"

McKinney threw back his head and laughed. The sound was full of genuine amusement despite the grisly subject they were discussing. "Oh, but she did. It was an accident. Before you were born, Aaron, and you were too little to remember it, Thad. She wanted to learn how to chop wood, so I was showing her." He chuckled again. "I should've just told her I'd take care of the wood chopping. Then that ax wouldn't have had a chance to miss. She sure was upset and embarrassed."

"That's all there is to it?" Thad said. "An accident while she was trying to chop wood?"

"Yep. They weren't cut off by an Apache or anything dramatic like that."

Aaron asked, "How come you never told us? You knew we were curious what happened to your fingers."

"Yeah, I know. You pestered me enough about it. But I just told you, your ma was embarrassed and upset. She made me promise I'd never tell anybody what happened. And I never did, until now."

They walked on in silence for several moments, then Aaron muttered, "That don't have anything to do with why you ran off and left us."

"No, it doesn't," McKinney admitted. "I never planned on doing that at all. But then . . . a fella I used to know showed up in Singletary and happened to see me walking out of the general store. He recognized me and came up to me, said it was good to see me again and that I ought to throw in with him and his pards. It wasn't much of a question. It was more of a threat."

"Creager," Luke guessed.

"What?" McKinney shook his head. "No, it wasn't Creager. It was a man named Abe Gibson. He's dead now. A posse killed him up in Utah less than six months later. Creager was part of his bunch, though."

"This Gibson, he was the boss?"

"Yeah. By the time he was killed, I was sort of his second-in-command, so when he went under, the other boys looked to me to take over."

Aaron said, "Now hold on. When Gibson came up to you in town, why didn't you tell him to go to hell?"

"There you go with the language again," McKinney said.

"But you didn't have to go back to bein' an outlaw," Aaron argued. "You could have told him no."

"I could have . . . and if I had, he was going to send one of those old wanted posters to Sheriff Collins and write on it where the sheriff could find me." McKinney shook his head. "Amelia . . . your ma . . . never knew the truth about what I'd been. I felt like I couldn't let her find out. I knew it would hurt her if I just up and disappeared, but I figured it would hurt her even more if the truth came out."

"That's bull," Aaron said without hesitation. "You just didn't want to be arrested and sent to prison."

Thad said, "You've got no call to talk to Pa like that, Aaron—"

"I reckon he does," McKinney said. "Maybe he's right. I never cottoned to the idea of being locked up, I know that. Maybe I was selfish and did things all wrong. But that's the way it was, and I can't change any of it now." His voice hardened. "But I can stop that bastard Creager from hurting your mother, and from hurting my friends in town as well." He increased his pace. "Come on. Let's cover as much ground as we can before it gets hot."

Despite that resolve, the sun came up, of course, and the temperature began to rise with it. Within half an hour after the rays first struck his back, Luke's shirt was soaked with sweat.

His head hurt, too, and he knew the growing heat would just make it worse. He wished he had his hat, but he supposed McKinney had left it where it fell when Creager shot him off his horse. It would have been uncomfortable to wear over the makeshift bandage on his bullet-creased head, anyway.

In addition to everything else, his boots weren't made for walking—none of their boots were—and each step had become painful. Luke knew he would have blisters on his feet by the time they reached Stanton. Unless some miracle provided four horses for them, or at least two, taking one step after another was the only way to get there.

About an hour after sunup McKinney called a halt for them to rest. They had come to some scrubby greasewood bushes, and when they sank down on the sandy ground on the west side of the bushes, the vegetation provided a little shade from the already relentless sun.

"I sure am thirsty," Thad said after he'd sat there panting for a few seconds.

"I reckon we all are," his father said, "but it's best not to think about it." He reached over, picked up a pebble from the ground, brushed the sand off of it, and tossed it to Thad. "Suck on that. It'll keep your mouth from feeling so dry."

"Really?" Thad sounded unconvinced.

"Yep. It's an old trick. I'll bet Luke knows it."

"I do," Luke agreed. He found a pebble of his own and popped it into his mouth. "Doesn't help all that much . . . but anything is better than nothing, right?"

McKinney and Aaron followed suit, picking up pebbles of their own. The four of them sat there, sweating and sucking on rocks.

It was a toss-up which of them was the most miserable, Luke thought with grim amusement.

Eventually, Thad spat out the stone into his hand and said, "I've got to take a leak."

"If you just wait, your body will suck up that moisture," McKinney said. "You may need it."

"Tell that to my bladder." Thad got to his feet and stumbled back around to the other side of the grease-wood clump.

After a moment, McKinney chuckled. "Yeah, it's mighty hard for a fella to win an argument with his bladder. Guess I'll surrender, too." He stood up and went around the bushes to join Thad.

"How about you?" Luke asked Aaron.

"I'm fine," the youngster snapped. He lowered his

voice until it was barely above a whisper. "But I do want to talk to you about something."

"Something you don't want your pa and your brother to hear?" Luke guessed.

"Yeah. It's about that story Pa told . . . about why he ran off and became an outlaw."

"You're thinking maybe you judged him a mite too harshly?"

Aaron glared at the ground in front of them and said, "No. He should've figured out somethin' different instead of going along with what that fella Gibson wanted and abandoning us. But . . . from the sound of it, he really did believe he was doin' the right thing for Ma and Thad and me. He didn't come right out and say it, but it could be that Gibson threatened to hurt us if Pa didn't do what he wanted. That seems like something an outlaw might do, don't it?"

"It certainly does," Luke agreed.

"Then if that was true . . . and it might have been . . . Pa would have thought he was protecting us by going along with Gibson."

Luke nodded. "It's a feasible theory."

"You mean you think I'm right?"

"You could be. Only one person really knows."

Aaron took a deep breath. "You think I ought to ask him?"

"That's up to you. It depends on how much you need to know before you forgive him, or if you even *want* to forgive him."

"I don't know what I want," Aaron said miserably. "But I sure wish I'd never got mad and made up all those blasted reward posters. If I hadn't, you never would have seen one of them and decided to go after the bounty on Pa."

As Aaron was speaking, Luke heard the soft scrape of boot leather on the ground and saw a shadow move into view next to the bushes, then the next instant an icy voice cut through the hot air.

"Is that true, Luke? You're nothing but a damned bounty hunter?"

CHAPTER 32

Luke looked up at Three-fingered Jack McKinney. The outlaw stood tensely, his hand close to the butt of his gun.

In a calm voice, Luke said, "We don't need to have a shoot-out, McKinney. I don't want to kill you, and I don't want to take a chance on either of your boys getting hit by a stray bullet."

"You ain't killin' anybody, mister," Thad said as he stepped around the other side of the greasewood clump and pointed his gun at Luke. He thumbed back the hammer. "Let me shoot him, Pa."

"Stop that," McKinney said. "Put your gun away, Thad. You're not shooting anybody. You're not a killer."

"But you heard him! He's not one of us. He's a bounty hunter! That's even worse than a lawman."

"Both of you just quit it!" Aaron cried. "This is my fault. All my fault!" He twisted his head to look at Luke. "I'm sorry, Mr. Jensen. I never should've said anything—"

"It's all right, Aaron. Your pa was going to find out sooner or later, wasn't he?"

McKinney snorted disgustedly. "Yeah, when you shot me in the back so you could collect the blood money on my head."

Aaron scrambled to his feet and glared at his father. "Mr. Jensen's only here because of me. *I'm* the one who put out a reward on you."

McKinney stared at him in obvious disbelief. After a couple of heartbeats, he said, "Why in blazes would you do that? And where'd you get the money?"

"It wasn't just money," Luke said dryly. "An almost new harmonica was involved, too."

McKinney glanced at him, looking angry and confused. "What the hell are you talking about?"

Aaron didn't wait for Luke to answer. "It was me, Pa. I put up wanted posters around the county offering all the money I've got to my name, hoping somebody would get curious enough to find out there are other rewards for you and go after you. I thought you needed to be brought to justice for your crimes . . . but especially for abandoning us."

With his gun still pointing toward Luke, Thad said, "The kid's always been a little off in the head, Pa."

"Don't talk about your brother like that," McKinney said sharply. "Aaron's smart as a whip. He's just not old enough to know all that much about how the world really works, that's all."

"I'm learnin' more all the time," Aaron said.

McKinney nodded. "Yeah, I can see that you are. Why did you trail along with . . . Jensen." He turned to Luke. "Is that your real name?"

"It is. Luke Jensen."

"Why did you come with Jensen?" McKinney asked Aaron again.

"Because I wanted to see the look on your face when he caught up with you and arrested you."

Luke heard the pain in McKinney's voice as the man said, "You really hate me that much?"

"I had a lot of time to learn to hate you. Five years."

Luke said, "I'm going to stand up, McKinney. Please tell your boy not to shoot me."

"Thad, lower that gun," McKinney said as he glanced at his older son. "I'll deal with Jensen."

"Don't trust him, Pa!" Thad exclaimed.

"I never said I was going to trust him. I said I'd deal with him." McKinney nodded to Luke. "Go ahead and get up if that's what you want, Jensen. But keep your hands away from those guns if you know what's good for you."

With a wry smile, Luke said, "That's the problem. Too many times in my life, I *haven't* known what was good for me. Or I've known but couldn't do it. But I've managed to muddle through anyway." He climbed to his feet, making sure he didn't do anything Thad would mistake for a threat.

The young man was nervous as a cat, and those nerves, combined with his inexperience, made him very dangerous indeed.

"You have to look at this situation from a practical standpoint," Luke went on. "If you're going to stop Creager and the rest of the gang from hurting people you care about, you're liable to need my help. Right now, I have a lot bigger grudge against Creager than I do against you, McKinney." Luke lifted a hand and touched the bandanna tied around his head. "Honestly, I might be willing to forget about those bounties on you if it meant I'd get another shot at that ugly ape."

McKinney narrowed his eyes and said, "How can I trust you?"

"You claimed to be a good judge of character. What does your gut tell you? Am I telling the truth or not?"

McKinney looked intently at him for a long moment and seemed to be pondering the question. He had finally opened his mouth to answer it when Luke suddenly left his feet and crashed into McKinney with a flying tackle that drove the outlaw to the ground.

A split second later, an arrow whipped through the space where the outlaw had just been. If Luke hadn't knocked him down, the arrow would have lodged deep in McKinney's side.

Thad hadn't seen that, though. He yelled, "Son of a bitch!" and pulled the trigger.

The bullet went through the air above Luke's head as he sprawled for a second on top of McKinney. Powering into a roll that carried him to the right, he drew one of the Remingtons and lifted it toward Thad. Flame spurted from the muzzle as he fired.

It was a close thing, mighty close. But the .44 slug from the Remington whipped past Thad and smacked into the chest of the Apache charging toward him from behind, holding a lance that he clearly intended to ram into Thad's back.

Luke's shot drove the attacking Indian backward off his feet. Blood welled from the wound on his bare chest as he dropped the lance and spilled onto the ground.

Luke came up on a knee and swiveled toward the Apache who had fired the arrow at McKinney. The warrior had a second arrow nocked and let it fly as Luke triggered a shot that ripped into him. The arrow sailed past Luke's right shoulder. He heard McKinney curse behind him and hoped the shaft hadn't hit the outlaw.

The Apaches seemingly had materialized from the ground, perfect examples of their uncanny ability to blend into the landscape and not be seen until they were ready to attack. Luke had barely caught a glimpse of the one aiming the arrow at McKinney. Another split second and it would have been too late.

Unfortunately, the two men Luke had shot weren't the only warriors who had closed in. Several more leaped to their feet, howling war cries as they charged at Luke and his companions. Thad and Aaron, both of whom had been totally confused by Luke's actions, realized they were in danger and whirled to open fire on the Apaches.

McKinney was up on one knee, too, blasting away at the renegades. One of his bullets smashed into an Apache's shoulder and knocked the man spinning off his feet. An instant later, an arrow struck McKinney in the left arm, passing through it halfway between the elbow and the shoulder. He grunted in pain and fell back on his butt.

A few feet away, Luke had both Remingtons out and coolly fired them in turn, left, right, left, right, placing his shots with deadly accuracy. Each time one of the long-barreled revolvers boomed, an Apache either stumbled or fell.

Too many were coming from too many directions at once. One of the warriors wielding a long-bladed knife sailed at Luke from the left. Luke twisted in that direction and used the Remington in his left hand to parry the blade, but the Apache's momentum carried him into Luke. The impact knocked Luke onto his back.

Suddenly, the Apache's screeching face was within a few inches of Luke's nose. He had to drop the Remington in his left hand to grab the Apache's wrist and hold off the knife. With his right hand, he rammed the butt of that Remington into the man's nose. Hot blood spurted across Luke's face as the Apache went stiff. The insane scream choked off, and the wide, black, hate-filled eyes turned blank. The warrior went limp. Luke shoved him off, realizing that he had struck hard enough to shatter bone and send shards of it slicing up into the Apache's brain.

Grabbing the revolver he had dropped, Luke rolled onto his belly and raised his head in time to see one of the Apaches kneeling on top of Aaron with a tomahawk raised high, ready to split the boy's skull. Luke triggered both Remingtons at the same time. The two bullets hit the Apache's head just above the right ear and blew the top of it off. He dropped the tomahawk and toppled to the side.

Thad was still on his feet to Luke's left, but as he pulled the trigger on his Colt, the hammer fell on an empty chamber. With no time to reload, he reversed the gun and used it as a club as an Apache closed in on him.

Thad was no match for the wiry, seasoned warrior. He knocked Thad's arm aside and jabbed a knife to sink it into his belly. Thad twisted aside just in time to avoid being gutted, but the blade raked along his side, causing him to scream in pain as a bloodstain bloomed on his shirt around the deep cut.

The Apache slashed backhanded at Thad's throat. Thad tripped over his own feet and fell backward as he tried to get out of the way, but that misstep saved his life as the knife's point barely missed him.

With Thad on the ground, Aaron had a clear shot at the Apache. With the Henry at his shoulder already, he squeezed the trigger and sent a bullet smashing through the Apache's torso.

The warrior didn't fall right away. He stayed on his feet somehow and leaned forward as he tried again to stab Thad. Aaron levered the Henry and fired a second time. The slug struck the Apache in the heart and dropped him.

Luke's Remingtons were empty. He jammed them back in their holsters and yanked his bowie knife from its sheath behind the left-hand gun. As two Apaches charged him, he stooped and picked up the tomahawk one of the warriors had dropped when Luke blew his head off. With the tomahawk in his right hand and the bowie knife in his left, Luke met the attack head-on.

Although he was deadly with a knife, he didn't have much experience using a tomahawk. But he allowed his instincts to guide him, and they had kept him alive for a long time in a dangerous profession. He whirled and lashed out with the weapons, parrying the Apaches' blows and striking some of his own. The point of the blade raked a bloody trench across the chest of one warrior, while the tomahawk struck the other renegade on the forearm and broke bone with a sharp crack.

Those injuries didn't stop either man. They crowded in. A knife ripped Luke's black shirt over his ribs but didn't find flesh. The Apache with the broken arm had deftly switched his tomahawk from one hand to the other, and Luke felt it stir his hair as it went by and narrowly missed braining him.

He kicked the tomahawk-wielder in the groin, slowing the man's attack for a few seconds. That gave Luke time to concentrate on the Apache with the knife and block another thrust. In a continuation of the move, he swiped the tomahawk back against the renegade's jaw, shattering bone and cleaving flesh. The lower half of the man's face sagged grotesquely and seemed barely hanging on to his head. He gurgled in pain, a sound that was abruptly cut short when Luke whirled the tomahawk around and struck him in the forehead, penetrating all the way into his brain.

Already dead on his feet, the Apache's knees buckled. As he fell, the tomahawk remained stuck in his skull, and that wrenched it out of Luke's hand. He let it go, knowing that he couldn't afford the time to pry it free.

He crouched and swung the knife as the man he had kicked in the groin tried to decapitate Luke with one mighty swing of his tomahawk. The miss left his belly open to attack. Luke rammed the bowie knife into it and heaved, causing a huge wound through which blood flooded and intestines spilled. Luke ripped the knife out and shouldered the screaming, dying man aside.

He looked around for another opponent but didn't see any. The ground around the greasewood clump was littered with the renegades' bodies.

McKinney and Thad were down, while Aaron stood there with the Henry held ready at his shoulder. He gazed around wide-eyed, jerking the rifle from side to side as he sought another target.

"Aaron," Luke said, recognizing someone who was completely caught up in the heat of battle.

The boy's nerves were drawn so tight, he needed only the slightest excuse to keep pulling the trigger.

Luke said it again. "Aaron. I think it's all over. We won, Aaron. You don't have to shoot anymore."

He knew that Aaron's rifle was what had turned the tide of battle. The Henry held fifteen rounds—sixteen if a cartridge was already in the chamber—and that firepower had taken a deadly toll on the band of renegades.

"The first time we met, you told me you were a good shot," Luke went on. "You've sure proven that. You maybe saved us all, Aaron."

The boy swallowed hard, then lowered the Henry a little. "They kept running at me, and I . . . I just kept shooting." His shoulders started to tremble. "Why didn't they stop?"

From where he sat on the ground with the arrow still through his arm, McKinney said, "Because they were too full of hate to stop, son. They wanted our blood too bad. But we stopped them. You did the right thing." His face was pale and drawn. He had to be in a lot of pain from the arrow wound, and he had lost quite a bit of blood, too.

Thad appeared to be hurt worse. He lay on his side with the knife slash. Blood soaked the shirt around it. Still conscious, he was shaking and staring straight ahead without actually seeming to see anything.

"Your brother and your pa need help, Aaron," Luke said with a sharp tone in his voice.

Aaron lowered the rifle the rest of the way and turned his head to look at Luke. "What should we do?"

"Help Thad first," McKinney said without waiting for Luke to answer. "I'll be fine."

Luke knew McKinney was right. McKinney might not be fine, but Thad was in even worse shape. Luke told Aaron, "Use your bandanna and put some pressure on that cut in his side. We need to stop the bleeding, or at least slow it down." He finished reloading his Remingtons and began to walk around the area with a gun in each hand. More than once in his life, he had seen an enemy feign death while waiting for a chance to strike again. In fact, it was a common tactic for wounded Apaches.

A few minutes of checking was all that was necessary to determine that all the renegades were really and truly dead. He was convinced that none of the war party had gotten away, only to return later with more allies.

As he holstered the revolvers, he walked to where Aaron was kneeling next to Thad and holding the folded bandanna on the knife wound. The thought occurred to him that they had been mighty lucky none of the warriors were armed with rifles or pistols. The fight might have had a different outcome if they had been.

Aaron looked up and said with no real conviction, "I think the bleeding is slowing down."

"Let me take a look," Luke said as he knelt on Thad's other side. He leaned over and tore the bloody shirt away more as Aaron lifted the bandanna.

The deep, sharp-edged cut was about five inches long. Blood oozed from it, but it wasn't running freely anymore.

"You're right," Luke told Aaron. "Put that bandanna back on there for now. I'm going to pull some leaves off this greasewood bush and crush them up. It would be better if we had some water to make a poultice out of them, but we'll do the best we can. We can cut some strips off your shirttail, put those leaves on the wound, and tie it up good and tight. That ought to keep it from festering too much before we get to Stanton."

"You think he's going to be all right?" Aaron asked worriedly.

"I don't see why not."

Luke got busy, and within fifteen minutes, they had the wound dressed and bandaged. Thad was still pale and his breathing was ragged, but he looked a little more coherent now that he wasn't losing so much blood so quickly.

"Stay here with him. I'll go tend to your pa."

Aaron nodded in acknowledgment of Luke's words.

Luke walked over to McKinney and hunkered on his heels beside the outlaw.

"I heard what you told the boy," McKinney said quietly. "How's Thad really doing?"

"He lost a lot of blood and he's mighty weak. He needs proper medical attention, a lot of rest, and plenty of water. If he can get those things—"Luke shrugged—"he's got a pretty good chance, I'd say. The wound itself isn't that bad; it's just a matter of the blood he lost."

"So we have to get him to Stanton."

"The sooner the better. But we need to get that arrow out of your arm first."

"I'm not gonna argue with you." McKinney managed a faint smile. "It hurts like blazes."

"It's about to hurt more," Luke warned him.

"Yeah . . . Damn, I wish I had a slug of whiskey about now."

Luke grasped the bloody shaft where it stuck out from the back of McKinney's arm and snapped it. With the arrowhead gone, he was able to pull the rest of the arrow back out of the wound. McKinney sucked in his breath sharply as Luke removed the arrow. The entrance and exit wounds bled, but not heavily.

Luke dressed the injury with crushed greasewood leaves as he had the one on Thad's side and bound them against the wound to help with their medicinal properties.

"Can you walk on your own?" Luke asked.

"You're damn right I can. You go ahead and help Thad."

Luke went to the young man and lifted him to his feet. "If there were any trees around here, we could build a travois and pull you. Not much chance of that, though, I'm afraid."

"I'll be all right," Thad rasped. "Let's just get out of here." He glanced at the corpses of the Apaches sprawled around and shuddered. "I don't like bein' around so many dead bodies."

Luke got on Thad's left side and slid an arm around his waist, being careful to avoid the injury. "I'll help you walk. Aaron, it's going to be up to you to go ahead of us a little and keep an eye out for trouble. Can you do that?"

"Yeah," the boy replied. "I can."

"You reload that rifle?"

"Yes, sir. It's got sixteen rounds in it."

"Good," Luke said, hoping they wouldn't need those rounds. "Let's go."

CHAPTER 33

"I'm thirsty." Thad's voice was thin and strained, not much more than a whisper.

"I know," Luke told him. "I thought maybe we'd come across a waterhole, but no luck on that yet."

They had been walking for an hour since leaving the site of the battle with the Apaches. Luke knew that far behind them, the buzzards were having themselves a feast. He couldn't bring himself to feel too bad about that since he knew the renegades would have been only too happy to leave him and his companions to the same grisly fate.

Several times during that hour, they had stopped to let Thad rest for a few minutes. He had no strength left, and judging by the dull, disoriented look in his eyes, he might not even know where they were or where they were going. But with Luke's help, he continued putting one foot in front of the other, so that was all that really mattered.

To Luke's left, Three-fingered Jack McKinney trudged along, keeping the arrow-skewered arm in the crude sling Luke had rigged with the outlaw's belt. He still wore the bandage around his head where Creager's bullet had grazed him. They really were the walking wounded, Luke thought with grim amusement.

Aaron was the only one who had somehow come through unscathed. He walked about twenty feet in front of the others, the Henry rifle held ready for instant use if he needed it. He slowed suddenly, looked back over his shoulder, and raised one hand to point. "Pa, I see something up ahead. Isn't that those hills that lie just this side of the settlement?"

"Glory be, I think you're right, son," McKinney said. "They're still pretty far away, but it's good that we can see where we're going, anyway."

The sight of the hills lifted their spirits, even Thad's. McKinney was right. Having a goal in sight made their ordeal easier. The sun beat down on them, draining the moisture from their bodies and along with it their strength, but on the other side of those hills lay shade and water.

Luke felt like he wouldn't mind lying down in the Colorado River and just staying there for a while. However, he knew there wasn't time for that. Creager and the other outlaws had too big a head start. Already, it was going to be impossible to catch up to them before they reached Singletary.

One shred of hope remained. It would be late in the day before the gang could make it to the town. Creager might decide to wait until the next day to hit the bank. At the very least, he would probably wait until the county seat was asleep. If Luke and McKinney rode hard, they might get there in time to prevent the raid.

But if Creager decided to pay a visit to the McKinney spread first, there was no way in the world for the outlaw and Luke to stop what would happen there.

Best not to get ahead of himself, he thought. They still had to make it to Stanton, get help for Thad, and find some horses. He had a little money in his pockets, maybe enough to rent a couple of mounts and saddle rigs.

They trudged on, and it seemed as if the hills that were their destination stayed just as far away as they had been when Aaron first sighted them. Familiar with that phenomenon, Luke didn't let it get him down.

After a while, Thad groaned and said, "Are we ever going to get there?"

"We will," Luke promised. "Just keep going a while longer."

"You can do it, son," McKinney urged. "Don't give up."

Through gritted teeth, Thad said, "I'm not . . . givin' up. But it sure would be nice . . . to get somewhere we could . . . sit down and get something to drink."

Luke sure as blazes couldn't argue with that sentiment.

They drew closer to the hills with every step, and eventually that became evident. Aaron led them toward a gap that would allow them to reach Stanton. The sun was almost directly overhead when they stumbled into sight of the settlement lying on the eastern bank of the Colorado River.

"I know we're not there yet," McKinney croaked

through dry lips, "but that sure is a pretty sight anyway."

"Amen to that," Luke said. "Come on, Thad. We'll be there soon."

When they limped into the settlement less than half an hour later, townspeople noticed the blood-stained, weary figures right away and hurried over to help.

"This boy needs a doctor," Luke rasped.

"So does my pa," Aaron said. "He took an Apache arrow through the arm."

One of the townies exclaimed, "Apaches! Where'd this happen, mister?"

"About five miles east of here," Luke explained. When he saw the worried glances the citizens exchanged, he added, "But we wiped out the war party that jumped us. You don't have to be concerned about them raiding the town."

That seemed to ease the minds of some of the settlers but not all of them. Still, they put that aside for the moment and two men took over the job of helping Thad to the doctor's office, which was located on the opposite corner from the bank. Luke glanced at that edifice as they went past it. The gold shipment that had been in there was gone now, steaming downriver on a paddle wheeler. The town was safe from an outlaw threat that they hadn't even known existed.

The medico was a short, stocky man with rumpled gray hair and spectacles. Watery blue eyes behind the lenses widened in surprise as the men helped

Thad into the office and Luke, McKinney, and Aaron followed.

"Good Lord," the doctor said. "Did somebody declare war and forget to tell me?"

"It was Apaches, Doc," a man said. "These fellas claim to have wiped 'em out, but who knows?"

"Well, I imagine they know," the doctor said, "since they were there and all. Bring that boy into the examination room and help him onto the table." He glanced at McKinney. "What happened to you?"

"Arrow through the arm," McKinney answered curtly. "I'll be all right. Tend to my son."

"Your son, is he?" The doctor looked at Luke and gestured toward his head. "And you?"

"Bullet graze. Nothing to worry about. The boy has a deep cut on his side and lost a lot of blood, so he needs help first."

"I'll take your diagnosis under advisement. You three look like you're done in. Sit down before you fall down." The doctor waved toward a sofa and a couple of chairs as he gave the order.

Luke, McKinney, and Aaron sank gratefully onto the seats as the physician hurried into the examination room to see to Thad.

After only a few moments, McKinney said, "We can't stay here long, Jensen. We have to get our hands on a couple of horses and go after Creager and the others."

"Three horses," Aaron said. "I'm coming with you."

McKinney shook his head. "You can forget about that," he told his younger son. "You're staying here where it's safe. Somebody will need to stay and look after Thad. He's not going to be in any shape to ride."

"He'll have the doc to look after him," Aaron argued. "Besides, you're the one who's wounded, not me. If anybody stays behind, it ought to be you." He snorted. "Not sure that'd be safe, though. You might take off and disappear again."

"Damn it, boy, don't talk to me like that."

"I reckon you gave up the right to tell me how to talk to you when you ran off."

McKinney stared at Aaron for several seconds, then sighed and shook his head. "You just can't let go of all that bitterness inside you, can you?"

"I want to, but it's mighty hard." Aaron sounded sincere, and Luke believed him.

"Bitter or not, you're not coming with us." McKinney leaned his head against the back of the sofa and licked his lips. "Damn, I'm dry. I think a big cup of cool water would do me more good than just about anything else."

"You're probably right about that. I'll see what I can find." Luke got to his feet, but before he could do anything else, the doctor bustled back into the room.

"That boy's your son?" He looked at McKinney.

"That's right." McKinney got quickly to his feet. "How's he doing?"

"Well, it's a good thing he didn't lose any *more* blood, because if he had, he never would have made it this far. But I've cleaned the wound, and I'm going to stitch it up. Who put the greasewood leaves inside the dressing?"

"That was me," Luke said. "I would have made a poultice of them, but we didn't have any water."

The doctor nodded. "You did well enough, it appears. I don't see any signs of infection yet. Of course, it could still set in. Only a few hours have passed since he was injured. But I'll sew up that gash, then let him rest and get a lot of fluids in him. He should be all right."

McKinney sighed again, a huge sigh of relief. "I'm mighty glad to hear that, Doc." Suddenly, he blew out a breath and swayed a little on his feet. "Sorry, got a mite lightheaded there . . ."

"I don't doubt it. Sit down again. I'll get to you shortly. In the meantime . . ." The doctor went to the doorway leading into the front room where several of the townspeople waited to see what was going to happen. "One of you rattle your hocks up to the café and tell Maudie we need a pot of coffee, a pitcher of lemonade, and some of her beef stew down here, pronto." He turned his head and dropped a wink at Luke, McKinney, and Aaron. "Best medicine in the world for what ails you fellows."

When the foodstuffs arrived Luke, Aaron, and McKinney quickly guzzled some lemonade. While the doctor, whose name was Linus Pettigrew, cleaned the arrow wounds in the outlaw's left arm and took several stitches in both to close them up, Luke and Aaron downed a bowl of beef stew. Luke washed his down with strong coffee. The headache that had plagued him all day had faded away to almost nothing, and he felt almost human again.

Pettigrew removed the bandanna, examined the

bullet graze on Luke's head, and cleaned it just to make sure it wouldn't fester, even though he proclaimed that it was starting to heal already. He sat next to McKinney, who was finally eating the beef stew and drinking coffee. "If you expect a family discount on all this work, don't get your hopes up.

"About that, Doc . . ."

Pettigrew snorted and said, "Let me guess. You don't have any money to pay me."

"I have a little money, but I need to get a horse and saddle."

Pettigrew frowned at him. "You're planning on riding with that arm?"

"I don't ride on my arm," McKinney said. His voice took on a grim note as he added, "And it's not my gun arm, either."

"We have to be somewhere, Doctor," Luke said. "And we don't have any time to waste, either."

"I'm surprised you'd want to leave while Thaddeus in there is recuperating. That is his name, isn't it? Thaddeus?"

"Yeah," Aaron said. "But we only ever called him Thad. He never liked the whole thing."

McKinney said, "That was your mother's grandfather's name. She picked it." He turned back to Pettigrew. "But you said he'd be all right, didn't you, Doc?"

"I believe he will be. Still, if it was my boy in such a shape, I wouldn't want to go gallivanting off."

"It's not that I want to," McKinney said. "I promise you that."

Luke said, "And I promise that you'll receive payment for your services, Doctor. I give you my word on it. But it may take a short period of time to deliver on that."

Most of the money Luke had collected for the bounties on the men he had brought into Singletary had been in his saddlebags, so that loss was one more score to settle with Creager.

"I'm a doctor, young man. Believe me, I'm used to waiting for my pay!"

With Luke and McKinney patched up and sporting fresh bandages on their injuries, it was time for them to hit the trail again.

Thad was sleeping, but McKinney stepped into the room where he had been carefully placed in a bed and bent down to rest a hand on the young man's head for a moment. "We'll be back, son," he said, even though Thad couldn't hear him.

He joined Luke and Aaron in the front room. Aaron glared stubbornly at him.

McKinney said, "If we ride off and leave you here, you'll just find a way to come after us, won't you? Even if you have to steal a horse to do it."

"I reckon I might," Aaron said tightly.

"All right. You can come along, but you're going to steer clear of any shooting, you hear me?"

"I didn't steer clear of it any of the times Apaches jumped us, did I?"

"You're just a kid, damn it. You've had enough fighting and killing to last you a lifetime."

"I just want to make sure Ma's all right," Aaron said. "If I can, I'll stay out of any trouble."

"I suppose that's the best I'll get out of you," McKinney said. "Come on."

The three of them stepped out onto the porch of

the doctor's house to find a man in a black suit, with a badge pinned to his vest, waiting for them.

"Hold on there," Stanton's marshal said. "I've been waiting to talk to you fellas."

McKinney had his left arm in a sling. Luke saw how the outlaw moved his hand a little to use the sling to conceal the lack of those two fingers. McKinney didn't want the lawman to notice it and maybe be reminded of some wanted poster he had seen.

"I've heard about your fight with the Apaches," the marshal went on. "Is there anything more you can tell me?"

McKinney shook his head. "I don't know what it would be. They jumped us, and we killed them. That's about the size of it."

"What about your horses?"

Without hesitation, Luke said, "The Apaches killed them, of course. They did that first to put us on foot so we couldn't get away from them."

"You didn't bring in your saddles?"

"We knew we had a long walk in front of us, Marshal, and three of us were injured. We didn't figure it was worth lugging heavy saddles all that way."

The lawman grunted and then nodded. "I reckon that makes sense, all right. Were you bound for Stanton to start with?"

"Actually, no," Luke said. "We were on our way down to Singletary. But we knew this place was closer and we needed to get medical help. So we made the jog over here."

"But now we have to get moving again," McKinney said, not doing a very good job of concealing his impatience. "It's important that we get to Singletary as soon as we can."

"How come?" the marshal wanted to know.

"No offense, but that's our business, isn't it?"

The lawman shrugged and said, "I suppose it is. As long as you're not plannin' on breakin' any laws there."

Luke said, "I can assure you, Marshal, lawbreaking is the furthest thing from our minds. Now, I was wondering . . . where can we rent or buy some horses? I'm afraid we're burning daylight."

CHAPTER 34

It took all the money Luke and McKinney had to buy three horses and tack for the ride to Singletary. The liveryman refused to rent the animals, saying that it would be too much trouble for him to get them back. Luke could tell he didn't really trust them, either.

When they pooled their funds, they had enough, and Luke didn't have to ask Aaron whether or not he had that nearly new harmonica with him. They didn't have to use that to sweeten the pot.

The horses were decent mounts, although Luke could tell they didn't have the stamina for a long run, day after day. McKinney set a fast pace, though. He was naturally anxious to stop Creager and to make sure his wife was all right. Luke insisted on several stops to rest the horses, pointing out that if they ran the animals into the ground, Creager would be able to do anything he wanted without anybody getting in his way. McKinney went along with that reluctantly.

By dusk, the horses were beginning to play out, but McKinney and Aaron had spotted some familiar landmarks.

"We're not far from the ranch now," McKinney said. "We're going there first."

"You're going home?" Aaron asked. "For good?"

"I didn't say that. I may have broken ranks with Creager and the rest of the bunch, but I'm still an outlaw. A wanted man."

"You could turn yourself in. Go to prison for a few years, and then when you get out—"

"I told you before," McKinney broke in, "I don't cotton to the idea of being locked up. And chances are, that's not how things would play out, anyway."

Aaron looked over at his father in the fading light. "What do you mean?"

"I mean they'd probably hang me, son."

"No! They couldn't do that!"

"Tell him, Jensen," McKinney said.

"Your father's wanted on some pretty serious charges, Aaron," Luke said. "It's entirely possible he might be sentenced to hang."

"But they only hang you if you kill somebody! Isn't that right, Pa? You never killed anybody."

When McKinney didn't respond to that statement, Aaron went on. "Did you?"

"Whether I actually pulled the trigger or not, people *were* killed in some of those bank robberies. A judge and jury might consider me to blame for those deaths, since I led the raids. What it comes down to, Aaron, is that they might decide to hang me, and even if they didn't, I don't intend to go to prison. That's just the way it is."

"You don't get to decide how it is for everybody else! You don't have the right! I know Ma wants you back, even after all this time—"

"I'd never bring all that pain back into her life,"

McKinney declared. He pointed to a ridge looming darkly in front of them. "That's why we're going up there to take a look around instead of just riding in. If everything's all right, we'll head on to town without stopping."

"You can't mean that," Aaron continued to argue. "You'd really be that close and not ride down to see her—"

"I'm doing what's best, boy," McKinney said, his voice hardening. "When you get older and meet some gal you care about, you'll understand."

Aaron shook his head. "I'll never understand you."

"Maybe not. Time will tell." McKinney urged his horse toward the top of the ridge. "Come on. I want to take a look around before it gets full dark."

Luke trailed father and son up the slope. They stopped and dismounted before they reached the crest.

McKinney handed his reins to Aaron and said, "Hold the horses while Jensen and I go the rest of the way."

"Tie 'em to a damn bush," Aaron snapped. "I'm coming, too."

McKinney shrugged, took the reins back, and fastened them to a scrubby bush growing out of some rocks. Luke and Aaron did likewise, then all three of them catfooted toward the top of the ridge.

Some brush grew along there, too, so they didn't have to get down on their bellies and crawl. The vegetation, as well as the gathering shadows of evening, gave them enough concealment that they likely wouldn't be spotted by anyone down below. They were careful anyway. If Creager and the gang were nearby, they had probably posted some lookouts.

Peering down the far slope toward the spread, they saw yellow light glowing in the ranch house's windows but no horses tied up anywhere nearby. As they watched, the back door opened and Amelia McKinney stepped out onto the porch. She had a bucket in her hand, lifted it and threw out some water, then turned and went back into the house, closing the door behind her.

Luke had heard the breath hiss between McKinney's teeth at the sight of his wife. The outlaw's eyes never left her during the brief moment she was in sight. Enough of an afterglow remained in the western sky for Luke to see the deeply pained expression on McKinney's face.

"At least I got to see her again," McKinney said hollowly. "And she seemed to be all right."

"How can you not . . . not go down there . . . and hug her, at least?" Aaron demanded.

"If I did that, boy, I might never leave . . . and then, sooner or later, things would be even worse for all of us." McKinney looked over at Luke. "Creager's not here. He doesn't appear to have *been* here."

"The money he can get by raiding Singletary is the most important thing to him right now," Luke said. "If they ride out of there with plenty of loot, it'll go a long way toward making his hold solid on leadership of the gang. They can stop by here while they're making their getaway, if that's what he wants."

"And take Amelia with them," McKinney said, his face and voice grim. "Well, that's one more reason for us to stop them, once and for all."

"We'd better head for town, then."

"In a minute." McKinney turned to Aaron. "You go on back down there to the ranch now, son. There's

no need for you to go to town with us. Go give your
ma a hug for me and tell her . . . Well, I guess it's too
late now to tell her much of anything except that I'm
sorry and that I always loved all of you. The two of
you can take the wagon and head back to Stanton to
get Thad and bring him home as soon as he's strong
enough to travel."

"What about you?" Before McKinney could answer,
Aaron went on. "No, there's not any need to wonder,
is there? After you settle things with Creager, you'll
just run away, the way you always do. Isn't that right?"

"Be best for everybody if I move on," McKinney
answered with a shrug.

"You promised Thad you'd be back for him!"

"I know. You can tell *him* I'm sorry, too."

Aaron stared at his father for a long moment, then
spat out words. "You're a coward. Nothing but a
damn coward. I reckon you always were."

"Aaron—"

The youngster turned away sharply, stalked back to
the horses, and jerked his mount's reins free. He
practically leaped into the saddle and then kicked the
horse into motion, sending it churning over the ridge
crest and then down the slope toward the ranch
house. Aaron didn't say anything or even look back
as he rode off.

After several seconds of taut silence, McKinney
said, "You told me before that you don't have any
kids, Jensen. In some ways, you're a lucky man."

"I've never particularly felt like it," Luke said.
"We'd better head on to Singletary. Once it's good
and dark, Creager's liable to make his move."

* * *

The stars were out by the time Luke and McKinney reached the town. Some houses were dark because their inhabitants had already turned in for the night. Most of the businesses along the main street were closed. A few stores were still open, and of course the saloons had customers. Luke would have liked to stop in at the Plainsman and say hello to Glenda Farrell, but it was more important for him and McKinney to scout for any sign of Creager and the gang.

"You think it would do any good for you to go talk to Sheriff Collins?" McKinney asked quietly as they rode along the main street, keeping to the shadows in the middle of it.

"The sheriff and I weren't on the best of terms when I was here before," Luke said. "I'm not sure he'd believe me. And you can't exactly come with me to back up the story."

A humorless chuckle came from McKinney. "No, Collins would throw me behind bars before I could get a word out. He'd like nothing better . . . unless it was leading me up the steps to the gallows."

"We're not going to let it reach that point. As soon as we've dealt with Creager, you can fade out of sight."

McKinney glanced over sharply at Luke. "You're not going to try to turn me in to the law? What about the reward? That's the reason you came after me to start with."

"I admit, it's hard to give up on that harmonica," Luke said with a chuckle, "but the real reason I came after you was to satisfy my curiosity. I've done that. I'm not saying I admire you, Jack, and we're not exactly friends, but in some ways you've gotten a raw deal. With what you've lost already—your wife and those boys—I think that punishment has to be taken into consideration, too."

A few seconds of silence hung between the two men, then McKinney said, "Maybe I was wrong about you, too, Jensen. Maybe all bounty hunters aren't just out for blood money."

"Just remember one thing . . . if we cross trails in the future, the situation may not be the same. If there *is* a future, for either of us."

On that grim note, Luke angled his horse toward the two-story brick building he remembered as being the bank. McKinney followed suit. To anybody watching them, their actions wouldn't appear suspicious. They appeared to be just two easy-riding cowpokes, maybe on their way to a night's drinking and gambling.

As they drew up at a hitch rack in front of a hardware store that was closed for the night, McKinney said quietly, "Creager never had an original thought in his life. He'll use the plan I had for the bank in Stanton. They'll go in the back and use dynamite to blow the door off the vault. It hasn't happened yet. The whole town would be in an uproar if it had."

"That's true," Luke said. "Maybe we'd better take a look in the alley back there."

They swung down from their saddles and tied the horses. Since Luke was dressed in black, he would blend into the shadows alongside the bank—except for the white bandage around his head. To cover it up, he took out the bloodstained bandanna he had used as a makeshift bandage earlier and once again wound it around his head, tying it in place so the white cloth was covered. The range clothes McKinney wore were brown and blue and gray, so they wouldn't stand out, either.

They eased through the gloom and into a narrow passage between the hardware store and the bank. Drawing their guns, they slipped toward the alley at the back. The bank building, solid and imposing, was at their left.

They were careful not to make any noise, placing each foot carefully in case there was any trash in the passage that could be knocked over. As they neared the far end, Luke's keen ears caught the faint sound of voices coming from the alley. At the same time, McKinney put out a hand to stop him. Evidently the outlaw heard the same thing.

McKinney put his mouth close to Luke's ear and breathed, "Somebody's back there. It's got to be Creager and the others."

"I agree," Luke whispered. "I'll take this side, you take the other. We'll stop at the alley and take a look around the corner."

They moved apart, pressing against the building on either side, and approached the end of the passage in complete silence. When Luke reached the corner, he leaned forward enough to peer along the rear wall of the bank to its door. On the other side of the passage, McKinney did the same.

The shadows were so thick and black it was difficult to see anything. Luke's eyes had adjusted to the stygian gloom, though, and after a moment he began picking out shapes in the very faint starlight. Counting them was impossible, but he estimated that at least a dozen men were clustered around the bank's back door. That left a handful of outlaws unaccounted for. Luke strongly suspected they were scattered around

to help cover the gang's getaway once the bank had
been looted.

A rasping whisper reached their ears, "Got the
dynamite, Donnelly?" That was Creager's voice,
Luke knew.

"Right here, boss," a man answered.

"Then let's get in there and get started. I want to
turn this town upside down and shake every damn
penny out of it!"

Something heavy crashed against the door. They
had some sort of battering ram, Luke realized. Probably a section of tree trunk. Whatever it was slammed
against the outside door again, and the door gave way
with a splintering of the wood frame around it.

That racket covered any noises Luke and McKinney
made as they stepped out into the alley and leveled
their guns at the bank robbers.

The outlaws knew they were there only when
McKinney shouted, "Creager! Fill your hand!"

So they weren't going to give the gang members a
chance to surrender, Luke thought fleetingly as he
raised the Remingtons. Well, it probably would have
been a waste of breath, anyway. The confrontation
had been destined to come down to lead and flame
from the moment Creager double-crossed Three-
fingered Jack McKinney.

Gun flashes split the night.

CHAPTER 35

The Remingtons roared and bucked in Luke's hands as he poured lead into the outlaws. A couple of feet to his left, McKinney's Colt blasted out a death song of its own.

They had taken the outlaws completely by surprise, so a pair of heartbeats went by before any of Creager's men could react. By that time, a hail of lead had scythed into them and smashed half a dozen of them off their feet.

But then the ones who hadn't been hit began to recover their wits. They clawed guns from holsters and returned the fire. Luke and McKinney had to scramble for cover. Luckily, the back alley provided some shelter. Luke dived behind a rain barrel while McKinney threw himself over a pile of crates and sprawled on the other side.

"Close in now, Sheriff!" Luke shouted over the gun-thunder.

The outlaws heard that and believed they were caught in the jaws of a trap, just as Luke intended. Several of them turned and threw shots blindly into the night. That took some of the heat off Luke and allowed him to aim his shots using the muzzle flashes directed away from them. A man screamed and another howled curses as Luke's bullets found them.

Boot leather slapped the hard-packed dirt behind Luke and McKinney. Luke knew there was a good chance the other outlaws who had been scattered around town were charging back to see what all the shooting was about. He rolled over and swung the Remingtons in that direction. Several shadowy shapes rushed along the alley toward him and McKinney, but Luke held his fire. He couldn't be sure who they were and didn't want to gun down any innocent, if foolhardy, citizens of Singletary.

"Kill 'em!" Creager roared from behind the bank. From the sound of his bellow, he hadn't been hit in the death storm of bullets. "Behind that barrel and those crates!"

The newcomers opened up, settling the question of whether or not they belonged to the gang. Luke triggered the Remingtons as slugs smacked through the air around him.

A normal man would have been at least half blinded by all the muzzle flashes, but Luke had been in many desperate gun battles and knew how to squint his eyes against the spurting jets of flame. His shots knocked down two of the fresh attackers, but that left three men on their feet, and as the Remingtons' hammers fell on empty chambers, Luke knew that he and McKinney were in a bad fix.

Then the sharper crack of a rifle sounded behind the outlaws. Men grunted and fell forward as .44 rounds smashed into their backs. At that moment, the back door of the hardware store flew open, spilling light into the alley.

An old man's quavery voice yelled, "What the hell is goin' on out here? Are the Yankees attackin' again?"

"Grandpap, get back!" a younger man's voice cried inside the building.

The light revealed five outlaws sprawled in the alley in various attitudes of death. Behind them, the Henry rifle still in his hands with a wisp of smoke curling from the barrel, was Aaron.

"That damn kid!" Creager shrieked from the other direction.

Luke rolled into the open and raised his head to see Creager charging toward them, the gun in his outthrust hand aimed at Aaron.

"No!" McKinney said as he leaped up. He reached his feet just as Creager started pulling the trigger.

Shots crashed and bullets thudded into McKinney's chest, driving him backward in a jittery dance.

Luke yanked the bowie knife from its sheath and threw it as he came up on one knee. The heavy blade revolved once and then buried itself in Creager's chest with a resounding smack. Creager stumbled. The gun in his hand sagged. His eyes widened in horror as he looked down at the knife protruding from his chest.

Then Aaron's rifle cracked again. Creager's head jerked back as a red-rimmed black hole appeared over his right eye. The back of his head blew out in a grisly spray of blood, brain matter, and bone fragments as the .44 round bored on through. Creager stayed upright for half a second, then pitched forward on his face, dead.

Aaron screamed, "Pa!" as he dropped the Henry and ran toward McKinney.

Luke wanted to get to McKinney, too, but first he

had to make sure the threat was over. He holstered the Remingtons and scooped up pistols dropped by the men Aaron had shot. A quick check showed him that several rounds remained in each one. He stalked among the fallen outlaws, ready to fire if necessary.

There was no need. All the men were dead.

The silence seemed to echo in the night air, now that all the guns had ceased talking.

That lasted for only a moment before shouts and running footsteps came from the street. The law and an aroused citizenry would be there shortly.

Luke stepped over beside Aaron, who had lifted McKinney's head and shoulders into his lap as he sat on the ground. McKinney was shot to pieces. Four or five of Creager's bullets had struck him. But he was still alive, and his eyelids fluttered as he tried to look up at Aaron, who bent over him crying.

"No . . ." McKinney rasped. "No, don't . . . cry . . . son. I'm not . . . worth the tears."

"Pa!" The word sounded like the cry of a wounded animal.

"You . . . you're all right?"

Luke hunkered beside McKinney. "He's fine, Jack. He's not hurt. You saved his life."

"He saved . . . ours."

"Yes, I believe he did. Again." Luke smiled. "He's a good boy. You can be proud of him."

"I am . . . proud of him . . . proud of both . . . my boys." Blood trickled from the corners of McKinney's mouth. "Aaron, you should've . . . should've stayed at the ranch . . ."

"I couldn't. I just couldn't. I had to see it through."

"Reckon I'm glad . . . you felt that way. Now you've got to . . . got to . . ."

"Anything, Pa," the youngster said, still sobbing.

"You tell . . . your ma . . . and Thad . . . how much I love 'em."

"I will," Aaron promised. "I swear I will."

"And don't ever forget . . . how much . . . I love you . . . too."

"I won't." Aaron swallowed hard. "I love you, Pa. I never stopped—"

McKinney's head fell back. The breath rattled in his throat.

Aaron leaned over him and cried again, "No! He . . . he can't be gone."

"He is," Luke said gently. He put a hand on Aaron's shoulder. "But he heard what you were trying to tell him."

Aaron raised his head and asked, "How . . . how do you know that?"

"Look at the smile on his face."

Seconds after Jack McKinney's death, Sheriff Ross Collins, carrying a lantern and a shotgun, came stomping along the alley, only to stop and stare in shock at the bodies littered everywhere.

One of the deputies following him muttered, "Ye gads, what a massacre."

"Jensen!" Collins exclaimed when he looked closer at Luke. "And . . . and Aaron . . . Is that your father?"

"It is," Aaron said, more composed now. "But you won't arrest him, Sheriff. He won't ever go to prison or be hanged!"

An old man with a long white beard down almost to his waist peered out the back door of the hardware store and asked, "It's not that damned Ulysses S. Grant again, is it?"

Collins shook his head, blew out a breath, and said, "You've got a lot of explaining to do, Jensen."

Luke did that for the next hour or so, while the undertaker and his assistants tackled the big job of cleaning up the mess in the alley behind the bank. While talking to Sheriff Collins, Luke found out that the old man in the hardware store was the grandfather of the owner, whose living quarters were in the back of the building. The old-timer had been wounded during the war when Yankee troops had marched through the farm he owned in Georgia and then had lost the farm to carpetbaggers after the war. He wasn't right in the head anymore, and his grandson took care of him.

The old man's timely opening of the back door had provided enough light in the alley for those left alive to see what was going on. If he hadn't done that, there was a good chance Aaron would be dead, gunned down by Creager.

Instead Jack McKinney was dead. Luke knew that McKinney had willingly sacrificed his life for his son. McKinney was a bank robber and a killer, but honestly, Luke had known worse men in his life.

He couldn't help but wonder if McKinney had experienced some sort of premonition on that ridge, looking down at his former home and seeing his wife for the last time. Maybe he'd had a hunch that he wasn't going to make it through alive.

The next day, with a new hat and freshly outfitted with supplies, Luke rode out to the McKinney spread and found Aaron hitching up a team of horses to a wagon. Luke had arranged with Sheriff Collins and the bank for most of the bounty money on Creager and the other outlaws to be deposited in Amelia McKinney's account. Luke felt that was only right, since Aaron had killed several members of the gang, and those funds would give Amelia and her sons enough of a cushion that they'd have a decent chance to make the ranch a success.

The bounties on Three-fingered Jack McKinney would go unclaimed. Luke knew Aaron wouldn't want them, and neither did he. Amelia and her sons would find out about all of that when they got back from Stanton with Thad.

Amelia came out of the house, dressed for traveling. "Mr. Jensen. I'm glad you stopped by. Aaron and I are about to start out for Stanton to bring Thad home, but I wanted to thank you before we go." She managed a smile. "My boys wouldn't be alive now if not for you."

Luke thumbed his hat back as he sat in the saddle. "I don't know, ma'am. Some might say I sparked the whole thing and that Aaron never would have been in danger if I hadn't come along."

"But Thad would have been, if he had stayed with his father. You know that's true."

Luke shrugged, unable to disagree with her.

Amelia went on. "Anyway, I think it's a mistake when people say, 'If only this thing had happened, this other thing would have happened . . . or wouldn't have.' Because we don't really know, do we? All we know is what life has given us. What we've made of it. Everything else is as insubstantial as . . . as a puff of dust in the wind."

"You're right, ma'am. I hope what you make of it is good from here on out." Luke glanced at the freshly mounded grave out beyond the barn, where Jack McKinney had been laid to rest that morning, then tugged his hat brim back down and nodded politely.

Aaron helped his mother onto the wagon seat and climbed up beside her to take hold of the reins. Before he got the team moving, he reached into his pocket, took something out, and tossed it to Luke. "You've got this coming, Mr. Jensen."

Luke caught it and looked down at what he held in his hand as the wagon rolled away. He grinned, lifted the harmonica to his mouth, and blew a single sweet, pure note on it.

Then he slipped the harmonica into his shirt pocket, turned his horse, and rode away.

Keep reading for a special exceprt of the new series by
William W. and J. A. Johnstone!

CUTTHROATS
A SLASH AND PECOS WESTERN

Two wanted outlaws. One hell of a story.
Not every Western hero wears a white hat or a tin star.
Most of them are just fighting to survive. Some of them
can be liars, cheaters, and thieves. And then there's a
couple of old-time robbers named Slash and Pecos . . .

After a lifetime of robbing banks and holding up
trains, Jimmy "Slash" Braddock and Melvin "Pecos
Kid" Baker are ready to call it quits—though not
completely by choice. Sold out by their old gang,
Slash and Pecos have to bust out of jail and pull one
last job to finance their early retirement . . .

The target is a rancher's payroll train. Catch is: the
train is carrying a Gatling gun and twenty deputy
U.S. marshals who know they're coming. They're
caught and quickly sentenced to hang, but then
their old enemy— wheelchair-bound bucket of
mean Marshal L. C. Bledsoe— shows up at the last
minute to spare their lives. For a price. He'll let
them live if they hunt down their old gang, the
Snake River Marauders. And kill those prairie rats—
with extreme prejudice . . .

Look for CUTTHROATS.
Coming in July, wherever books are sold.

CHAPTER 1

In the early morning hours, the bounty hunters gathered around the remote mountain cabin, crouched in a shadowy clearing. They were thirteen in number—a dozen-plus wolves on the blood scent.

Ray Laskey walked up to where Jack Penny crouched in the pines roughly fifty yards from the cabin, running an oily rag down the barrel of his Henry repeating rifle.

"All the boys are in position, boss," Laskey said, slicing a hunk of wedding cake tobacco onto his tongue and chewing.

Penny turned to Laskey and winked in acknowledgment with the rheumy blue eye that always seemed to roll to the outside corner of its socket and that always made Laskey feel vaguely uneasy, for some reason. That wandering eye seemed like some separate living thing, rolling and bobbing around in Penny's ugly, bearded head . . . like some ghastly thing that lived inside a log at the bottom of a murky lake and only came out to rend and kill. . . .

Both men crouched lower behind their covering pine when the cabin's front door latch clicked.

Laskey drew a sharp breath as he turned to see the door open. He squeezed his Spencer tightly but then eased his grip when he saw that the person stepping out onto the cabin's small stoop was a woman with long, thick, copper-red hair.

The woman, nicely put together and clad in a man's wool shirt and tight denim trousers, turned toward the split firewood stacked against the cabin's front wall. When she had an armload, she straightened, turned back to the door, and stopped abruptly.

No, Laskey thought. *Don't do that. Keep goin'. Get back inside the cabin, dearie. . . .*

The woman turned ever so slowly to stand staring straight off into the trees, directly toward where Laskey and Penny crouched behind a stout ponderosa.

Laskey's gut tightened.

Had she heard or in some other way sensed the killers crouched in the forest around the cabin? Had she smelled their unwashed bodies made even whiffier from their long, hard ride over the course of the long night lit only by a small and fleeting powder-horn moon?

Penny glanced at Laskey. The bearded bounty hunter smiled darkly, then raised his Henry to his shoulder. He slid the barrel up over a feathery branch and leveled his sights on the woman. He crouched low over the long gun, resting his bearded cheek up snug against the stock.

Slowly, almost soundlessly, he ratcheted back the hammer with his thumb.

Laskey looked at the woman. His heart thudded. She appeared to be staring straight at him. Straight at Penny steadying his sights on her chest.

No, no, no, dearie. You didn't hear nothin'. You didn't smell nothin'. No one's out here. A coyote, maybe. A rabbit, maybe—up and out too early for its own damn good . . .

That's all.

Go on inside, stoke your stove, start cookin' breakfast for them two cutthroats in there. It's them we want. Not you, purty lady.

We got other plans for you . . . dearie. . . .

As though obeying Ray Laskey's silent plea, the woman turned slowly, stepped back toward the door, nudged it open, and stepped inside. She turned to look outside once more, then closed the door and latched it with a soft *click.*

Penny eased his Winchester's hammer down against the firing pin.

Laskey released a breath he hadn't realized he'd been holding.

Penny turned to him, spreading his ragged beard as he grinned. "She almost joined the angels."

"When, uh . . ." Laskey said, pressing the wedding cake up tautly against his gum, "when do you want to . . . ?"

"Start the dance?"

"Yeah, yeah. Start the dance."

"As soon as they show themselves. Best odds, that way. Won't be too long now, most like. We got time."

"What, uh . . . what about the woman?" Laskey said.

"What about her?" Penny asked him.

Laskey shrugged, toed a pine cone. "She's too purty to kill. Outright, I mean . . ."

Laskey grinned, juice from the wedding cake bleeding out from between his thin lips.

Penny scowled down at the shorter man. "We came here to kill, an' that's what we're gonna do, Ray, my boy. She's with them cutthroats, so she dies with them cutthroats. Hell, there's a reward on her head, too. Dead or alive. Same as them."

"Oh, boy," Laskey said. "The woman, too, huh? Seems a shame's all."

Penny placed a big, strong, gloved hand on Laskey's shoulder and squeezed. "The woman, too, Ray. We ain't here for none o' that nonsense you're thinkin' about, you randy scoundrel."

Penny brushed his gloved fist across Laskey's pointed chin.

He winked his weird fish eye again, and it rolled like that living thing in the dark lake, fleeing back to its log after feeding.

CHAPTER 2

"What you two old cutthroats need is a job," said Jaycee Breckenridge.

James "Slash" Braddock lifted his head from his pillow, frowning at the pretty woman forking bacon around in the cast-iron skillet sputtering atop her coal-black range. "Jay, honey, please don't use such nasty language so early in the morning. Pecos an' me got *sensitive ears*!"

"What'd she say?" asked Melvin Baker, better known for the past thirty years of his outlaw career as the Pecos River Kid.

He lay belly down on the cot on the far side of the small cabin from Slash Braddock. His blue eyes were open, regarding his longtime outlaw partner in shock and disbelief. "I didn't just hear her use the bad word again—did I, Slash?" He closed his hands over his ears. "Oh, please, tell me I didn't!"

"Now, look what you done, Jay! Poor ole Pecos is beside himself over here! He's likely ruined for the whole dang day! I might have to hide his guns from him, so he don't blow his brains out!"

Pecos buried his face in his pillow and pretend bawled.

At the range, one hand on her hip as she continued to flip and shuttle the bacon around in the same pan in which potatoes and onions fried, Jay shook her long, copper-red hair back from her hazel-eyed face and laughed. "Look what time it is, you old mossyhorns!"

She glanced at the windows behind her through which slanted the crisp, high-altitude sunlight of the Juan Valley of southern Colorado Territory. "It's nigh on midmorning and you two are still lounging around like a pair of eastern railroad magnates on New Year's Day!"

"Lounging around—nothin'!" Pecos lifted his head from his pillow and looked over his shoulder at Jay. "I was dead asleep not more'n two minutes ago. You done woke me up with your foul language. You oughta be ashamed of yourself, woman. What would Pistol Pete think of such talk?"

"Ha!" Jay threw her head back, laughing. "Whenever I mentioned the word 'job' to that old rascal—as in he might want to quit ridin' the long coulees and try an honest job for a change—he'd howl like a gut-shot cur an' skin out of here like a preacher caught in a parlor house. He'd run clear across the yard and throw himself in the creek. Didn't matter what time of year it was. Spring, summer, winter, or fall—that's just what he'd do, Pete would."

Jay threw her head back again, laughing.

But then she turned a thoughtful look over her shoulder, gazing out the window toward the lone grave standing on a knoll about sixty yards out from the cabin, in a little pocket of ponderosas and cedars. Jay's shoulders, clad in a plaid work shirt tucked into tight denims, rose and fell slowly, heavily. Her lower lip trembled. She stifled a sob, clamping her hand over her mouth, then wheeled from the range and hurried to the cabin's front door.

"Excuse me, boys!" she said in an emotion-strangled voice as she opened the door and stepped out onto the small front stoop. She slammed the door behind her.

Through the door, Slash heard her sobbing.

He turned to his partner, scowling, and said, "Pecos, what'd you have to go and do that for?"

"Ah, hell!" Sitting up now, clad in his wash-worn longhandles that clung to his big, rawboned frame, Pecos slapped the cot beside him and hung his gray-blond, blue-eyed head like a young man fresh from the woodshed. "I reckon Pete's name just slipped out. I mean, hell, he *was* her man. And, hell, we rode with him for nigh on thirty years before he . . . well, you know . . . before he got himself planted over there in them trees."

Pecos turned a disgruntled look at Slash. He kept his voice down so he wouldn't be heard on the stoop from where Jay's sobs pushed softly through the door. "Come on, pardner, Pete's been dead almost five years now. We should be able to mention his name from time to time."

"Dammit, Pecos." Slash tossed his animal skin covers aside and dropped his bare feet to the timbered floor still owning the chill of the crisp mountain morning. "You an' I both know Pete didn't get himself planted in them trees over there. *I* did!" Slash jabbed his thumb against his chest that bore the hooked knife scar that gave him his nickname. "I'm the one that got him planted. My own damn carelessness did."

"It was a bullet from the gun of one of Luther Bledsoe's deputies that killed Pete, Slash, you stupid devil. Don't you start in with all this old Pete stuff now, too!"

"I didn't," Slash said, rising in disgust and grabbing his brown whipcord trousers off a chair. "You did!"

"Ah, hell!" Pecos twisted around and flopped belly down on his cot, burying his head in his pillow. His big Russian .44, snugged inside its brown, hand-tooled leather holster, hung by its shell belt hooked over elk horns mounted on the wall above his head, within an easy grab if needed. Such a move had been needed more than a few times in his and Slash's long careers as riders of the long coulees, or the owlhoot trail, as some called the life of a professional western outlaw.

Slash quickly stepped into his pants. Then his boots. He left his blue chambray shirt on the chair but he strapped his twin, stag-butted Colt .44s around his waist, which was solid as oak at his ripe age of fifty-seven, which he was not above crowing about to Pecos, who'd grown a little fleshy above the buckle of his own cartridge belt.

Slash rarely walked more than five steps without either the revolver or his Winchester Yellowboy repeater. As he grabbed his hat off the kitchen table his bone-handled bowie knife, also strapped to his shell belt, rode high on his left hip, behind the .44 positioned for the cross-draw on that side. He swept a hand through his dark brown hair, still thick, he was proud to know, but well streaked with gray—especially up around the temples and in his long sideburns that sandwiched a broad, strong-jawed, brown-eyed face—the face of a handsome albeit middle-aged schoolboy.

One who'd spent the bulk of his life out in the blazing western sun.

That he was no longer a schoolboy, however, made itself obvious once again as it always tended to do upon his first rising. As he tramped across the kitchen, his hips and knees and ankles popped and cracked, stiff from too long in the mattress sack after too many years forking a saddle and sleeping on the hard, cold ground of one remote outlaw camp or another. An old back injury, the result of being thrown from a horse during a run from a catch party nearly twenty years ago, made Slash curse under his breath as he lifted the popping skillet off the range and slid it onto the warming rack, so the vittles wouldn't burn.